FLINTLOCK
HELL'S GATE

FLINTLOCK
HELL'S GATE

William W. Johnstone
with J. A. Johnstone

PINNACLE BOOKS
Kensington Publishing Corp.
www.kensingtonbooks.com

PINNACLE BOOKS are published by

Kensington Publishing Corp.
119 West 40th Street
New York, NY 10018

PUBLISHER'S NOTE
Following the death of William W. Johnstone, the Johnstone family is working with a carefully selected writer to organize and complete Mr. Johnstone's outlines and many unfinished manuscripts to create additional
novels in all of his series like The Last Gunfighter, Mountain Man, and
Eagles, among others. This novel was inspired by Mr. Johnstone's superb
storytelling.

All Kensington titles, imprints, and distributed lines are available at special
quantity discounts for bulk purchases for sales promotions, premiums,
fund-raising, educational, or institutional use. Special book excerpts or cus-
tomized printings can also be created to fit specific needs. For details, write
or phone the office of the Kensington sales manager: Kensington Publishing
Corp., 119 West 40th Street, New York, NY 10018, attn: Sales Department;
phone 1-800-221-2647.

PINNACLE BOOKS, the Pinnacle logo, and the WWJ steer head logo are
Reg. U.S. Pat. & TM Off.

ISBN-13: 978-0-7860-4008-7
ISBN-10: 0-7860-4008-4

First printing: September 2017

10 9 8 7 6 5 4 3 2 1

Printed in the United States of America

First electronic edition: September 2017

ISBN-13: 978-0-7860-4009-4
ISBN-10: 0-7860-4009-2

CHAPTER ONE

In a raging thunderstorm any shelter is welcome, and the cabin set among the foothills was a pleasing sight to Sam Flintlock. He said as much to O'Hara, his half-breed sidekick, who agreed that the place fit the bill.

But the bullet that kicked up a startled V of dirt a foot ahead of Flintlock's horse was less than welcoming, and the racketing roar of a heavy rifle was warning enough to stay the hell away.

Flintlock drew rein, waited until lightning scrawled across the sky like the signature of a demented god and thunder boomed over the blunt peaks of the Carrizo Mountains to the west, and then said to O'Hara, "Do you think that bullet was meant to scare us?"

The breed looked around him, at an empty, untamed landscape and said, "I reckon so. There's nobody else in sight but us two."

Rain ticked off the brim of Flintlock's hat and ran down the front of his slicker. "That there shot didn't come from a friendly party," he said.

O'Hara said, "Sam, I'm always amazed at your grasp

of the obvious." Then, "I guess we should try and find a place out of the rain to make camp."

"We got no coffee, no grub and I'm too damned wet for a cold camp," Flintlock said.

"So what do we do?" O'Hara said, his eyes scanning the cabin. "The traveling preacher we met told me there's a stage station to the north of us at Rock Creek on the old Oregon Trail."

"You mean the feller with the one arm?" Flintlock said.

"The very same. He said he lost that arm at Chancellorsville and maybe he did."

"How far?" Flintlock said.

"How far what?" O'Hara said.

"Damn it, you can be annoying by times, Injun," Flintlock said, scowling. "How long away is the stage station?"

"It's a few years since I've been this far west, but I reckon we're about four miles south of the trail, maybe less."

"And then when we get there we have to hunt around for a stage stop in a wall-to-wall downpour," Flintlock said.

O'Hara nodded. "Yeah, there's always that."

"Well, we got a cabin right in front of us with smoke coming out the chimney and I'm sure I can smell coffee on the wind. I say we"—a thunderclap that shook the ground obliterated Flintlock's words—"and we'll be made right welcome."

"I missed that," O'Hara said. "What did you say?"

Flintlock shook his head and rain cascaded from his hat brim. "You don't pay attention—that's always been your trouble, O'Hara, you just don't listen. I said we'll ride on in a-grinnin', like we're visiting kinfolk. Nobody's gonna gun grinning kinfolk, especially in a thunderstorm."

"We ain't grinning kinfolk and he'll know it," O'Hara said. "Try it and we're dead men."

"Trust me, O'Hara."

"Remember all the times I've trusted you before?"

"And you're still alive, ain't you? Anyways, this time will be different."

Flintlock kneed his horse forward and again a bullet kicked up dirt a couple of feet ahead of him and put an exclamation point at the end of the warning to steer clear. A cloud of gray gunsmoke drifted from the cabin's cracked open door and Flintlock caught the glint of a rifle barrel. He felt the burn of O'Hara's hostile gaze and said, "If the party in the cabin wanted to kill us he'd have done it by now. We can ride in real slow, a-grinnin' like a bushel basket of possum heads, and we'll be just fine."

O'Hara glanced at a turbulent sky as black as mortal sin and said, "Whoever he is, he ain't going to invite us in for cake and ice cream and that's a natural fact."

Rain driven by a gusting north wind drummed on the shoulders of Flintlock's slicker and his wet horse tossed its weary head and made the bit chime. "We'll give it another try," he said.

"Suppose he shoots again?" O'Hara said.

Flintlock's eyes narrowed. "Well, then he'll make me good and mad and I'll go in there a-hollering and a-shooting."

O'Hara grimaced. "Hell, Sam, he'll blow you

right off that buckskin before you even cover half the distance."

"Maybe he's been trying to hit us and missed every time. Ever think of that?"

"No, I never thought of that. I've thought of other things but that never crossed my mind."

Flintlock kneed his buckskin forward. "Let's go, O'Hara. The coffee is bilin' in the pot and maybe there's a stack of bear sign cooling on the plate."

"And maybe pigs will fly," O'Hara said.

Thunder crashed and lightning scraped across the sky but there were no more shots.

"Only a pair of damn fools would ignore two warning shots from a Sharps fifty," the man on the cabin porch said. He was a scrawny, tough-looking old coot, the white stubble on his right cheek parted by a wicked knife scar. The muzzle of his rifle was pointed right at Flintlock. "Did Nathan Poteet send ye?" he said.

"Never heard of the man, and you're less than hospitable, old-timer," Flintlock said. "In fact you're one unfriendly cuss."

"Man and boy, I never was a friendly cuss," the old man said. His Sharps didn't waver. "State your name and your intentions."

"My only intention is to come in out of the rain. My name is Sam Flintlock. There are them who know it and others who fear it."

"Big talk, mister." The old-timer cradled his rifle, reached into the pocket of his vest and produced a pair of pince-nez spectacles that he clamped onto the bridge of his nose. He craned his head forward and stared at Flintlock for a long time and then said, "Ach, I ken ye fine. You're old Barnabas Feeney's grandson, a right homely kid turned into a homelier man. You still got the thunderbird on your throat?"

"It's there," Flintlock said. Rain lashed at him and lightning gleamed on the shoulders of his slicker but the oldster was a talking man and didn't seem to be in a hurry.

"I mind the time back in '42 me an' Barnabas an' Kit Carson joined John C. Fremont's expedition to survey the Platte and the Sweetwater as far as the South Pass. That was the time Barnabas fought a mounted rifle duel with Black Faced Dave Cosgrove over an Arapaho woman. Dave got a bullet into Barnabas but he cussed off the wound, rode straight at Dave and shot him in the belly. Dave hollered in pain and said he was done but Barnabas drew his pistol and put a bullet in his head. Well, sir, Dave lingered for a while but his brains were running out of his skull so he didnae last long." The old man cackled. "But after all that, the Arapaho woman spread her blankets next to a Yankee surveyor and Barnabas lost out. He was all for killing the surveyor, mind, but Fremont brandished a horse pistol and said he needed all his surveyors alive. And that was the end of that. He was a rum one, was ol' Barnabas."

The old man lowered his rifle and said, "My name is Jamie MacDonald, Scotland born and bred as ye probably can tell. There's a barn around the back where you can put up your horses. There's hay but if you want oats it will cost you fifty cents an animal, so think carefully on that. And be careful of my mule, she does not care for strangers."

* * *

"Your ankle is bruised but it's not broke," MacDonald said. "She kicked you, you say?"

Irritated but mindful of the weather outside, Sam Flintlock bit back a sharp retort and said, "Yeah, that's what I say, damn mule kicked me, all right."

"Well, let that be a lesson to ye, never get behind a cantankerous mule," MacDonald said. "Now ye'll be wanting coffee, you and the Hindoo?"

"His name is O'Hara and he's half Irish," Flintlock said. "But as far as I know, when it comes to religion he's all Indian."

"Ah, weel, the Scots and Irish are brothers under the skin separated by differing views of Christianity, so you're welcome to my home, Mr. O'Hara."

"That's most gracious of you," O'Hara said. Flintlock gave the old man a sidelong look, surprised at his politeness.

"And now I'll get the coffee and later I'll boil us up a mess of porridge, or as some say, oatmeal," MacDonald said.

Flintlock and O'Hara exchanged horrified glances and the old mountain man laughed. "I always say that to my guests just to see their faces. You need not be alarmed. I've got a nice beef stew on the stove that will stick to your skinny ribs."

The old man cackled and busied himself with the coffee, and Flintlock looked around him. The cabin was small but the wood floor was meticulously swept and MacDonald's few sticks of furniture glowed from polish and much elbow grease. A fire burned in the stone fireplace and above the mantel was a painting of a self-assured young man wearing armor, a blue sash over his shoulder, and a fancy powdered wig.

"That's Prince Charles Edward Stuart, known to Scots the world over as Bonnie Prince Charlie," MacDonald said, seeing Flintlock's interest in the painting. "He should have been the king of Britain but his cause was lost." The old man shook his gray head. "He risked all on one final battle against the English, was defeated and had to flee Scotland, never to return. Forty-two years later he died in exile in Rome, of the drink, they said." MacDonald raised his cup to the portrait. "To you, my prince, and a tragic but noble figure you were."

MacDonald took a chair beside the fire opposite Flintlock. O'Hara, as was his habit when no other chairs were available, sat cross-legged on the floor.

"So, young Sam, tell me how Barnabas fares? Does his shadow still fall on the earth?"

"No, he's dead," Flintlock said. "Well, more or less."

MacDonald looked puzzled but he never asked the question framed on his face because from outside in the rain a man's voice called out, "MacDonald! Jamie MacDonald! Show yourself and make an accounting."

The old man rose to his feet, grabbed his Sharps from the gun rack beside the mantel and yelled, "Nathan Poteet, is that you?"

An answer from outside, "You know it's me, old man. You've had your week to decide if a map is worth dying for. Speak up now. What conclusion have you reached?"

MacDonald stepped to the door and yelled, "Poteet, there is no buried gold. There never was any buried gold. Mechan Cully died penniless. All he had left was the big house. He drank and gambled away the rest and there are some say he lay in sin with fallen women."

"Get out here, old man," Poteet said. "My talking is done."

To emphasize that statement a bullet shattered through one of the top panes of the cabin window, hit Bonnie Prince Charlie and sent him crashing to the hearth, and then thudded into the far wall, splintering timber.

"Damn ye for a scoundrel, Poteet, you broke my window and shot my bonnie prince," MacDonald said. "And twice damned to ye for a rogue!" The old man flung the door open and Flintlock yelled, "No!"

Too late.

Jamie MacDonald angrily stomped onto his porch, raised his rifle and was immediately hit by a volley of bullets that punched great holes in his thin frame. Flintlock heard a thud as the old man fell, and he pulled his Colt from the waistband.

"Easy," O'Hara whispered. He stared through the open door. "I see six but there could be more."

"You, in the cabin!" This from Poteet.

"What do you want?" Flintlock said.

"Step outside and identify yourselves. My quarrel is not with you."

"Damn you, you murdered the old man," Flintlock said.

"He had been notified," Poteet said. "Come out now or we'll shoot the cabin down about your ears."

O'Hara hollered, "We're coming out!" Then, "For

God's sake put the gun away, Sam. There's too many of them and I think I see Hogan Lord out there."

"You're seeing things. Hogan never leaves the Brazos River country," Flintlock said. "It isn't him."

"Even if it isn't him, there's still too many guns out there," O'Hara said.

He stepped out the door into teeming rain that hissed like an angry dragon. Reluctantly, Flintlock shoved his revolver back into the waistband and followed.

Six men wearing yellow rain slickers sat their horses in the downpour, Winchesters at their shoulders. Flintlock saw no friendly faces but then one of the gunmen lowered his rifle and said, "Hell, it's Sam Flintlock. I'd recognize that beak of a nose and sour disposition anywhere."

Flintlock now remembered the face and a shooting scrape from a few years before. "Howdy, Hogan," he said. "It's been a while."

"Four years to be exact," Lord said. Rain dripped from his hat brim. "That time we both went after the same mark. Remember?"

"Yeah, I remember. His name was Link Liddell and we caught up with him in Ciudad Juárez down Chihuahua way. He was wanted for rape and murder and you scattered his brains all over the front door of the church of Christ the Redeemer. As I recollect the priest got real mad over that."

As always Lord's smile was wide but without warmth. "That town was a dung heap."

Flintlock nodded. "So was Link Liddell. Sorry I didn't stick around to share the reward with you,

Hogan. I took one look at the money and decided that three thousand pesos just wasn't enough for two people. Doesn't go very far, like."

"If I'd found you that day, Sam, I would've gunned you," Lord said.

"You were always too quick to go to the gun, Hogan. I always considered it a character flaw in you," Flintlock said, staring at the gunman, thinking about things.

Could Hogan Lord shade me on the draw and shoot? Damn right he could and on my best day.

"Well, now that we're all reacquainted, tell us what you're doing here, Flintlock," Poteet said. "Be honest and straight up, like a white man."

"What I'm not doing here is murdering old men," Flintlock said.

"Self-defense, Sam," Lord said. "McDonald was fixing to cut loose with the Sharps. Mr. Poteet here was in fear for his life."

"It took six of you to kill one old man?" Flintlock said.

Poteet shrugged. "That's the way his hand played out." He looked past Lord to the other riders. "All right, boys, go earn your day's pay."

Now that his quick anger had subsided and he no longer saw through a red haze, Flintlock realized that the four men who'd climbed out of the saddle and stepped onto the porch were of a different stripe than Poteet and Lord. Low-browed and coarse, these were common thugs, dark-alley specialists, skull-and-boot fighters more at home with a sap, billy club, brass knuckles or a knife than a Colt. All four wore plug hats and the townsman's lace-up boots and when they talked to one another their accents were not of the West but of the rank, violent slums of the big northern cities. They were trash, but hideously dangerous and they'd attack in packs.

"Tear the cabin apart, boys," Poteet said. "If the map's in there find it." He stared at Flintlock, his eyes hard as stone. "You thinking of taking cards in this game?"

"I reckon not," Flintlock said. "I know when I'm facing a stacked deck."

"You, breed?" Poteet said as crashing, smashing and splintering sounds came from the cabin.

"I'm not the law," O'Hara said. "I've got no call to be involved."

"Wise man," Poteet said, dismissing O'Hara with a disdainful glance reserved for anyone not of the white race.

Poteet and Lord sat their saddles for the best part of an hour while the cabin was wrecked. They ignored the torrential rain as though it was a matter of no consequence.

Finally, one of the thugs stepped out the door onto the porch and said, "It ain't there, Mr. Poteet."

Poteet didn't hide his disappointment. "You sure?"

"Look for yourself, we tore the place apart. Two hundred dollars in a cigar box but no map." The thug shook his head. "It just ain't there."

Poteet, a big man whose claim to handsomeness was sabotaged by the cruel hardness of his mouth and his dead gray eyes, said, "Dave, you and the others share the two hundred among you, a bonus for getting wet."

"Obliged to you for that, Mr. Poteet," the scarred

bruiser named Dave said. Then, as the others three joined him, "You want us to ride to Mansion Creek with you?"

Hogan Lord answered that question. "No. You four got too many wanted dodgers on your back trail and you could be recognized. And that goes for you too, Nathan. Stay close to town and I'll send for you when I need you."

"Need him for what, Hogan?" Flintlock said. "Does he have more old men to kill?"

Poteet's face hardened into hewn rock. "Take my advice, don't push it, Flintlock," he said.

"Listen to the man, Sam," Lord said. "Mr. Poteet will take only so much."

"And then I get the urge to kill somebody," Poteet said. "Keep that in mind."

"Sam, let it go," O'Hara said, his voice urgent. "This isn't the time or place."

"Listen to the breed, Sam," Lord said. "If you stop in Mansion Creek look me up. I'll buy you a drink."

"Poteet, you didn't put the crawl on me," Flintlock said. "What's your opinion on that? Sum it up, now."

"We broke even, Flintlock," Poteet said. "That's my opinion."

"Sam, you can live with that," O'Hara said.

Flintlock nodded. "So be it." But there was a rage in him that scalded like acid.

CHAPTER TWO

"We done well by the old man, buried him decent," O'Hara said.

Sam Flintlock nodded. "I reckon. He had two mourners and a marked grave, that's more than most mountain men could hope for."

The rain had stopped during the night and Flintlock and O'Hara had buried Jamie MacDonald by lantern light, neither feeling much inclined to sleep. Now, as they took to the trail again, the sky was serene and white clouds drifted across its blue depths like lilies on a pond. The air smelled fresh after the rain had settled the dust and was heavy with the scent of pine and juniper. An east wind rustled in the grass like the whispers of dead Navajo. Ahead of the two riders rose the twin peaks of the Pastora and Zibetod mountains. Nestled between them in a grassy meadow ringed by stands of juniper, pine and mountain oak, lay a one-street settlement that Flintlock decided must be Mansion Creek.

O'Hara was of the same mind. "Maybe we can get

breakfast. I should've shot the ranny who tipped out MacDonald's stew."

"But you didn't," Flintlock said, drawing rein.

O'Hara smiled. "I've lived among white men for a long time, but I'm still not completely crazy. Hogan Lord is not a man to antagonize."

"Unless you have to," Flintlock said. "You're the banker. How much money do we have?"

"Enough for coffee, bacon and eggs, and then we're done."

"Maybe we can find some work."

"Maybe. Saloon swampers are always in demand."

Flintlock grimaced. "I was thinking more of something in the restaurant trade. At least we'd eat regular."

"Dishwasher?"

"If that's all I can get."

O'Hara shook his head. "I'd rather rob the town bank."

"It may come to that," Flintlock said. He kneed his horse forward. "Did you see Barnabas at the graveside?"

"I saw him," O'Hara said. "He didn't seem to be cut up about MacDonald's death."

"For Barnabas it's way too late for sorrow," Flintlock said. He shrugged. "Or maybe when he was alive he didn't like the old man. Barnabas didn't like many people."

O'Hara smiled. "Who did he like?"

"Beats the hell out of me. I only know that whoever they were, I wasn't one of them." Flintlock's eyes rose to the sky above Mansion Creek. "Hell, look at that, there's buzzards drifting above the town."

"A bad omen for somebody," O'Hara said.

Flintlock sighed. "You know, I have the strangest feeling that we're not heading into a happy time."

"But maybe your ma is there in town, Sam," O'Hara said. "There's always that possibility."

"Something is there, all right," Flintlock said. "But I don't think it's my ma. I don't think she'd turn the air black."

"What is it then?"

"Wicked things," Flintlock said. "Like hell has emptied out and all the devils are right there in Mansion Creek."

CHAPTER THREE

Sam Flintlock mopped up a smear of egg yolk with a piece of bread, popped it in his mouth, chewed thoughtfully and then said, "Well, that hit the spot."

"I'm glad you enjoyed it," O'Hara said. "It could be a long time before you taste bacon and eggs again."

Flintlock shook his head and frowned. "O'Hara, what half of you makes you so darned depressing, the Indian or the Irish?" Because of the pretty young lady who sat at another table, he'd gone out of his way to say *darned* instead of *damned*, but the girl didn't seem to notice.

O'Hara spoke again. "Sam, you haven't seen depressing yet. If we don't find some work and earn money soon both halves of me will really be woebegone."

"Woebegone? Where did you dig up that word?" Flintlock said, irritated that he didn't know what it meant.

"It means to feel unhappy. Heard a snake-oil salesman say it one time to some ladies. He said if they felt woebegone they should buy a bottle of his remedy, guaranteed to make them happier . . . instanter!"

Flintlock was intrigued. "And did it?"

"Since the stuff was about nine-tenths rotgut I guess it did." O'Hara saw a glint in Flintlock's eye and said, "Forget it, Sam. It takes money to start a business like that and we don't have any."

"Well, maybe there's some ranny with a fat reward on him on the scout in Mansion Creek," Flintlock said. "That Nathan Poteet now, and the four with him look like they're on the dodge, to say nothing of Hogan Lord. He's killed more than his share and not all of them legal."

"My advice at the MacDonald cabin was not to take on six killers at a time," O'Hara said. "It still stands."

"Maybe I'm overreaching at that," Flintlock said. "But it's something to keep in mind. Well, that and as you said, there's always the town bank if things don't start shaking our way soon."

A big-bellied man wearing a stained white apron stepped to the table and began to pick up the plates. He grinned and said, "You boys must have been almighty hungry on account of how you ate the flowers right off the plates." He held up a dish. "Look, it's down to white."

"Yeah, that's a good joke," Flintlock said. "But unless we can find some work real soon we'll be mighty hungry all over again."

The restaurant owner shook his head. "If it's honest work you're looking for there's nothing in this town or in the whole of Apache County," he said. Then, looking wise, "You boys should head north, pick up the Old Spanish Trail and follow it west all the way to California. Plenty of work there for a man."

"We'd starve to death before we got to California," Flintlock said.

"You could kill your chuck along the way," the man said.

"Thanks," Flintlock said. "You've been a big help."

"Anytime. Happy to oblige."

Flintlock sat back in his chair and decided that his search for his mother was rapidly going nowhere, thwarted by a lack of funds. But then a man's voice at his elbow gave him new hope. "Excuse my intrusion, I couldn't help overhearing and I may be able to help you, young fellow."

Flintlock turned and saw the jowly, florid face of the man who sat at the next table. Opposite him was the pretty girl Flintlock had noticed earlier, a petite brunette with the wide dark eyes of a startled fawn. "Do you have work?" he said.

"Possibly. Would you care to join us?" the man said. His thin black hair was combed over a bald crown, and his belly hung between his thighs like a sack of grain. Whereas the girl's eyes were a lustrous golden brown tinged with green, the fat man's were almost black, the color of Louisiana swamp mud.

"Don't mind if I do," Flintlock said. He dragged his chair over to the man's table and O'Hara did likewise. "This here is my friend, O'Hara, and I'm Sam Flintlock."

The girl stared at O'Hara, at the long black hair falling over the shoulders of his beaded Apache vest and the holstered Colt on his hip, and then to Flintlock, her gaze moving from his great hooked nose to his stained buckskin shirt and finally lingered on the thunderbird tattooed across his throat. She seemed alarmed, almost fearful, and the fat man smiled and placed his huge, pudgy hand over hers.

"Don't be distressed, my dear," he said, purring like a cat at the cream bowl. "I realize they look a pair of frontier ruffians but surprisingly their kind can be quite gentlemanly, even the half-breed savage. But just to set your mind at rest . . ." The man reached under his coat and produced a short-barreled Colt that he laid on the table. "You'll be quite safe now, Lucy."

The girl had the good grace to blush. "I don't think that will be necessary, Tobias," she said. Then to Flint-lock, "I meant no disrespect, sir. I . . . I fear I am not yet used to the ways of the West. My name is Lucy Cully of the Philadelphia Cullys."

"And I'm Tobias Fynes, this town's only banker and Miss Lucy's lawyer," the fat man said. He glared at O'Hara. "You disapprove of me?"

"I disapprove of any man who draws a gun on me," O'Hara said, thoroughly disliking the fat man. "I make it a rule never to shoot women, children and most animals, but I got no trouble gunning a banker or a lawyer, come to that."

"O'Hara is a tad testy this morning, but he's right pleased to make your acquaintance, Tobias," Flintlock said. "Now, you said you could help us. Do you have work?"

"In a manner of speaking, yes." Fynes tore hostile eyes away from O'Hara and his smile was practiced and as slick as oil on water. "But let Miss Lucy give you a little background first."

"What I have to tell you is most singular in its

content, so much so that I can scarcely believe it myself," the girl said. She took a sip of coffee, composed herself and continued, "To the north of town there is a mesa, a remote spot of much beauty and tranquillity. After he retired from gold prospecting, it was near there, on a lofty crag or rock, that my grandfather Cully built a mansion in what is called the Gothic style."

"Mechan, Miss Lucy's grandfather, didn't build the mansion from scratch," Fynes said. "He had the house moved from Philadelphia, brick by brick, and then hired workers to reassemble it on the very edge of the crag."

"When Grandfather died last year I discovered that he'd left the house to me in his will," Lucy said. "I was his only living relative."

"There was no money, only the house," Fynes said. "Mechan was penniless when he was killed."

"He was killed?" Flintlock said.

"Murdered," Fynes said. "His feet were burned and he was almost decapitated by an ax and viciously cut about with a knife. The killer was never caught."

Lucy dabbed tears from her eyes with a scrap of lace handkerchief, and Fynes reached over the table and patted her on the shoulder. Flintlock noticed that the fat man made the gesture in such a way that the heel of his hand lingered a few seconds too long on the topmost swell of the girl's breast.

"May I continue, Mr. Fynes?" Lucy said, her cheekbones tinged pink, aware of what the lawyer had done to her. "After all, my present situation is of the greatest moment."

"Yes, my dear, please continue," Fynes said. "You do indeed have a harrowing story to tell."

Lucy said, "Mr. Flintlock—"

"Call me Sam."

"Sam, I fear that when my grandfather moved his house out here he brought something else from Philadelphia besides bricks, tiles and paneling . . . something evil, something wicked."

"I sensed that when I rode into town, but it sounds like nothing a Colt can't get rid of," Flintlock said.

"Sam," Lucy said, "you can't shoot what's not alive."

"What do you think of all these ha'ants and sich, Fynes?" Flintlock said.

"Indeed, there have been rumors of strange happenings in and around the house," the fat man said. "All of them started after old Mechan died." Fynes smiled. "But it's a very old house, floorboards creak, loose windows rattle, unlatched doors bang open and shut and the wind sighs around the eaves. It's just that and nothing more."

"Have you spent a night in the house, Fynes?" O'Hara said.

"No, I haven't. The house is not mine, though I fervently wish Miss Lucy would sell it to me."

"Sam, when I arrived in Mansion Creek a week ago I was told the house was haunted and that the couple that Mr. Fynes had hired as housekeepers had spent only two days in the old place before they fled into the night, leaving their belongings behind them."

"Did you speak with them, Fynes?" Flintlock said.

"I didn't get a chance. As far as I know they're still running."

Flintlock grinned. "Now I get it. You want me and

O'Hara to go into the house and chase off the ghosts or whatever they are. How much will you pay?"

Lucy said, her pretty face troubled, said, "It's not that simple. Being of a somewhat timid nature I'm hesitant to take possession of the house. My plan had been to inspect the property and then return to Philadelphia to wed my fiancé, Roderick, a Romantic poet of considerable renown. But he has weak lungs and both his doctor and Roderick's best friend, Walt Whitman, advised him to return to the West with me where the clean air would soon make him strong again. But now I'm not so sure of my plan. If the house is really haunted by evil spirits, I will sell it to Mr. Fynes and return back East, hopefully to happier times."

"And I will purchase at fair market value, my dear," the banker said, sweat beading the blue jowls of his eager face. "You may rest assured of that." Tobias Fynes sat back in his chair, studied Flintlock over the tips of his steepled fingers and then said, "And now we come to the crux of the matter, the very essence of the problem, and you, Mr. Flintlock, could well be the solution."

"How much does being the solution pay?" O'Hara said.

"Five hundred dollars," Fynes said. "Cash in your hand."

"It's thin," Flintlock said. "Five hundred will not go far."

"Ah yes, perhaps so, but for a week, seven full days, you will live in luxury in a beautifully appointed house stocked with plenty of grub, tobacco and whiskey. I know that a loose woman or two would help seal the deal with men of your stripe, but there are none to be had."

Lucy Cully gave Flintlock a sympathetic glance as he said, "You want men of our stripe, me and O'Hara, to spend the week in the Cully mansion?"

"Exactly. At the end of that time you will either tell Miss Cully that her house is free of ghosts and other evils and she will take possession, or you will declare that the home is indeed haunted and on no account should she live there, especially with an ailing husband." The fat banker stared into Flintlock's eyes. "So, will you do it? Come now, speak up, give me a yes or no."

"When do we get the five hundred?" O'Hara said, his dislike for Fynes so palpable that the harsh tone of his voice made others in the restaurant turn to look at him.

"You will take residence tomorrow," Fynes said. "Seven days later, when the job is done, you will be paid in full."

"If we're still alive?" Flintlock said.

"Indeed, but I see no earthly reason why you should be otherwise," Fynes said.

"It's the unearthly reasons for being dead that worry me," Flintlock said.

Fynes was insistent. "Will you take the job? Speak up now, be blunt and don't shilly-shally. I can't abide a man who dawdles."

"Since it's the only offer we've had today, yeah, we'll take the job," Flintlock said.

Lucy Cully smiled. "Oh, thank you, Sam. I feel safer already."

That last obviously didn't set well with Fynes. He

scowled and said, "You two might as well ride out to the Cully mansion now. Just follow the wagon road west for a couple of miles and you'll find it. The road cuts through a stand of ponderosa pine and beyond that is a mesa of no great height. The house sits atop the rock crag to the north."

"My grandfather called the crag the Ravens' Nest and it is reached by a switchback trail that climbs that neighboring mesa," Lucy said. She smiled. "Getting to the house is not quite as difficult as it sounds. The plateau is not very high, much lower than the crag, and the switchback trail is wide and sits on a solid foundation."

"I'm sure the boys will find their way," Fynes said. "My dear, to men like these it's just another robbers' roost in the wilderness." Then to Flintlock, "You may bed down in the house tonight, but your week will not start until tomorrow when a wagon will arrive bringing your supplies." He waved a hand like shooing a fly. "Our business is concluded for the moment and you may go."

Flintlock, finding no reason to linger, stood and O'Hara followed him out of the door into the street.

Tobias Fynes watched them leave, then said, "Lucy, those are a couple of desperadoes and low-down, but they will help you make up your mind."

"I'm sure they will, Mr. Fynes," the girl said. "And now we must talk. I have something to say that will surprise you."

CHAPTER FOUR

"Bitch took me by surprise. She's decided to spend the week in the house with Flintlock and the breed," Tobias Fynes said. "Now, why in the hell would she do that?"

"Maybe she doesn't trust you, Tobias," Hogan Lord said.

Fynes's great weight made his office chair creak in protest as he sat back and considered what the gunman had just said. Finally, he said, "No, that's out of the question. Of course she trusts me, I've no doubt about that. But Lucy very much wants to marry her puny, puking poet and play happy honeymooners in grandpappy's house." Fynes's fleshy lips widened in a grin that was not pleasant. "I have other honeymoon plans for that little lady."

"What about the house?" Lord said.

"How do you mean?" Fynes said.

"Do you think it's really haunted?"

"Hell, no, it's not haunted. The story I told her about the couple who fled the place was a big windy to help make her feel uneasy. No one has lived in the house since old Mechan Cully died so tragically. But when the two latest custodians are found dead, and I mean Flintlock and the breed, Lucy will be convinced the place is cursed and she'll be glad to sell it to me for any price. Naturally, I'll be very sympathetic and more than willing to take it off her hands for say, ten cents on the dollar, since the mansion is evil and must be torn down."

"And that's when we'll find the treasure map. If such even exists. Old Jamie MacDonald swore to Nathan Poteet and me that there is no map."

"I never liked that damned Scotsman, too independent-minded by half," Fynes said. "I thought either old Mechan had given MacDonald the map or told him exactly where it was. You didn't find it in his cabin so that means it must be in the Cully house, as I first suspected. He was lying to you, Hogan. MacDonald knew where the map was hidden. It's in the house somewhere, has to be. Before he died, old Mechan told me he'd hidden the map where I wouldn't find it and dying men don't lie."

"Maybe he'd have told you exactly where it was but you went too far with the torture, Mr. Fynes, all that burning and cutting. You killed the old man too soon."

The banker said, "How the hell did I know he was going to turn up his toes so easily? But, looking back, I do admit it was a miscalculation on my part."

Lord shrugged. "He was a frail old man with a bad ticker." The gunman locked eyes with Fynes. "The one and only time I was at the big house I saw something."

Fynes showed surprise. "Saw something?"

"At an upstairs window. It was looking down at me and Nathan Poteet."

"What was it?"

"I don't know. I saw a pale face and then it was gone."

"Man or a woman?"

"I don't know. I only saw it for a split second."

Fynes grinned. He rose from his chair and stepped to the drinks trolley and poured bourbon into a couple of glasses. He handed one to Lord and said, "The wind blows hard up there on the crag. You saw a curtain move."

Hogan Lord drained his glass and shuddered. Then he said, "The place has all those windows and turrets and spires and even in sunlight it looks dark. The house was old when Mechan bought it, so who knows what took place within its walls back in the day?"

"Bloody murders, you mean?"

"As I said, who knows?"

Tobias Fynes leaned over the gunman and poured more whiskey into his glass. It was a small movement but he wheezed from the effort. The banker grinned, his pouched eyes alight, and said, "This is perfect, Hogan, just perfect. If the place makes you afraid, imagine what it will do to Lucy Cully and her custodians."

"It didn't scare me and it won't scare Sam Flintlock or the breed," Lord said. "Those two have been up the trail and back again and they don't scare worth a damn."

Fynes said, "If we can send Lucy fleeing out of the

house screaming, it will be enough. And there opens up another tantalizing possibility."

"What's that?" said Lord, a handsome man wearing expensive broadcloth and clean linen. He looked more like a prosperous big-city businessman than a hired gun.

"Although I very much want her for my own enjoyment, Lucy Cully could die suddenly," Fynes said. "Then I'll spread the word that she was raped and murdered by the known gunman, outlaw and bounty hunter Sam Flintlock and his savage accomplice. Afterward, I'll be most happy to report that both culprits were later killed by my gallant associate Hogan Lord."

"I don't kill women," Lord said. "That's a line I don't step over, Tobias."

"And you won't have to, my dear Hogan. You and Nathan Poteet take care of Flintlock and the O'Hara breed and I'll do what needs to be done to the girl. If things don't work out the way I hope, this will be a foolproof option."

Lord couldn't hide his disgust. "You'd murder the girl?"

Fynes spread his hands and shrugged. "Why not? She's of little account after all and can only render me some passing pleasure. Now when I think about it, I wouldn't want to keep her. There's nothing she can give me that I can't buy from a two-dollar whore."

Hogan Lord decided he didn't want any more of Fynes's whiskey and he needed to get away from the fat man's fetid odor and breathe fresh air again. He rose from his chair and said, "I'll be around when you need me, Tobias."

The gunman stepped to the door but Fynes's voice, smooth as oil on water, stopped him.

"Hogan, there can be no bleeding hearts in this great venture. There is too much at stake, a fortune in gold, no less. You're either with me all the way or not at all. Do I make myself clear?"

"While you're paying my wages you can count on me," Lord said, his face stiff. "I ride for the brand."

Fynes nodded, sat back in his chair and talked over his steepled fingers. "And you can count on me, Hogan . . . to make you a very rich man."

CHAPTER FIVE

"Oh, Mr. Flintlock! Can I speak with you for a minute?"

Sam Flintlock tightened his saddle cinch and turned to look out the livery door. Lucy Cully stood in the sunlight with a carpetbag at her feet. She wore a plain blue dress with white collar and cuffs that made her look like a fourteen-year-old runaway from an orphanage.

"What can I do for you, Miss Cully?" Flintlock said. He smiled. "And I told you to call me Sam."

"Sam . . . you still intend to stay at the house tonight?" Lucy said.

"That's where me and O'Hara are headed," Flintlock said. "Right at the moment we have nowhere else to bed down."

"I want to come with you," the girl said.

"Do you have a horse?"

"No, I don't."

"Then you can't come with us," Flintlock said.

"Sam, she can ride behind me," O'Hara said.

"Miss Lucy, I don't trust your lawyer," Flintlock said.

"He's got sneaky eyes and a way of talking that worries me. I reckon where we're going could turn dangerous almighty sudden. You stay right here in town and do some knitting and we'll chase away the boogermen for you. After that, why, you and your new husband can move right in, cozy as can be, and he can write all the poetry he wants."

Lucy tilted her little chin at a stubborn angle. "May I remind you, sir, that Cully mansion is mine and I can go there anytime I want, and that as of tomorrow you and Mr. O'Hara are my employees." Her cheeks flushed, the girl said, "And I want to make it abundantly clear that I don't knit and never will."

The livery stable owner, a bearded man named Lawson, had been listening to this exchange. Now he stepped out of the stable and said to Lucy, "Can you ride, young lady?"

"I ride very well," the girl said.

Lawson nodded. "Good. Then I got a nice grulla mare you can rent. She's only half broke but a good rider can handle her."

Flintlock said, "She ain't riding a half-broke pony, not where we're going." He glared at O'Hara as though he were the cause of the problem. "All right, since you seem so keen to drag her along, take her up behind you."

Now it was Lawson's turn to glare at Flintlock. "You ain't very good for the hoss-selling business, mister," he said.

"Better you lose business than the lady breaks her neck riding a green horse," Flintlock said.

Lawson looked angry and opened his mouth to speak, and it was an accurate measure of Flintlock's irritation that he now said, "Not another word, livery-man, or I'll shoot you in the belly. I was gonna shoot you anyhow for charging two bits for a stingy scoop of oats."

Lawson, refusing to be intimidated, said, "Go to hell," and stomped back into the stable.

His face sour, Flintlock sat his saddle and watched Lucy Cully climb up behind O'Hara, her unwieldy carpetbag bumping into both horse and rider. "I'm so sorry," Lucy said. "That was clumsy of me." O'Hara told her to think nothing of it, and Flintlock said, "Now can we dispense with all the niceties and ride?"

Lucy sitting astride O'Hara's paint showed a considerable amount of slim, shapely leg, and Flintlock mentally berated himself for taking time to notice.

Delayed by rapidly deteriorating weather conditions, it took Flintlock and the others an hour to reach the switchback that led to the top of the butte and by then the high country was blanketed in mist. Pine, cedar and juniper grew on the slope in addition to greasewood and a host of flowering plants. When they reached the top of the mesa Flintlock let the horses take a breather while Lucy Cully pointed out the rock crag that jutted from the top of the rise like the prow of an ironclad. "The house is there, at the end of the promontory, invisible in the mist," she said. "Oh, what a poem Roderick could write about this most melancholy scene."

Flintlock let that last go without comment and slid his Winchester from the boot. "All right, you spotted the tracks, O'Hara. Maybe you should go take a look-see," he said.

The breed nodded, helped Lucy off his horse and dismounted himself. Like Flintlock, he retrieved his rifle and then said, "If you hear shooting come a-running."

Flintlock grinned. "What about screams?"

"Them too," O'Hara said.

He walked away, silent on moccasin feet, and disappeared into the gray, hanging mist.

"I'm sure there is no danger," Lucy said, lifting her eyes to Flintlock. "The house has lain empty for weeks but lawyer Fynes's people have visited the place a time or two and they could have left the tracks."

Flintlock pointed with the Winchester. "Look ahead of us there, and there. Them horse tracks are not old. Looks like four riders on shod horses, so they were made by white men, not some wandering blanket Apaches."

"What would four men be doing all the way up here?" Lucy said.

"When O'Hara gets back I'm hoping he can tell us," Flintlock said. Then, his face serious, "Lucy, if anything happens to me and O'Hara in the next few minutes, you take O'Hara's paint and skedaddle off this mesa right quick. Understand?"

"But . . . but what could happen to you?" the girl said. She looked alarmed.

"We don't know who made those tracks," Flintlock said. "They might be honest travelers who lost their way and took refuge in the house. But in this wild country there's always a chance that the tracks were left by outlaws on the scout."

"I thought I might be scared by ghosts, not outlaws," Lucy said, shivering.

"You've a right to be afraid, young lady. Most outlaws are a sight scarier than ghosts," Flintlock said.

Fearing that he might have to charge into the mist to help O'Hara, he remained mounted. Lucy found a rock to sit on, her carpetbag on the ground beside her. She looked very young and vulnerable and Flintlock found himself hoping that when the time came her betrothed would take good care of her.

A long ten minutes passed . . .

The mist grew thicker and swollen rain clouds dropped lower in the sky as though they'd grown too heavy and planned to rest on the mesa cap rock. The sunless, gray, grim, dreary and somber morning gave way to afternoon but the transition went unnoticed and the cheerless gloom remained. Lucy sat on her rock and the skin of her face was so pale it seemed that she wore a paper mask. Flintlock's horse tossed its head and the bit chimed. Then, from somewhere in the murk, an owl hooted.

CHAPTER SIX

Sam Flintlock slapped the forestock of his Winchester into the palm of his left hand. He returned the call of the great horned owl and like the bird itself his mouth barely moved.

A few moments later O'Hara stepped out of the mist like a gray ghost.

As Lucy Cully rose to her feet, her face framing a question, Flintlock beat her to it. "Well?" he said.

"Four of them," O'Hara said. "There's a barn out back and their horses all wear a U.S. brand and have McClellan saddles.

"Soldiers all the way out here? Or could they be deserters," Flintlock said.

"Deserters, would be my guess," O'Hara said. "Now the Apache are gone there's nothing out this way to interest the army." He looked at Lucy. "That is a wondrous house. I have never seen a dwelling with so many levels and windows."

"The house was built in 1830 in the Gothic Revival style, or so Roderick told me when I described it to him," Lucy said. "Walt Whitman told us that Gothic houses were designed to blend into the terrain, that's why most were built in remote areas."

"Right now I think the intentions of four army deserters occupying the house is more important than how and why it was built," Flintlock said, irritated again.

O'Hara said, "There's a sheer drop on three sides and not much room for a person to walk around the place. It's a long way to fall, Sam. A man could read his newspaper before he hit the ground."

"We don't have to go anywhere near the edge," Lucy said. "I'll just walk up to the front door and tell those four deserters, if that's what they are, that I'm the owner and order them to vacate the premises, instanter!"

"I'm betting they're deserters and not regular cavalrymen," Flintlock said.

O'Hara said. "I'm with you on that, Sam. I'd swear the ranny I saw through a window was wearing civilian duds."

"Well, we ain't getting anywhere standing here cussin' and discussin'," Flintlock said. "We'll go talk with those gents and as the young lady said, order them to vacate the premises."

"Instanter," O'Hara said. He shook his head. "Sam, I'm sure this is going to end up in a gunfight."

"You having them Indian visions again?" Flintlock said.

"No, but I have an Irish foreboding telling me that all is not well."

"Then we'll go and make talk and ask them boys to state their intentions," Flintlock said. "If they're running from the army they'll listen to reason. I'm sure they're not looking to get into a shooting scrape."

"And we'll ask them if they've seen any ghosts," Lucy said. "We might as well get this adventure started."

"Young lady, by the time this day is over we might all be ghosts," Flintlock said.

Sam Flintlock shuddered as he led his horse through the dank, dreary day toward the mist-shrouded mansion. When the building appeared through the gloom, Flintlock stopped and his eyes lifted to a soaring edifice built much higher than it was wide. The rambling structure used the pointed arch everywhere, for windows, exterior doors, porches, dormers and roof gables. The house had a steeply pitched tile roof and front-facing gables with carved, gingerbread trim. An extensive porch with decorative turned posts connected by flattened arches ran the full width of the building. Withal, Flintlock thought the towering, spiky house looked like a fantastic mountain fortress more suited to robber knight or wicked sorcerer than a crazy old coot like Mechan Cully. There was nothing cheerful about the mansion, nothing bright and friendly, rather it was a dark, for-bidding, brooding presence with no welcome mat outside the front door. It was a dwelling out of time and place, torn from a long-settled land of white fences, green lawns, clipped hedges and planted shade trees, and plunked down in the middle of a mountainous county of fanged rock, soaring crags and deep canyons where nothing was decided, nothing settled, the only constant the breathtaking beauty of the untamed landscape itself.

O'Hara tore his eyes from the house, turned to Flintlock and said, "Hell, what do we do? Knock?"

"It's my house and I will do no such thing," Lucy said. She gave O'Hara a sidelong look. "Knock, indeed!"

The closer the girl had gotten to the mansion the more assertive she'd become, and while Flintlock admired her pluck, to just storm into the place would be foolhardy, to say the least. He grabbed Lucy by the arm and halted her in her tracks just as O'Hara said, "Sam, up there on the peak of the house."

Flintlock looked up and saw old Barnabas, his dead grandfather, perched like a gargoyle on the sharp spine of the V-shaped roof. The wicked old mountain man glared at Flintlock, made an obscene gesture at him and then vanished.

"Well, we know there's at least one spook in this place," O'Hara said.

"Barnabas isn't a spook," Flintlock said. "He's a damned nuisance . . . and I mean damned."

Lucy looked confused. "What do you see, Sam? I don't see anything."

Flintlock was spared having to answer because just then the front door of the mansion swung open and four men walked onto the porch. One of them stepped to the edge, peered into the crawling mist and said, his voice sounding hollow, "Who goes there? Identify yourself. I can see you."

"I'm with the owner of this house," Flintlock said. "She wants you to leave."

"Instanter," O'Hara said.

A laugh from the porch, then, "The hell you say? Git away from here."

Flintlock walked forward. He had no rifle but his Colt was shoved in his waistband. Now the men on the porch could see him clearly. "Name's Sam Flintlock and I'm here to see justice done."

"The Texas bounty hunter?" a man said.

"Texas and other places," Flintlock said.

"Seems I heard about you a time or two," the man said. "I'm Shade Pike and I'm one mean son of a bitch. Name mean anything to you?"

"I would've remembered that name and the natural fact that you're a son of a bitch," Flintlock said. "No, I never heard of you."

"There's a pity," Pike said. "You should have."

He was a tall man, hatless, who wore a black frock coat and pants of the same color tucked into knee-high boots. The boots and his wide cartridge belt that supported two holstered Colts and a sheathed bowie knife were all of the same color, a deep mahogany brown. He also wore a Colt in a shoulder holster, and his left hand rested on the silver knob of a walking cane, a vanity he'd stolen from Bat Masterson.

Flintlock thought Pike a cheap, tinhorn imitation of a better man.

His three companions were not so well dressed but they weren't shabby either and their boots, gun rigs and revolvers were all of good quality. How sudden they were with the iron and whether or not they would stand and get their work in, Flintlock didn't know. But by the hard, confident look of them he guessed they were game enough.

Lucy pushed past O'Hara and said, "Mr. Pike, I want you to please vacate the premises."

"Instanter," O'Hara said, enjoying the word.

Pike grinned. "All right, little lady, you're as pretty as a field of Texas bluebonnets and I'll deny you nothing. So here's what's coming down—you can claim your house but we'll linger for a spell and you and my boys can get acquainted, like." As the other men let loose with a vulgar chorus of ribald laughter, Pike said to Flintlock, "As for you and the breed, light a shuck before I cut that bird off your throat and use it for a hatband."

Unfazed by the man's threat, Flintlock said, "What the hell are you doing here, Pike? And why are you riding army horses?"

"The horses we got from four Yankee soldier boys who don't need them anymore," Pike said. "We were on the scout after a bank job we pulled in Texas, and our mounts just tuckered out on us. Lucky them soldier boys were close. Then we heard about this house from a lawman in El Paso. He said he'd heard the story in Mansion Creek, a pissant burg west of here," Pike said.

"What did he hear?"

"That there was gold hidden in every room, he said. Make you rich overnight, he said. Well, we've been all over this pile and there's no gold to be found. We was duped into coming here by a no-good law dog who wanted rid of us, but now"—Pike smiled as he stripped Lucy naked with his eyes—"maybe it's been a worthwhile trip after all."

Lucy's face flushed. She was used to lustful looks from men and she dismissed Pike's hungry eyes with contempt, but she was angry nonetheless. "Who was the officer of the law who lied to you that there is gold in my home?" she said. "Give me his name and I'll see that the proper authorities deal with him."

Pike said, "It doesn't matter who told me. Hell, when there's gold involved everybody knows about it anyhow."

"Yeah, it's hard to keep talk of gold and treasure maps secret," Flintlock said. "Seems like somebody in Mansion Creek spread the good word."

"Well, there ain't a treasure map either," Pike said. "Me and the boys have been all over this place and all we found was damned spiderwebs." He glared at Flintlock. "Answer me a question, tattooed man."

"Ask away," Flintlock said. "But be polite when you're asking it."

Pike said, "I told you to light a shuck. So why the hell are you still here?"

It was then that mistakes began to be made that would have deadly consequences.

"I'm here because I intend to throw you and your boys out of this house," Flintlock said. He was tense, ready. "Are there any Texas dodgers out on you, Pike? A dodger for a big-enough reward would make it worth my while keeping you alive, at least for a while. Understand?"

Then came the first mistake to be made . . . and Pike's boys made it.

The three were frontier thugs, brave enough when the chips were down, but they were former cowboys, not Texas revolver fighters. They stood in awe of Shade Pike's speed on the draw and shoot and figured him in the same class as fast guns like John Wesley

Hardin and Wild Bill Longley. It was a mortal error, but a grinning, not-too-bright bunch, as they urged Pike to "gun the son of a bitch," the three toughs were unaware of it.

Then Shade Pike made another mistake. Sure, he was a fast gun with five kills to his credit. But none of the five were named men. A couple had been drunk punchers and another a fifty-five-year-old gambler whose reactions had slowed ten thousand whiskeys before. The only man who'd even came close to being a gun was a Nacogdoches livery station owner called Denham or Denning who had a local rep as a bad man to cross. Pike outdrew and killed the man, consulted his watch and then went to breakfast. Like his companions, Pike believed his own brag that he occupied the elite tier of the revolver fighter hierarchy. But when he made the mistake of drawing down on Sam Flintlock he instantly realized that there was only one top-class shootist present . . . and it sure as hell wasn't him.

Shucking his iron from the waistband Flintlock shot Pike between the eyes even as the gunman cleared leather. Pike staggered back, his face white with shock at the time and manner of his death, and the men with him knew that mistakes had been made. They'd set store by the man's flashy, two-gun draw and now they didn't want to make another blunder. One of them, a bearded man with alarmed eyes, yelled, "Flintlock, we're out of it!"

Gunsmoke drifting around him, Flintlock said. "You're out of it when I say you're out of it." He stepped to Pike's body and said, "Yup, he's as dead as he's ever gonna be."

A younger man with freckles all over his face like a sparrow's egg stared openmouthed at Flintlock and said, "But . . . but Shade was fast. Everybody said he was fast."

"Who was everybody?" Flintlock said.

"Folks . . ." the youngster said, confused.

"Folks were wrong," Flintlock said. "He wasn't near fast enough, and the proof of that is lying right there at your feet." He took a step back, his Colt in his hand. "Anybody else object to my presence here?" He waited and then, "Anybody? All right, I got no answer. Now, you men mount up and get the hell away from here. If I see you around this house again, hell, if I see you anywhere in the Arizona Territory, I'll shoot you on sight." An unforgiving enemy, Flintlock motioned to Pike's body. "And take that with you."

The bearded man said, "Mistakes were made here today."

"And you made them," Flintlock said.

CHAPTER SEVEN

The mist that had shrouded the crag throughout the day thickened as darkness fell and lapped around the ground floor of the house like a gray, primordial sea. Uneasy on its rocky foundation the mansion creaked and groaned constantly, and from his refuge in what seemed to be the library Sam Flintlock fancied that from upstairs he heard heavy curtains flap like the wings of gigantic bats.

Lucy Cully tilted her head to one side, listened for a while and then said, "I hear that. It's only the wind."

Flintlock smiled. "There is no wind."

"Yes, that's right, there is no wind." Lucy shivered and hugged herself. "I wish O'Hara would get back." Since the killing of Shade Pike the girl had kept her distance from Flintlock, staying close to the solid, reassuring presence of the breed.

It seemed that old Mechan Cully had no time for newfangled oil lamps but there was a plentiful supply of candles and candlesticks to hold them. The light in the parlor came from a couple of four-armed candelabras that cast a fitful yellow glow around the table where Flintlock and Lucy sat but deepened the shadows in the corners where the eight-eyed spiders lived and spun.

Flintlock had earlier made a foray around the kitchen and found a couple of cans of meat and one of peaches. Lucy had dismissed the former as "greasy, gristly and most unappetizing," but had eaten some of the peaches. Now she pushed her plate away from her and said, "Sam, why did you kill that man?"

"He gave me no choice," Flintlock said. "As to whether or not Shade Pike needed killing, I don't know. But when he drew down on me I didn't have time to ponder the question."

Lucy shook her head. "All day I've been blaming you for the man's death but now I begin to realize that it was myself who was responsible. If it wasn't for me, Shade Pike would still be alive. Now I wonder if I made a big mistake coming here. Maybe I'm not cut out to live on the frontier and it would be better for everybody if I'd never left Philadelphia."

"This is your house, Lucy, and you didn't make a mistake," Flintlock said. "This is the West, where sometimes both men and women must fight to keep what is theirs. Don't make any decisions until the coming week is over. By then I reckon you'll feel better about living here."

"Will I feel better?"

"Yeah, because you'll know the old place isn't haunted and that you and your intended belong here."

"I hope so, Sam. I really do," Lucy said. "But I don't want to be the cause of any more deaths."

Flintlock nodded. "That's a good way to be. Killing

a man takes its toll on a person and the memory of it never goes away." He shrugged. "But there are some men who need killing, so there it is."

The grandfather clock that stood in the hallway outside the kitchen chimed twice, one of a number of clocks in the house that, with considerable dedication, O'Hara had wound and set to the right time.

Lucy Cully yawned. "I'm all used up, Sam. I think I'll retire."

"I'll see you to your room," Flintlock said.

The girl smiled. "Thank you, Sam. I'm so nervous tonight that I declare, if I saw a ghost on the stair I'd go into a most aromatic faint."

Flintlock picked up a candelabra. "Miss Lucy, the only ghosts in this house are the ones in our own imaginations," he said. It was a small lie. Old Barnabas was around and he could feel his unwelcome, malevolent presence.

Flintlock led the way upstairs, each guttering candle a dim halo of light in the darkness. The floorboards creaked as he and Lucy walked to the door at the end of a hallway that smelled of mildew and old age. Paintings of important people lined the wall opposite the balustrade, most of them dead Confederate generals with startling amounts of facial hair. Surprisingly in such a reb gallery, there hung a portrait of the gallant Custer draped in black crepe, his disapproving blue eyes following Lucy's and Flintlock's every move.

Holding the candelabra high, Flintlock opened the door and stepped inside the master bedroom. Large and sparsely furnished, it contained a fireplace, a huge four-poster bed, a couch and two chairs of wine-colored leather and a much worn Persian rug that covered the floor. Opposite the door were a pair of casement windows with latticed panes, and Flintlock guessed that their view would be of the sky and the dizzying drop of the crag's sheer cliff to the jagged rocks below. The room smelled of burned pine logs, pipe tobacco and dampness, a dark, dead, dreary, empty, echoing space, the life that once dwelled within its walls long gone.

There was no bed linen, only a worn, patchwork quilt and a pair of blue-and-white-striped ticking pillows. Flintlock held the candelabra in his left hand as he tested the bed with his right. "It's soft enough, Lucy," he said.

The girl nodded. "I'll be quite comfortable here."

"You don't walk in your sleep, do you?"

"No, I never have."

"Good. Don't go near those windows. If you fall, you'll drop for a mile."

Lucy smiled. "A singularly unpleasant thought, Sam. But I'll make a point to steer clear of open windows, I assure you."

"Then I'll leave you," said Flintlock, mildly disappointed that there was no invitation to stay. Then a pang of guilt. Lucy was a respectable woman and soon to be wed, not the kind of loud, brassy and obliging female he was used to.

"Can you find your way down in the dark, Sam?" Lucy said. "I'd like to keep the candles here."

Flintlock smiled. "Sure, I'll be just fine. In my time I've walked down a lot of staircases in the dark."

"I fell down the stairs, that's why," Sam Flintlock said, irritated that O'Hara had noticed his limp.

Then, by way of explanation, "It was as dark as night under a skillet."

"Some folks can't see in the dark," O'Hara said. "You're probably one of them, Sam. Not a good way to be, but if you stick to walking down stairs in the daylight you'll be just fine."

"I can see in the dark as well as you can, maybe better," Flintlock said, groaning as he sat at the table, the pain in his back, hips and right leg nagging at him. "Why the hell were you gone so long? And why did you take my Hawken?"

"Who left this?" O'Hara said, picking up a plate of greasy canned beef and peaches.

"Lucy. She didn't like the meat."

"Then I'll eat it," O'Hara said, digging in with the girl's discarded fork.

The breed's long black hair fell over his shoulders and in the gloom of the kitchen Flintlock thought he looked more like a bronco Apache than a half Irishman. O'Hara looked up from the plate and said, "I took the Hawken because it always brings me luck." He chewed energetically on a piece of gristly beef. "I didn't expect to pull the trigger on the old smoke pole."

"And did you?" Flintlock said.

"No, I was strictly an avant-courier."

O'Hara had used the mountain man words for scout, something he may have picked up from the specter of wicked old Barnabas, who'd spent much time around the French trappers who'd first used the term. Flintlock thought O'Hara was showing off but he didn't press the matter. "What were you doing wandering around out there for hours? You might have fallen over the side of the crag and broke your fool neck."

O'Hara let his fork drop onto the empty plate. When he leaned across the table his breath smelled of canned peaches. "I got news, Sam. Shade Pike's boys are all dead," he said.

Flintlock let his surprise show. "You done for them?"

O'Hara shook his head. "Not me. Somebody else." He reached out, took the makings from Flintlock's shirt pocket, and his eyes sought the other man's in the candle glow. "Or some . . . *thing* . . . else."

Not by inclination a smoking man, O'Hara made a mess of the papers and tobacco and Flintlock said in irritation, "Here, let me do that." Then, "You don't smoke."

"Do you have any brandy? No? Then tonight I'm smoking."

Flintlock built the cigarette, had O'Hara lick the paper and then he rolled it closed. He thumbed a match, lit the smoke, waited until O'Hara's coughing fit had passed and said, "Tell me."

Wheezing out his words, the cigarette smoke coiling in his fingers, O'Hara said, "After darkness came down I felt uneasy about Pike's boys. I figured they might come back here looking to even the score for ol' Shade."

"Thought that my ownself," Flintlock said. "But I didn't reckon it was likely. Those three boys seemed mighty beaten down when they left."

"I didn't want to take a chance on them," O'Hara said. He inhaled deeply on the cigarette and immediately went into a paroxysm of coughing.

"Give me that damned thing," Flintlock said. He

grabbed the cigarette, dropped it on the floor and ground it into shreds with his boot heel. "Don't let me catch you smoking again, O'Hara. Tobacco sure don't fit your pistol."

"Doctors say (*cough*) that smoking (*cough*) is good for your (*cough*) health," O'Hara said. "Strengthens the chest and clears the lungs."

"Yeah? Well, doctors don't know everything," Flintlock said. "Now take a deep breath and tell me what happened."

It took O'Hara a few moments to recover, and then he said, "I found them all dead on the switchback. Sam, they were naked and it looked like they'd been cut about by somebody using one of them meat cleavers you see in a butcher's shop."

Flintlock was stunned. "Tell me that again," he said. "Slower this time."

O'Hara did, and then summed things up when he said, "They were cut to the bone, Sam. Just about all their flesh was gone."

Flintlock said, "A bear? There's black bear in these parts and maybe a big grizz or two wandered off the Mogollon Rim. Or a hungry cougar? Plenty of those around."

"It was dark but the mist was gone and I swear there were no animal prints," O'Hara said. "But I did see human tracks, hard-soled moccasin tracks and a lot of them. Only the Apache make moccasins with a rawhide sole."

"The Apaches are long gone, O'Hara, penned up in Florida," Flintlock said. "You must be mistaken about the meat cleaver. It was some kind of animal tore into those four men."

"No mistake, Sam," O'Hara said. "I saw what I saw."

Flintlock thought things through and said, "We'll scout the switchback come morning. I want to see those bodies for my ownself."

O'Hara nodded. "Then we'll leave at first light, Sam, before the supplies get here. Only there are no bodies, just skulls and skeletons with scraps of meat clinging to them." He looked around him. "Where is Miss Lucy?"

"Sleeping like a baby upstairs in her room," Flintlock said.

A moment later a woman's terrified scream echoed around the mansion and shattered the tranquility of the breathless night.

CHAPTER EIGHT

Still hurting from his fall, Sam Flintlock let O'Hara sprint up the stairs while he followed at a limping pace. He heard Lucy Cully's voiced raised to an almost hysterical pitch and then O'Hara's reassuring drone.

"What happened?" Flintlock yelled, his voice hollow on the stairway.

"Miss Lucy saw a ghost," O'Hara answered.

"What kind of ghost?"

"The scary kind."

"Damn it," Flintlock said, hobbling to the bedroom. "I knew she shouldn't have eaten them peaches so close to bedtime."

"There, in the corner, Sam," Lucy said, pointing. O'Hara had lit a candle and she sat bolt upright in bed, wearing a white satin nightgown that had more frills and froufrou than a wedding cake and left her shapely shoulders and the upper swell of her breasts bare. Flintlock thought the revealing gown odd in such a prim young lady and he decided to study on it later, but right then he had a specter to contend with.

"What did it look like—the ghost, Miss Lucy?" O'Hara said. He had his Colt in his hand.

"An old man with long gray hair falling over his shoulders," the girl said. "He wore a coat . . . it looked like leather and it had fringes all over. And he held a mask in front of his face, a hideous, grotesque kind of mask. And he said, 'Boo!' And then something else."

"Boo?" O'Hara said.

"Boo," Flintlock said. "It was Barnabas."

O'Hara stared hard at him. "You think?"

"I don't think, I know," Flintlock said. "The old coot is around. I can smell him."

Lucy was shocked. "Sam, you . . . you know the ghost?"

Flintlock quickly backtracked. "He wasn't a ghost, Lucy. I saw an old man hanging around the place and figured he was looking for a place to bed down so I didn't run him off. He must have found his way into the house and sneaked into your bedroom by mistake."

"But he disappeared like a puff of smoke," Lucy said.

Without any success, Flintlock searched his mind for a logical explanation but O'Hara came to his rescue.

"Miss Lucy, this room was very dark," he said. "I bet the old man slunk out and—"

"But you would have passed him on the stairs," Lucy said.

"Yeah, that's right, O'Hara," Flintlock said. "How come the old man didn't pass us on the stairs?"

O'Hara gave Flintlock a sidelong look, then said,

"There are doors opening onto balconies and widow's walks all over the front of the house. In the darkness he could have easily made his escape that way."

Flintlock nodded as though O'Hara had fairly stated the case. "That's what happened, all right," he said, looking wise.

"But, Sam, how did he get down?" Lucy said. "Did he jump?"

"How *did* he get down, O'Hara?" Flintlock said. "Did he jump?"

That question was met with yet another withering look, but O'Hara rose to the occasion. "In his panic the old man probably did," he said. "Come morning, we might find him out there nursing a broken ankle or leg."

"Oh, the poor man," Lucy said. "We must search for him at once."

As the girl swung her slim legs over the side of the bed, Flintlock said quickly, "Better we wait until first light, Lucy. If the intruder has an injury and crawled into the brush like a wounded animal we'll never find him."

"Sam's right. Wait until daybreak," O'Hara said.

"You mean at cockcrow?" Lucy said. "Isn't that what they always say in the ghost stories?" Her left eyebrow was raised and a shadow of a smile played around her pretty mouth.

"Yeah, that's what we mean," Flintlock said. "Now you get back to sleep, Miss Lucy. And don't you worry about a thing, we'll find that trespasser and let the law deal with him."

"Good night, Miss Lucy," O'Hara said. He blew out the candle and stepped out of the bedroom.

Flintlock followed but Lucy's voice from the darkness stopped him.

"Sam, I think the intruder might be related to you," she said.

Flintlock heard the smile in her voice and became alarmed. "How come?"

"I told you he said, 'Boo!' and then something else, didn't I?"

Wary now, Flintlock said, "Yeah . . . you did. What did the old man say?"

"He said, 'Tell my grandson he's an idiot.'"

Flintlock swallowed hard and then said, "Nah, it sounds like he's one of O'Hara's kin, the Irish side."

"Perhaps that's the case," Lucy said. She lay back, adjusted her pillow, then said in a quiet voice, "I saw a ghost tonight, Sam, but it didn't scare me, not really." Then, turning on her side, "Sweet dreams."

CHAPTER NINE

The hoarse croak of ravens quarreling around the upper levels of the mansion woke Sam Flintlock from sleep. He'd drifted off at the kitchen table, his head resting on his arms, Colt within reach. When he sat up his neck hurt, his shoulders hurt, his leg hurt and the sight of Barnabas sitting opposite hurt worst of all.

Irritated beyond measure, Flintlock said, "You played hob, old man. Why are you haunting a haunted house?"

"You mean that thing with the pretty young lady?" Barnabas said.

"Yeah," Flintlock said. "That thing with the pretty young lady."

"I was just having some fun."

"You said 'Boo,' and be damned to you for a crazy old coot."

"Well, isn't that what ghosts say? Boo?"

"You're a ghost and I never heard you say it until last night."

"I'm not a ghost, Sammy. I'm more what you'd call an ambassador from the infernal regions." Barnabas grinned and held up an ugly, snarling painted mask. "I scared her with this. It belonged to a cannibal chief from the South Seas who had a taste for young virgins. He's now an honored guest of You-know-who and I got his mask. Scary enough to raise the hair on a bearskin rug, ain't it?"

"Why are you here, Barnabas?" Flintlock said. "Apart from scaring young women?"

"Got something for you, what detectives call a clue, Sam. Your ma is west of the Painted Desert, doing fer an old farmer and his wife."

"West of the Painted Desert takes in a lot of country," Flintlock said.

"Maybe so, but it's the only clue I'm allowed to give. You-know-who says you should use the girl for your own villainous pleasure and then kill and rob her and go after your ma. Sound advice from the master of suggestion, Sam."

"That kind of advice I can do without. O'Hara and me will be here for a week and prove to Lucy that this house isn't haunted. Then we'll move on. I don't want to see you or your cannibal mask around here again, Barnabas. You are not welcome here, or any other place, come to that."

The old mountain man shook his head, his gray locks brushing his buckskinned shoulders. "I raised an idiot. Boy, do you know how boring it is to haunt a house? No? Well, it's pretty damned boring. That's why the restless dead don't do it. Tried it myself once, haunted a hotel in Denver and boogered a few folks but I gave it up. There's just no future in it."

"You have no future, old man," Flintlock said. "You're dead and damned, remember?"

For a moment Barnabas's eyes glowed red and then he said, "You're impertinent, Sam. I blame myself. I should've taken a stick to you more often."

"You did, until the day I was man-grown and took the stick from you and broke it over your hard head," Flintlock said. "Now get away from me and this house."

"I mind that well," Barnabas said. "It was up in the Oregon Willamette Valley country when you snuck up on me and took my stick. I always believed in spare the rod, spoil the child. And that ain't from your precious Bible, stupid. It was written in a poem by Samuel Butler in 1664, another one of them sniveling poets you set such store by, Sammy. Ah well, let bygones be bygones, I say. I'm glad You-know-who didn't hear me say that. He's one to hold a grudge, is Old Scratch. Now afore I go, listen up. You're as dumb as a snubbin' post, Sammy, so concentrate on what I'm about to tell you: There are no ghosts in this house. The real terrors, the ones that can kill you stone dead, are all outside."

"What are they, Barnabas?" Flintlock said.

The old man smiled, put the mask over his face and said, "Boo!"

Then he vanished and only the acrid stench of brimstone remained.

"Barnabas is not to be trusted, Sam," O'Hara said. "He may be lying about there being no ghosts in the house."

Flintlock nodded. "Barnabas lies about a lot of things. Hell, no, he lies about everything."

O'Hara took a while before he said, "But I don't

think he was lying about all the real terrors being outside."

"You mean the killing of Shade Pike's boys?" Flintlock said.

"Wait until you see the bodies and make that decision for yourself," O'Hara said.

Flintlock stared at his companion. O'Hara was not an easy man to scare, but in the dawn light as they took the switchback down the rise he seemed shaken, as though he'd seen something that had disturbed him and would take a long time to forget. As a distraction Flintlock glanced at the sky and said, "Looks like it could rain again. Clouding over to the north."

O'Hara, his eyes fixed on the trail ahead, made no answer.

They were about three hundred feet below the crest of the crag when the switchback took a turn north through a stand of juniper and century plants, then widened so considerably a pair of wagons could easily pass each other. The trail here was mostly gravel and sand and heavy brush grew in every break and hollow of the rock face . . . the reason why Flintlock at first saw only dried, black pools of blood but no bodies.

O'Hara swung out of the saddle, glanced up at the still-mounted Flintlock and said, "Over here. Looks like the dead men have been dragged into the brush."

Flintlock dismounted and followed O'Hara to a wide fissure in the rock, its interior hidden from view by a tangled growth of bunchgrass and greasewood. O'Hara kicked aside brush and the shock of seeing three pale, mutilated skeletons grabbed Flintlock's breath and sweat popped out on his forehead. "My God," he said, "they've been butchered."

"Looks like, don't it?" O'Hara said. His face was expressionless but there was real fear in his eyes. "Let's get them out of there."

It took a while until the headless, slashed and torn skeletons were laid out on the gravel. O'Hara leaned against his saddle until the dizziness that beset him had passed and then in a strange, hollow voice he expressed the horror that Flintlock felt. "The killers took heads and butcher meat, Sam. What kills like this? A man-animal? What kind of man-animal? A man-cougar? A man-bear? A man—"

"O'Hara!" Flintlock yelled. "Damn it, that's enough!"

For a moment O'Hara was stunned, as though he'd just received a blow to the gut. He stood silent, blinked himself back to sanity and then said, "Sorry." He searched his mind for something else to say that would explain his moment of madness, but Flintlock put his hand on his shoulder and said, "You've got no call to say sorry to me, O'Hara. This is a sight no Christian man should ever see."

"What do we do with them?" O'Hara said. "We can't just leave them here."

"We bury those boys without telling Lucy. That's what we do, O'Hara."

"Not an easy task, Sam. We'll need shovels, maybe picks, to say nothing of when we can get it done. Day or night, it seems to me Miss Lucy is sure to notice."

"Yeah, I know," Flintlock said. "I reckon she notices everything."

His eyes went to the fissure and then lifted higher. He rubbed his stubbled chin, thinking something through. After a while he nodded to himself. Yeah, it just might work. *Might* being the operative word. The V-shaped fissure in the rock was narrow but fairly deep, as though the crag had been hit by a gigantic ax back in the olden times. But what interested Flintlock most was the thick slab of limestone that tilted across the top of the fissure like an ill-fitting lid. The slab supported the weight of a haystack-shaped mound of talus that had slid from the steep slope of the crag, the accumulation of centuries. The limestone shelf looked none too secure, the massive weight of its shingle and rock burden beginning to tell. Now if he could bring that down . . .

"O'Hara, we'll drag the bodies back where we found them," Flintlock said.

"Those boys will soon stink, Sam. What's left of them," O'Hara said. "Anyone passing this way is sure to notice."

"Not if they're covered by a rockfall," Flintlock said.

O'Hara shook his head. "I'm not catching your drift."

Flintlock pointed out the slanted slab of rock and described his plan. O'Hara was skeptical and said it would never work, that it would take a squad of laborers with sledgehammers to bring down the limestone block.

"We can try," Flintlock said. "The land around here is three inches of topsoil on top of a thousand feet of rock. I don't fancy digging a grave without dynamite, and even if we had any, the boom would bring Lucy running." Flintlock pointed to an exposed corner of the limestone. "I can dab a loop on that and have my horse pull it down. The dead men will be buried

under tons of rock and then we . . . you . . . can say a
prayer and we'll have done our duty."

"Won't work, Sam," O'Hara said. "The ledge up
there must weigh a couple of tons at least. You'll never
budge it."

"I'm sure going to give it a try," Flintlock said.

After he and O'Hara dragged the three headless,
flensed skeletons into the cleft Flintlock stepped into
the saddle, shook out his rope and eyed the slab, calculating distances. He'd had never worked as a puncher
but in the past he'd known one or two who'd been
bored enough to teach a stick-horse cowboy the way
of the thirty-foot lariat. Now he was about to put that
skill to the test. He threw for the projecting corner of
the slab, but the rope slipped off the smooth limestone and had no effect. A couple of more tries didn't
do any better and Flintlock cussed under his breath.
Damn it all, this was going nowhere.

Meanwhile O'Hara had been intently studying the
underside of the slab where it projected from the wall
of the crag. He stepped to his horse, slid his Winchester from the boot and racked a round into the
chamber. Unless he was very much mistaken the slab
was supported by only a thin layer of limestone rubble
that in turn lay on, of all things, an ancient and rotted
tree trunk that had fallen and wedged itself across the
top of the fissure. The whole teetering shebang was
ready to come down, but it needed more encourage-
ment than Flintlock's loop . . . an incentive that
O'Hara was getting ready to provide.

Flintlock's noose slid off the slab again and this
time he turned the air around him blue with his

cussing. The limestone block remained as impassive and unmoving as the Sphinx. There is no greater irritation on earth than the perversity of an inanimate object. Ask any man who ever dropped a collar stud or woman an earring only to have it scuttle away and hide under the heaviest piece of furniture in the darkest corner of the room.

Flintlock was frustrated, all used up. His rope dangled limp and useless from his hand and he stared at the slab with unrelenting hatred in his eyes.

O'Hara threw his Winchester to his shoulder and said, "Sam, move your pony back. This thing is gonna come tumbling down like the walls of Jericho!"

There was alarm in Flintlock's voice. "O'Hara, what the—"

O'Hara fired, fired again, fired rapidly, levering the rifle from his shoulder, aiming for the trunk. There was no uncertainty about results that were beyond O'Hara's wildest hopes. Bullets smashed into dry, rotten wood and it disintegrated. For a moment the slab teetered and then collapsed, bringing down the talus that seemed to explode into hundreds of fist-sized rocks that blasted across the trail like shrapnel. Flintlock's horse reared, tossed him from the saddle and then galloped out of the way of the avalanche. As a thick column of dust rose from the fissure Flintlock staggered to his feet. He was already hurting from his tumble down the stairs and now, battered and bruised by rocks, he felt as though he'd just gone ten rounds with John L. Sullivan.

O'Hara looked from the rockfall to Flintlock,

grinned and said, "Well, that was some fandango, huh?"

Like a man in a blizzard, Flintlock's eyebrows and mustache were white with limestone dust and his attitude was icy. "O'Hara, you're crazy and you're dangerous, a one-man wrecking crew. Do you want me to shoot you now or later, just out of spite, like?" he said.

"Hell, Sam, we buried them poor boys decent under tons of rock like we set out to do," O'Hara said. "They will lie there sleeping in their tomb as long as the mountains last."

Flintlock removed his shapeless hat, once black now white with dust. "Say the words, O'Hara, redeem yourself."

"What words?"

"Damn it, any words fit for a white man's funeral."

O'Hara thought for a while, bowed his head and said, "When it comes your time to die, be not like those whose hearts are filled with the fear of death, so that when their times come they weep and pray for a little more time to live their lives over again in a different way. Sing your death song, and die like a hero going home."

Flintlock turned his bowed head to look at O'Hara. "Who said them words?"

"A wiser Injun than me," O'Hara said.

Flintlock nodded, replaced his hat and said, "I reckon they'll do."

O'Hara didn't comment. His eyes moved beyond Flintlock to the trail and he said, "Wagon coming. Looks like our supplies." Then, a devil in him, "Sam, maybe Tobias Fynes heard about your miseries and is sending liniment."

"And maybe I really should shoot you now," Flintlock said, irritated, scowling through each word.

The freight wagon's two-horse team made hard work of the switchback's incline but when it finally arrived the freckled, teenage driver kicked on the brake, eyed Flintlock and said, "Seen your smoke from a long ways off, old-timer."

"It was dust," Flintlock said, stung by the greeting. Then, "We had a landslide. Name's Flintlock. Are the supplies in the wagon for us?"

"If Flintlock's your name, then yes, they are, old fellow."

O'Hara decided to head off Flintlock's slow burn and grabbed the canteen from his saddle. "Give me your bandanna, Sam," he said.

"Why?"

O'Hara held up the canteen. "Because you need to wash your face. It's covered in dust."

Flintlock untied his bandanna and O'Hara wet it down good and handed it back. "And scrub your eyebrows and mustache."

It took only a few moments for Flintlock to rub his ashen face back to its homely normality and the young wagon driver was surprised. "Hell, I took ye fer an old coot," he said.

"Limestone dust can age a man real quick," O'Hara said, grinning.

"You boys mind clearing the rocks out of the way so I can get the wagon through?" the driver said. "I'm running behind schedule."

Flintlock had taken an instant dislike to the youth

and his voice was edged as he said, "You work for Tobias Fynes?"

"No, sir. My name's John Tanner and I work for the Mansion Creek Freight and Packing Company. Mr. Fynes hired us to take supplies to the haunted Cully place and said we'd meet a couple of mighty rough fellers up there."

"We're the mighty rough fellers," Flintlock said. "Who told you the Cully place is haunted? Fynes?"

"No, sir. As far as I know, Mr. Fynes didn't mention it but everybody knows spooky things go on around this neck of the woods."

"What kind of spooky things?" Flintlock said.

"If you plan on staying here for a spell you'll find out," Tanner said. Suddenly his eyes were guarded. "Didn't they tell you in town about Jasper Orlov?"

"No, nobody mentioned him," Flintlock said.

"I hope you never meet him," Tanner said. He looked around him, intent on the landscape, and then said, "They're around here someplace, Jasper and his clan. Or so folks say."

"He an outlaw?" Flintlock said.

The youth nodded, "Yeah, he's that, and a whole lot worse. He's a legend that some will tell you doesn't exist, but how to account for all the people who've disappeared in these mountains? Half a hundred, maybe, one of them a Ranger who came in from Texas and boasted that he'd nail Jasper's hide to Governor Fremont's front door. He rode out of Mansion Creek with a Colt on his hip and a Winchester under his knee and was never seen nor heard from again. Mr. Fynes, the town banker, says Orlov probably done for old man Cully, and Mr. Fynes always knows what he's talking about."

O'Hara said, "Tell us more about this Jasper ranny."

"I'm telling you nothing else, best you never know, but I do have some advice for you boys—get the hell off this mesa as soon as you can."

"And if we don't?" Flintlock said.

"Then you'll leave your bones here," Tanner said.

CHAPTER TEN

"I planned to offer the driver a cup of coffee but he just turned his wagon around and left without saying good-bye," Lucy Cully said to Flintlock as she stood in front of the house.

"Yeah, he had to get back to town in a hurry to pick up another delivery," Flintlock said, smoothing out his lie.

"Where did you and Mr. O'Hara go so early this morning?" Lucy said. "I thought I heard gunshots."

"That was O'Hara fooling around shooting at rocks. We wanted to make sure Shade Pike's boys were long gone."

"And were they?"

Flintlock nodded. "They won't be coming back this way ever again."

"Are you sure, Sam?"

"Sure I'm sure. They're long gone and in a different place by now."

Lucy's concerned face brightened. "Well, Mr. Fynes did us proud on the provisions. I'm going to cook us all a fine dinner tonight."

"Are you a good cook, Lucy?" Flintlock said.

"Yes, I am. At least no one I've cooked for ever had a complaint."

"I'm a pretty good cook myself," Flintlock said. "At least when it comes to trail grub, bacon and beans and the like."

Lucy smiled. "Well, tonight I'll do better than bacon and beans." Concern clouded her face. "Sam, I've noticed that you're moving very stiffly. Are you feeling quite well?"

Flintlock thought on his feet, unwilling to tell the girl that he'd taken a header down her stairs, had recently fallen off his horse and had part of a mesa collapse on him. Finally, he said, "It's a touch of the rheumatisms. I'll be fine in a day or two."

"Come inside, Sam, and sit down for a while," Lucy said. "I have a fresh pot of coffee on the stove."

Flintlock was sitting at the kitchen table with Lucy, trying to act genteel as he balanced a cup and saucer of thin china that were too small for his big, hard-knuckled hands when O'Hara stepped inside. He answered the question on Flintlock's face and told him that all was quiet.

"So now we settle in for a week and convince Lucy that her place isn't haunted," Flintlock said. He smiled at O'Hara. "I found a pack of cards and some poker chips in the parlor that will help pass the time. Don't worry, I'll take your IOUs and you can pay me later."

"Suppose I win?" O'Hara said.

"Now, that ain't likely, is it?" Flintlock said. Then, as though the matter was not worthy of any further discussion, "Lucy, did you see anything strange when we were gone this morning?"

"No. But I felt I was being watched the whole time, especially in my bedroom where I saw the ghost last night."

"You told me it didn't scare you," Flintlock said. The china cup rattled on the saucer as Flintlock gingerly put it down.

"No, it didn't scare me," Lucy said. "Perhaps I felt a little uneasy, but it soon passed."

"Miss Lucy, if the ghost didn't scare you, then why are we here?" O'Hara said.

"Because we need the money, O'Hara, remember?" Flintlock said quickly. "As far as Tobias Fynes is concerned, it will take the whole week for us to convince Lucy that she has nothing to fear."

"Perhaps I do have something to fear," the girl said. "If there's one spirit here there may be others that are much more frightening."

Flintlock beamed and said, "Now you're talking. That's good thinking, Lucy, very good thinking. When it comes to ha'ants like this one, I reckon it will take me and O'Hara a full seven days to roust out the boogermen."

O'Hara's reaction was more measured. "Woman, you say you are not scared yet I see fear in your eyes. Why is this?"

Lucy did not answer directly. A scion of a Philadelphian patrician family, she'd been taught to keep her emotions in check, and her face was expressionless when she said, "I do so very much want this house to be the home of Roderick and me and I want to raise our family here, if the good Lord chooses to bless us with children. But—"

Flintlock and O'Hara waited.

"But the house has to want it too," Lucy said.

"Give it a week and the old place will come around to liking you, Lucy," Flintlock said. "Hell, I think it likes you already. Don't it, O'Hara?"

"Seems like," O'Hara said. "I haven't heard it raise any objections to you being here."

"And that's a natural fact," Flintlock said. "Truer words was never spoke."

"The house makes strange noises and talks to me all the time," Lucy said. "But I don't understand what it's saying."

"It's saying, 'I like you being here, pretty woman,'" Flintlock said. He smiled. "Trust me, that's what it says. I've heard it myself a time or two."

"I do hope so," Lucy said. She looked around her and shivered. "Oh, how I so very much hope so."

Perched as it was on the lofty pinnacle of the crag where the winds blew strongest, gusts from the north-east wind buffeted the Cully mansion and rattled windows and banged doors as it sighed and blustered around the eaves and sought out every rambling nook and cranny to explore. As it always did the house creaked and groaned on its foundation and distressed ravens fluttered around the high upper floors and cawed in alarm.

"Beginning to blow some, huh?" Flintlock said to no one in particular as he used a piece of bread to sop up the last of the roast beef gravy on his plate. He sat back in his chair and said, "That was an elegant meal, Lucy. The best I've ate in many a year."

"And that goes for me too," O'Hara said.

"You're too kind," Lucy said, "both of you." She drew her shawl closer around her shoulders and said, "When the wind blows like this I find it most distressful, in this house or in any other. I fear that one day a strong gust is going to lift the house all the way up to the clouds and bear me to India or Cathay or some such foreign place and then set me down on a high mountaintop."

Flintlock smiled. "Lucy, if that ever happens, just hold on tight and enjoy the trip. That's the ticket."

"Listen up. Do you hear that?" O'Hara said.

"Hear what?" Flintlock said. Constant practice with revolvers in his early life had left him slightly deaf.

"Music," O'Hara said. "I hear it on the wind."

As a gust shook the house, Lucy said, "Yes, now I hear it. A fiddle."

"And a tin whistle, maybe," O'Hara said.

"Hell, I can't hear a thing," Flintlock said. He stood and said, "I'm going outside to take a listen."

Lucy and O'Hara followed as he stepped out the front door. All three stood still for a moment, letting their eyes grow accustomed to the darkness. The wind molded Lucy Cully's skirt against her legs and long strands of hair laced across her face. The ravens fluttered high among the tall chimneys and peaked roofs and were never quiet.

Flintlock listened into the night and then said, "I hear it. Sounds like some folks are having a hootenanny."

The fiddle music came and went with the surging wind, sometimes thin and distant, other times louder.

"'Little Liza Jane,' for sure," Flintlock said, his head

cocked, listening. Then, in his deep baritone, "*I got a beau and you ain't got none, Little Liza Jane.*"

Lucy smiled and sang, her toe tapping, "*Hambone hammer, where you've been, down by the river, making gin. I know a man that's three feet tall, drink his liquor and have a ball. Saw him just the other day, he had a horse and a bale of hay.*"

Flintlock took up the chorus again, "*Little Liza Jane, Jane, little Liza . . .*"

The tune came to an end and then the fiddle, distant but distinct in the wind, took up the lively "Whiskey Before Breakfast."

"Some feller is giving his fiddle licks and he's pretty good," Flintlock said, grinning, his foot tapping as he sang, "*Lord protect us, saints preserve us, we been drinkin' whiskey afore breakfast.*"

Flintlock held his hands out to Lucy and she stood, fell into his arms and they began to dance a lively reel around the open ground at the front of the house. O'Hara grinned and clapped the measure as the dancers two-stepped, dipped and spun and laughed. Flintlock, high-stepping, thudded his booted feet onto the dirt, and Lucy's swirling yellow dress glowed in the darkness.

The dance finally came to an end when the wind changed and the music faded away into silence.

Lucy whooped, flopped onto the porch steps, threw up her hands and said, "Lawdy, I'm all out of breath, Sam." She smiled. "My goodness, I haven't had that much fun in ages. You're a fine dancer."

"I surely enjoyed it myself, Lucy," Flintlock said, breathing hard. He grinned and said, "I hurt all over but I'll be just fine directly."

"Where did you learn to dance like that?" the girl said. "You are such a cavalier, Sam."

"From old Barnabas. Mountain men sure loved to dance and when there were no womenfolk around, they'd cut a caper with each other."

"Tonight, where did the music come from?" Lucy said.

"Hard to tell," Flintlock said. "I'd say north of the mesa, back in the timber country."

"How far?" Lucy said.

"A couple of miles, maybe less," Flintlock said.

Lucy stood in silence for a few moments, then she said, "The music was wonderful and I took great joy in it, but listen to the ravens. Why are they so afraid?"

"I guess they don't like to see folks dancing," Flintlock said.

Lucy said, "It's been a wonderful evening but I'm going back inside. Suddenly I don't like being out here in the darkness."

The girl walked into the house and when she was gone, Flintlock said, "What's ailing them damned ravens? Why are they kicking up such a racket?"

O'Hara tilted his head and stared up at the birds. The ravens kept up with their noisy agitation and flapped around the house like pieces of charred paper blowing in the wind. "I don't know why," O'Hara said.

"Well, they shouldn't be scaring womenfolk," Flintlock said. "Tomorrow I'll load up the Hawken with buckshot and drive them away."

"Leave them be, Sam," O'Hara said, his long hair tossing in the rising wind.

Flintlock gave him a puzzled look and O'Hara said, "The Apache believe the raven is a bearer of magic and it brings messages from places beyond time and beyond this earth. The messages are carried on the midnight wings of the raven and only come to those in the tribe who are worthy of the knowledge."

"All right, then, are you worthy, O'Hara, being half Injun an' all?" Flintlock said.

"No, I am not, Sam. But the ravens have brought us a warning, so leave them be."

"What kind of warning?"

"That, I do not know. Their message is not for me."

Flintlock's eyes lifted to the dizzying heights of the mansion and for a while he stood still, but then he cried out, stumbled back and almost fell. "Well, damn," he said. "Does that not beat all?"

"What happened?" O'Hara said.

"Nothing happened. But for a moment I thought I saw the house move, as though it was going to come crashing down on top of me."

"The music has stopped," O'Hara said. "Let us go inside, Sam."

Flintlock grabbed the other man's arm. The colors of the thunderbird tattoo on his throat seemed alive in the gloom. "O'Hara, why did I think the house was going to fall on me, huh?"

O'Hara shook his head. "Sam, I have a feeling it's going to be a long week," he said.

And that was the only answer Flintlock was going to get.

CHAPTER ELEVEN

By candlelight, casting moving shadows on the walls, Flintlock and O'Hara were allotted quarters upstairs. O'Hara's bedroom was close to Lucy Cully's, within calling distance, as Flintlock noted. But his own boudoir, a small, cobwebbed space under the roof, had a narrow iron cot, a dresser and not much else. It had obviously been intended as a bedchamber for a servant, and a low-ranking one at that.

Flintlock laid his Colt on the floor beside the cot and then stripped off his buckskin shirt, revealing a stocky, muscular body that bore the puckered scars of two bullet wounds and the jagged mark of a knife that seared red across the ribs of his left side. He'd known going in that the life of a bounty hunter could be nasty, brutish and all too often short. But when a man joins the dance he must be prepared to pay the fiddler. Flintlock pulled off his scuffed, down-at-heel boots, let them thud one by one onto the wood floor and then stepped on sock feet to the dresser mirror. Staring back at him in the candlelight was a strong, square face and blue-gray eyes that measured a man. His reflection

confirmed what he already knew, that he had no claim
to handsomeness and was ill equipped to cut a dash in
front of the ladies. At first sight of him, feminine
hearts did not flutter and they didn't flutter at second
sight of him either.

Flintlock stripped to his long johns and then lay on
the cot, the lumpy mattress promising him no com-
fort. He stared gloomily at the ceiling and closed his
eyes. An hour passed but sleep refused to come and
it was not the fault of the bed. He'd slept in worse
places, in all kinds of weather, usually cold or wet on
ground that grew rocks as a crop and rattlers as live-
stock. Then he realized with certainty what was
troubling him . . . he was under scrutiny . . . somebody
was watching him, and with hostile eyes.

Flintlock rolled off the cot and lit a candle. He
grabbed his Colt from the floor, held the candle high
and looked around the tiny room. Shadows moved as
he explored the dark corners, the ceiling, the floor.
Nothing. Only the spiders watched him. He shook his
head. Damn it all, he was acting like an old maid
who hears a rustle in every bush.

But then Flintlock turned quickly as he heard a
dull *thump . . . thump . . . thump . . .* that seemed to
come from beyond the narrow, latticed window opposite the bed. Flintlock raised his revolver and padded
across the creaking floor on bare feet. Cobwebs hung
from the window frame like the thin, gray hair of a
hag, and the diamond-shaped glass was old and
opaque. A raven fluttered against the window, beating
with its wings as though trying to force its way inside.

"It was you making the noise, huh? Were you spying
on me, bird?" Flintlock said.

The lattice window frame was stiff from age and mold and Flintlock had to push hard on it to get it open. The raven had perched on a narrow ledge but the opening glass pushed it off and the bird cawed indignantly and flapped away on the blustering wind.

Flintlock was not familiar with the ways of ravens and dismissed the incident as the bird's attempt to get inside out of the wind and nighttime cold. He leaned forward to pull the casement back in place and then stopped as something outside caught his eye, a glint of yellow light on the ground below. Flintlock stuck his head out of the window, blinked and looked again. A human figure stared up at him that he finally recognized as a man wearing a floppy black hat and an ankle-length cloak. A lantern had been at the man's feet and now he lifted it and raised it high so that half his face was illuminated. It was a long, narrow face, the eye sockets and the hollows of the cheeks in deep shadow. The man smiled, and in the lantern-lit darkness Flintlock saw the gleam of exceptionally white teeth.

"Hey, what are you doing down there?" Flintlock yelled. "State your name and your intentions."

The cloaked man did something strange. Something very strange and unnerving. He reached under his cloak, grinned and produced a large carving knife that he proceeded to hone on a sharpening steel. Even from his perch at the top of the house Flintlock heard the harsh, rhythmic rasp of metal on metal, a sound Flintlock associated with a butcher's shop, not a cloaked man in the wilderness in the middle of the night.

"You wait right there!" Flintlock yelled. "I want to talk with you."

The grandfather clock in the hallway chimed three as he ran down most of the stairs and, as was fast becoming his habit, tripped and noisily fell the rest of the way. His Colt was dashed out of his hand and skittered across the marble floor. Hurting bad, Flintlock rose and retrieved the errant revolver. Above him on the stair landing he heard Lucy Cully's sharp cry of alarm and O'Hara cursing in English and Apache.

Flintlock didn't pause to speak to them. He sprinted for the door, threw it open and ran outside into the night. But he slowed considerably when the soles of his bare feet came in contact with gravel not unmixed with vicious sandburs. As he grimaced in pain and danced a little jig, O'Hara, wearing boots, hat and gunbelt with his long johns, ran up to him and said, "Sam, what happened? I heard you fall down the stairs . . . again."

"Other side of the house," Flintlock said. "Man in a cloak. Hurry."

O'Hara didn't wait for further explanation—he took off at a run and Flintlock watched him go.

"Sam, are you all right?" Lucy said. Her hair was tied back by a blue ribbon and she wore a demure cotton robe over a low-cut nightdress that showed considerable cleavage, and once again Flintlock was struck by how contrary was this woman.

"Burrs," Flintlock said. "I need my boots."

"What happened, Sam?" Lucy said. "You poor thing, I heard you fall down the stairs."

Using as few words as possible Flintlock told the girl

about the man in the floppy hat and cloak. He didn't mention the raven or the butcher's knife.

Lucy frowned. "This is a most singular mystery," she said. "What would he be doing all the way out here on the crag in the dead of night? Oh, here is Mr. O'Hara come back. Maybe he can tell us."

O'Hara had little to say other than that the strange visitor was definitely a grown man wearing hard-soled moccasins. There were other tracks, possibly of two men, back toward the edge of the crag, both of them wearing moccasins.

"The cloaked man had no way of knowing that I was in the room at the top of the house," Flintlock said. "Why did he stand where he did?"

"He hoped to be seen by anyone looking out a window," O'Hara said.

"Why?" Flintlock said.

"To put a scare into him or her," O'Hara said. "Whoever he was, I think he wants us out of the house."

"Was he a ghost, a restless spirit?" Lucy said, her pretty eyes wide.

"Ghosts don't leave behind moccasin prints," O'Hara said. "Depend on it, he was as human as you or I, Lucy."

The girl shivered in the night air, the thin stuff of her robe no protection against the cold and keening wind.

"I think we'd better get inside," Flintlock said. "Whoever he was, I ran him off and he won't be back tonight."

O'Hara helped Flintlock back into the house by clearing gravel and burrs out of the way with his boots.

Lucy went to bed immediately, making her way with a candelabra that cocooned her in a rising halo of light.

"I need to talk with you, O'Hara," Flintlock said after the girl's bedroom door closed. "Come into the kitchen."

Both men sat at the table and Flintlock took time to build and light a cigarette before he told O'Hara about the cloaked man's butcher's knife and sharpening steel.

O'Hara took in this information without a visible reaction and then said, "Those boys we buried under the rockfall—"

"Had all the flesh cut from their bones," Flintlock said. "Maybe the man with the big knife is the ranny who done the cutting. It may have been Jasper Orlov himself I saw out there. And you saw hard-soled moccasin tracks, the same ones that were at the killing of Pike's boys."

"The Tanner kid says Orlov might be a legend," O'Hara said. "But maybe he's not. He could be as real as you and me."

"If Orlov is real and not just a big story, I'm willing to bet there are dodgers on him. He killed a Ranger, and the Texas rewards could be huge," Flintlock said. "When we get done here we'll go look him up."

O'Hara rose to his feet. "We'll talk about that another day, Sam," he said. "I'm going back to bed."

"You got a thin, lumpy mattress like mine?" Flintlock said.

"No. Mine is about a foot thick and soft as swan's down," O'Hara said. "When Lucy showed me to my room she said the bed was a four-poster and had the second-most comfortable mattress in the house, hers being the first."

"Am I hearing right? She showed you to a room that has her second-best bed and a mattress a foot thick?" Flintlock said.

"She sure did," O'Hara said. "And a feather comforter. She said a cavalier like me needs his rest."

Flintlock was silent and glared at O'Hara, too damned irritated to speak.

CHAPTER TWELVE

Everybody in Mansion Creek knew about Tobias Fynes's kept woman and how he abused her, but he was too rich and powerful to be openly criticized. Half the people in town owed him money, including the publisher of the *Apache County Herald*, the newspaper that could have given any such censure a voice. Editor and reporter Roland Ives was a hopeless morphine addict, a dependency he'd carried home from the War Between the States after he lost his left arm at Vicksburg, and he stepped warily around the fat banker. Fynes had the power to break him by ordering the town merchants to withhold their advertising. Such as it was, the income from adverts announcing ice cream socials or women's shoes at cost was a pittance, but it covered Ives's simple needs. The town physician, Dr. Theodora Weller, like Ives, a piece of driftwood cast up on an uncaring frontier shore, supplied him with his morphine and when their separate pains became too much for either of them to bear, got drunk with him.

"It was the usual thing, he told me, to tend to Estelle

and then keep my mouth shut," Dr. Weller said. She was a tall woman, somewhere in her midthirties, with beautiful, wonderfully expressive black eyes and a finely boned face that was too gaunt to be pretty. "Someday I'll kill him, Roland."

"Not that, Theo," Ives said. "Why would you hang for such a man?"

Theodora managed a thin smile, showing good teeth. "What do I have to lose? My brilliant career as a failed female physician?"

Ives let that go and said, "Was Estelle hurt bad this time?"

"He never hits her where it shows. Her ribs were badly bruised and she had trouble breathing."

"What was the excuse, this time?"

"Fynes accused her of making eyes at Hogan Lord. But he doesn't need an excuse. The fat hog beats her because he enjoys it."

The interior of the newspaper office smelled musty, of ink, newsprint and dust. "Estelle can never return your feelings, Theo," Ives said. "She's not . . . what you are."

"My love, you mean? I know that. Sometimes I drink too much because I know that."

Ives said, "How is Fynes's wife?"

"Ruth is bedridden and wants to die, but she won't give him the satisfaction. She hangs on even though her breast cancer is down to the bone and causes her unimaginable pain."

"She takes morphine?"

"Yes, but to totally ease her suffering I'd need to inject her with five hundred milligrams every fifteen minutes. There isn't that much morphine in the territory, so she suffers. Ruth will turn twenty-seven this month but she looks like a ninety-year-old woman. She won't see her next birthday."

"When I first came to Mansion Creek I thought she was the most beautiful woman I'd ever seen," Ives said. He smiled. "I think I fell a little bit in love with her."

"She's beautiful no longer and Tobias badly wants rid of her."

Ives reached into his desk drawer and produced a bottle of Old Crow and two glasses. He poured for Theodora and himself and then said, "There's a new gal in town, Lucy Cully, old Mechan's niece."

"I saw her, very pretty. Tom Singer over at the hardware store said she's the new owner of the mansion out there on the mesa. Tom was pretty confused about what's happening, but he said Fynes hired a couple of ruffians to guard the girl while she looks over the place and makes her mind up about whether or not she wants to live there. Apparently her intended is a musician or artist of some kind and he'll join her later."

"Her husband-to-be is a poet, a friend of Walt Whitman, but he has a weak constitution and Lucy thinks the clean Western air will do him good," Ives said.

"Another patient," Theodora said. "If he can abide seeing a female doctor." She sampled her bourbon, lit a thin black cheroot and then said, "They say old Mechan's troubled spirit haunts the place. Maybe the girl is afraid of ghosts."

"She needn't be," Ives said. "One of the ruffians Fynes hired is a well-known troublemaker by the name of Sam Flintlock. The other is a murderous half-breed who goes by the name O'Hara. According to what Hogan Lord says, Flintlock is a bounty hunter and sometime train robber. He ran with the James boys and then John Wesley Hardin and that hard Texas crowd and the moccasin talk is that he's killed sixty white men, though Lord says he doubts that's true."

"Why would a gunman like Hogan Lord tell you all this, the pot calling the kettle black, perhaps?" Theodora said. "I treated his broken ankle a while back and he said he doesn't mind seeing a woman doctor. I thought that was big of him."

"It's my job to interview everybody in town," Ives said. "Especially a famous gunslinger like Lord, the man who put the crawl on Buckskin Frank Leslie."

"Did Lord ever tell you why he came to Mansion Creek in the first place?"

"Only that he's working for Fynes in an advisory capacity."

"Advising him about what?"

Ives smiled. "Well, since Fynes is acting as Lucy Cully's lawyer, maybe it's how to find the treasure that's rumored to be buried near her place."

"I treated Mechan Cully for an eye infection once and he didn't have two pennies to rub together. I doubt there's a treasure of any kind up on that cap rock," Theodora said.

Ives smiled. "Only an old, rickety house."

Theodora nodded. "That just about sums it up. Why anyone would want to live there is beyond me." She shrugged. "Unless it's for the view."

When Tobias Fynes got there, red-faced and sweating, Hogan Lord was already seated in the office at the rear of the Mansion Creek Bank & Trust.

The fat man threw himself into the leather chair behind his desk and wiped off his face with a red bandanna. "Sorry I'm late, Hogan," he said. "I had some trouble with Estelle."

"Again?" Lord said.

"She's never learned that I will not stand for sass and backtalk from a kept woman."

"From a whore," Lord said.

"Yes, she was a whore before and she'll be one again after I've had enough of her," Fynes said. "And the way things are going, that will be very soon."

"If you don't kill her first," Lord said.

"The thought has entered my mind a time or two, but I won't swing for her."

Fynes nodded to the drinks trolley. "Pour yourself a whiskey, Hogan, and one for me. My damned women have me all used up."

"That's the trouble of living with two of them," Lord said as he poured the drinks. "I've always found one woman at a time is hard enough to handle."

The chair creaked as Fynes shifted his massive bulk, his stomach as big and round as a beer barrel. He mopped his face again, his breath wheezing. The thick gold watch chain across his belly could have supported a farmer and his family for several years. "Estelle does little things for me," he said. "It's the only reason I keep her around." A brewer's dray rumbled past the office window and from somewhere children yelled and screamed in play. Fynes took a glass from Lord and said, "I'm not a patient man, Hogan. I want the Cully house torn apart and the treasure map found."

The gunman smiled. "Tobias, it's only been one

night. Give it a few days. Lucy Cully hasn't had time to get scared yet."

"She's stubborn, Hogan." He jabbed a finger at Lord. "I warn you, I've read the signs and I think she's stubborn."

"She'll come around. A few days and nights in that place and she'll be running to you, begging you to buy it. The only person crazy enough to live on the top of that crag was old Mechan. Hell, come a big storm and the place might blow away."

"Not before I find the map," Fynes said. A pretty woman in a plain cotton day dress who held a parasol above her blond head against the afternoon sun, walked past the window, hesitated for a few moments, long enough to force a smile for Fynes, and then walked on, her face flushed with humiliation. The banker touched the tip of his tongue to his thick top lip. The woman's name was Edith Cooke and she lived a mile out of town with her sodbuster husband. Fynes held the mortgage on the farm and after two bad growing seasons and no payments he'd threatened to foreclose. Desperate, Mrs. Cooke had traded mattress time for a few more months to pay. Fynes smiled as the woman continued along the boardwalk. He'd enjoyed the dear lady for a while but now was getting bored with her and he planned to foreclose anyway.

"Tobias?" Hogan Lord said.

The fat man turned his attention to the gunman. "Sorry, I was woolgathering. Now, where was I?"

"The treasure map," Lord said.

"Ah, yes, the treasure map. As I told you I'm an impatient man and giving Lucy Cully seven days to make up her mind is too long. Another couple of days will suffice, and if she doesn't come screaming back to town by then I will take other measures."

Lord knew exactly what Fynes meant by "other measures," but he asked the question anyway. "You mean kill her?"

"There may be no other way, Hogan." Fynes steepled his fat fingers and said, "We searched and searched and failed to find the map, remember?"

"I remember."

"Why, of course you do, Hogan. It was a waste of time. The only way is to start at the top of the house and dismantle it board by board until the map is found. There are plenty of loafers we can hire for that kind of work, especially when I offer a substantial bonus to whoever finds it."

"You're taking a lot on trust, Tobias," Lord said. "A man could find it and just stick it in his pocket." Without a trace of irony, he said, "Plenty of crooks out there."

"Every worker leaving the job for the day will be searched," Fynes said. "That will be a condition of employment and where your friend Nathan Poteet and his cutthroats come in. They will do the searching. Any man who objects or looks suspicious will be shot and his body thrown from the crag." The banker's grin was not pleasant. "The luckiest one will land on top of Lucy Cully. Hah!" He waited a few moments and frowned at Lord. "Hogan, I made a joke."

"And a good joke it was, Tobias," Lord said, smiling. "I'm laughing inside."

Fynes's scowl betrayed the fact that he was not satisfied with the gunman's answer, but he had to move on to other, more pressing business. "Of course

Flintlock and the other thug, the breed, will have to go before demolition starts. That is very important, don't you think?"

"Important enough that I was about to mention it," Lord said. "But Sam Flintlock is no bargain and neither is O'Hara."

The banker's impatience grew. "Will Poteet take care of things?"

"If the money is right."

"He'll be well paid." Fynes made a gun of his forefinger and said, "Bang, bang." He performed a credible throwing motion. "And then it's over the side for Mr. Flintlock and the breed."

Lord nodded and rose to his feet. "I'll get in touch with Poteet."

A moment later Hogan Lord proved to Tobias Fynes that he was worth every penny of the money the banker paid him.

A riot of shouts and a woman's scream erupted from the front of the bank and a split second later a young, wild-eyed man carrying a Greener scattergun burst through the office door. He ignored Lord and yelled at Fynes, "My name is John Cooke and you lay with my wife, you damned animal!"

Cooke's finger tightened on the trigger and Lord reacted with lightning speed. As he drew, his left hand fanned across the hammer and raked it to full cock. He leveled his Colt, his finger found the trigger and he fired. Later a gape-mouthed, bug-eyed teller who'd watched from the doorway said that Lord's hand blurred as he drew and fired in a fraction of a second, less time than it took Cooke to trigger the Greener. Lord's bullet slammed into the young man's left temple and Cooke staggered, already dead. His shotgun blast went high and blasted a hole the size of a dinner plate in the timber wall six inches above Fynes's head.

"By any measure, Hogan Lord's speed on the draw and shoot was magnificent," Fynes would later say to a crowd outside the bank. And there wasn't a soul present who thought otherwise.

But the one thing Lord would remember most about the scrape was the fat man's primal shriek of terror when he first saw Cooke charge through the doorway. Lord hated Fynes because of his treatment of women, but he tolerated him because he paid his wages and men in Lord's profession rode for the brand. But after that day he despised Fynes for his cowardice with an intensity that would soon threaten to consume him.

To this day it has never been determined if Edith Cooke was so numb with shock that afternoon that she fell into some kind of dazed trance. What is known is that her blank eyes were dry, her face expressionless as she watched her husband's lifeless body carried to her farm wagon after insisting that she would bury him herself.

Better documented, because so many townspeople saw him, is that Tobias Fynes stood on the boardwalk and loudly cursed the woman as she drove away. He yelled after Edith Cooke that her mortgage was foreclosed and be damned to her.

A week later, in its widely read County Jottings column, the *Herald* mentioned that the widow Mrs. Edith Cooke had left the territory to live with relatives in Missouri and that the long trip had been financed by an anonymous benefactor. Privately, Roland Ives suspected that Hogan Lord had funded Mrs. Cooke's journey but he did not investigate further.

CHAPTER THIRTEEN

That morning when Sam Flintlock rode away from the Cully mansion, Lucy was singing as she did her kitchen chores, all thoughts of ghosts and mysterious midnight visitors seemingly banished from her mind. The reassuring presence of O'Hara with his quietly steady ways and Colt revolver probably helped.

Flintlock was worried about the night visitor and his pantomime with the butcher's knife and sharpening steel and he harbored the nagging feeling that the caped man and the dance music they'd heard were somehow connected. He intended to find out.

As he rode off the crag the morning air was as fine as crystal and in the distance a few white clouds drifted across the blue sky like waterlilies on a pond. It was good to be alive, Flintlock decided, strong as a horse and still young enough to make future plans. Not that he had any of those, at least not yet. After he found his mother and she gave him his name, he'd plan his future then, though he'd always held more than a passing fancy that he might prosper in the dry goods business. Of course he could choose to continue in his chosen profession as a hunter of other men. Time and inclination would tell.

At a distance, Flintlock was an imposing figure. He sat his buckskin well, straight-backed, like one of those statues of whiskery reb generals astride a bronze horse. Under his right knee he carried a Winchester, in the buckled brown leather case under his left, the old Hawken, and in his waistband he wore a Colt with its barrel cut back to the length of the ejection rod. He was competent with all three weapons and a fair hand with the bowie sheathed on his rawhide belt. Flintlock had known some of the best shootists, Wes Hardin, Wild Bill Longley, Dallas Stoudenmire, King Fisher, that wild Billy Bonney kid and a dozen more, but he did not consider himself a member of that distinguished fraternity. In actual fact he was faster on the draw and shoot than most of them.

Flintlock crossed the mesa, scouted around and found an ancient talus slope on the north face of the rise that provided a way off the plateau. Once on the flat, away from the sunbaked cap rock, the air was cooler and he was surrounded by trees, juniper, crab apple, and Arizona cypress and here and there stands of honeysuckle. He drew rein in a patch of dappled shade and built a cigarette, making little sound as he stood in the stirrups and studied the landscape around him. There was no breeze and nothing moved, not even the lizards. Flintlock's eyes restlessly scanned the ground, seeing as far in the clear air as trees and brush would allow. He looked for a circle of blackened grass that would mark the campfire of the fiddle player who was possibly Mr. Butcher Knife or one of his kinfolk. Or better still, he might come upon the man himself. Whoever he was he had some explaining to do. But he saw nothing, only the sky, trees with tall greenery between them, and in the branches of a juniper some roosting blackbirds spread out at different levels like notes on a sheet of piano music.

Flintlock finished his smoke, stubbed out the butt on his boot heel and let it drop to the ground. He kneed his horse forward and for the next hour scouted north until he was stopped by a wall of rock with no clear way around it and he turned his horse and backtracked his way south again.

Nothing. He found nothing. No trace of the fiddle player or the butcher knife man. Finally, as the sky rose to its highest point in the sky, Flintlock swung out of the saddle, grabbed the paper-wrapped sandwich Lucy had prepared for him and sat in the shade under a tree, his back against the trunk. The sandwich consisted of a thick slab of ham between a couple of slices of sourdough bread and he ate it to the last crumb. He then built another cigarette and smoked, thinking things through.

The fiddle playing seemed to come from this direction, but sound is a funny thing and the music could have come from many miles away. Flintlock smiled at the thought. Maybe they'd heard a fiddle being played in El Paso, Texas, or in a saloon in the New Mexico Territory. But the questions still remained: Where did the man in the cloak go? What were his intentions? Did he just vanish off the face of the earth?

Flintlock shook his head. He had questions without

answers and for now that's where the matter must remain.

But then he saw the old man and in a few moments everything changed.

Warily Flintlock rose to his feet, his hand on his Colt, and watched the oldster come. The man rode a gambler's ghost mule with a short-coupled, choppy gait, and from a distance the silk top hat on the rider's head was his most prominent feature. When the man rode closer at the trot, bouncing in the saddle, Flintlock saw a Winchester held upright on his right thigh and a Colt belted high on his waist over a brocade vest and wide-collared white shirt open at the neck. Tan canvas pants tucked into knee-high boots completed his apparel.

And then Flintlock realized the rider wasn't an old coot at all, but a younger man with lank, shoulder-length hair, dirty white in color. The pallor of his skin matched his hair and he wore round, dark glasses, and Flintlock reckoned the eyes behind them would be pink. The man was an albino and on his white mule he looked like a bloodless centaur.

Meeting an albino out there in the wilderness, only the second one he'd ever seen, unnerved Flintlock and he kept his hand close to his gun as the pale man drew rein and said in a pleasant, well-modulated voice, "Why have you come to this place?"

"Looking for a man," Flintlock said. "And I could ask you the same question." Suspicion clouded his face. "Were you anywhere near the Cully mansion last night? It's a big house, sits on a crag on the t'other side of the mesa."

"I've heard of it," the albino said. "But I've never been there. I do not wander far."

"A man visited the place last night, wears a cape and a wide, floppy hat and is partial to butcher knives," Flintlock said. "Ever hear of somebody like that around this neck of the woods?"

"Perhaps," the albino said. He stepped out of the saddle and cradled his rifle in his arm, showing no threat. He extended a thin, white, almost fragile hand. "Well met. My name is Jeptha Spunner. I'm a maker of magic."

Flintlock's big mitt enveloped the albino's slim hand like a grizzly shaking hands with a sparrow. "Sam Flintlock." Then he winced as he felt the steel in Spunner's fingers as they closed around his palm and ground bones together. Flintlock withdrew his hand quickly and shook out the numbness.

"I'm sorry," Spunner said. "Sometimes I forget my own strength."

Irritated, Flintlock said, "Don't forget it again. For a minute there I thought my hand was caught in a bear trap."

Spunner smiled, his teeth as white as the rest of him. "Let me at least try to make amends." He stepped to the mule, reached into a saddlebag and produced a squat black bottle. "Jamaica rum," he said. "A pleasant libation on a lazy fall afternoon such as this."

After Spunner laid his Winchester aside, he and Flintlock passed the bottle back and forth a few times and then the albino said, "I think the man you seek is a disciple of Jasper Orlov, the cannibal."

"I've heard of him," Flintlock said. "You reckon it could be Orlov who visited us last night?"

"No, not Orlov but I'd say one of his butchers. It would not surprise me if that's true," Spunner said.

"But why?"

"A hungry man studies the menu, does he not?"

Flintlock didn't like that. He didn't like it one bit. "Spunner, if that's your idea of a joke, I don't appreciate it," he said.

"It is no joke. In God's name, who can make a joke about men who eat other men?"

Flintlock, stunned into silence, watched a hawk drift against the blue sky, a predator of incredible beauty, wings, body and tail all sharply angled, as though it had been cut from black paper with a razor. Suddenly the bird folded its wings and dived into the bunchgrass . . . and something small gave up its life to feed a nobler and therefore more worthy creature than itself.

"Why hasn't Orlov eaten you, Spunner?" Flintlock said.

"I am a maker of magic and he and his clan fear me," the albino said.

Anger flared in Flintlock, sharpening his tongue. "Where is this Orlov son of a bitch? I'll put a bullet in him, what I call six-gun magic."

"He's behind you," Spunner said.

Flintlock drew from the waistband as he turned, the smooth, graceful motion of the shootist that cannot be learned. His heart pounding in his chest, his gun pointed into empty greenery.

"No, Flintlock, to your right!" Spunner said.

Again Sam Flintlock moved and again he saw nothing.

Furious, he said, "Spunner, are you funnin' me? If

you are, go for your iron and get your work in. Damn you, we'll have it out right here and now."

The albino raised a placating hand and smiled as he said, "I'm not making fun of you, Flintlock."

"Seemed like it to me," Flintlock said, still mad clean through and right then unpredictably dangerous.

"In my clumsy way I was trying to tell you that Jasper Orlov's people can be anywhere," Spunner said. "They move through the trees like phantoms and if you do see them, well, you're already a dead man."

Suddenly, as his anger cleared, a thought occurred to Flintlock. "Did Orlov or his people kill old man Cully?"

"Probably," Spunner said. Then, "No, wait. An old man, you say?"

"Yeah. He owned the Cully mansion I was talking about."

"A few months ago I did see the body of an old man hidden in brush at the northern edge of the mesa. He had been tortured with fire and cut with knives—"

"Orlov!" Flintlock said through gritted teeth.

"No. It was not Orlov. The body was badly decomposed but the knife cuts on the man's face and chest were still visible. Orlov would have taken his flesh."

"Then my guess is that he was tortured by someone who wanted to know where his treasure map was hidden," Flintlock said. He frowned in thought and then said, "There's one man I know who could have done that."

"Who?" Spunner said.

"A man called Tobias Fynes. He owns the bank in Mansion Creek and I don't trust him. Of course, this is a wild guess. It seems that a lot of people knew about the map and wanted it."

"I stay clear of towns," Spunner said. "I have never met the man, Fynes."

"You're not losing anything by that," Flintlock said. He corked the rum bottle, handed it back to Spunner and said, "I was thinking about gunning you earlier and I feel real bad about it. If you got nothing better to do why not come back to the house for supper? Miss Lucy Cully, the new owner, is a mighty fine cook."

"Well, thank you for not gunning me, but I fear I would be imposing," the albino said.

"No, you wouldn't and Miss Lucy would make you very welcome. Maybe you could show us some magic tricks, huh?"

"It would be my pleasure," Spunner said.

Flintlock hesitated a few moments, then said, "Here, you ain't afraid of ghosts, are you? The house is supposed to have a few."

The albino gave his shy smile. "Look at me, Flintlock. Look at my mule. Perhaps we are the ghosts."

CHAPTER FOURTEEN

As soon as he entered the Cully mansion Jeptha Spunner unbuckled his gunbelt and hung it on the hatstand to the left of the door, a gesture that won Sam Flintlock's unspoken approval.

Lucy Cully stepped out of the room she now called the library, a small book in her hand. If she was surprised at the albino's appearance her good breeding did not allow her to let it show. "You brought us a guest, Sam?" she said.

Flintlock nodded. "Met him at the other side of the mesa. His name is Jeptha Spunner and I told him he could join us for supper."

The man smiled and gave a little bow. "I am a maker of magic, ma'am, and I'm at your service."

"A maker of magic?" Lucy said. "How *très intéressant.* I have never met one of those before." She stared hard at Flintlock. "What were you doing so far from home, Sam?"

"It's not far, Lucy," Flintlock said. "The walls were closing in on me and I felt like riding."

"Well, you can tell me all about your adventure later," Lucy said, smiling. Her tone was light but her smile was forced. Then to the albino, "Do come into the library, Mr. Spunner, and let me get you a drink."

The man bowed again. "You are very gracious, dear lady."

Flintlock stepped back outside to put up his buckskin and the mule in the small barn behind the house, and O'Hara joined him there.

"Why did the old man build a stable so close to the edge?" Flintlock said. "I'm glad the horses don't know there's a sheer drop only a few yards away."

"They know, it just doesn't trouble them," O'Hara said. "Tell me about the white, white man."

"There's not much to tell. I was scouting for the ranny with the butcher's knife and Spunner showed up. I studied on the idea of gunning him just on general principle but invited him to supper instead." Flintlock said, "The strange thing is I think I've seen Spunner before, but I can't remember where or when."

"Not an easy man to forget, Sam," O'Hara said. "Like the white buffalo, a man like Spunner is close to the spirit world. It is well that you didn't shoot him. It would bring you bad luck." He handed Flintlock a brush. "Barnabas was here."

Flintlock began to brush his buckskin's back. "I figured he'd show up again sooner or later. He's a bad penny."

"He said to tell you that you're an idiot."

"Yup, just like he always does."

"He says to either kill the girl or take her with you and sell her someplace and then go find your ma."

"I wonder who gave him that advice?" Flintlock said.

O'Hara smiled. "I can guess, but I won't say his name."

As Flintlock and O'Hara talked, the west wind that always seemed to rise in the evening lashed the crag, and the ravens cawed and flapped and fussed in their usual state of alarm. The white mule tossed its head and seemed uneasy.

Flintlock ran the brush down the buckskin's glossy flank and he said, "Spunner told me about Jasper Orlov. He eats people."

"He's a cannibal?"

"Generally speaking that's what rannies who eat people are called. That's why he cut the flesh off Shade's boys and carried it away."

"Where the hell is his home range?" O'Hara said.

"Around here, Spunner says."

"Where?"

"Everywhere, Spunner says. He says if you do see him, you're a dead man."

O'Hara said, "There is a tribe of Indians called the Mohawks who two hundred years ago were eaters of human flesh. They were the most feared of all the red men, so terrifying that whole villages would flee at the approach of just a few Mohawk warriors."

O'Hara stopped speaking and Flintlock waited for more. After a while, irritated, he said, "And?"

"And what?" O'Hara said.

"What's the moral of the story, for God's sake?"

Flintlock said. He moved to the other side of his horse.

"No moral. I say only that cannibals make terrible enemies."

Flintlock paused in his grooming, laid his forearms on the buckskin's back and stared into O'Hara's eyes. "Then listen up," he said. "There's only one way to handle a man-eater and that's to put a bullet in his belly. Starting tomorrow, you and me are going to track down Jasper Orlov and if he's what folks say he is, we'll cut his suspenders for good."

"Sam, we can't leave Lucy in the house by herself," O'Hara said. "We're being paid to stay with her, day and night."

"Well, I don't want anything to happen to her," Flintlock said.

"Neither do I," O'Hara said.

"We'll only be gone a day, two at most," Flintlock said. "Maybe I could talk Spunner into staying in the house for a couple of days. He's got a Colt."

"We know nothing about him, Sam. Leaving Lucy with Spunner could put her in even more danger. Him and this Orlov ranny could be in cahoots for all we know. You don't hire a fox to guard the chicken coop."

"Then what do you suggest?" Flintlock said. "And don't give me no more flannelmouth talk about foxes and chicken coops."

"I say we wait until the week is over and then, if you're still in a mind to, we'll got after Jasper Orlov, if he even exists."

"I reckon he exists, all right, and a week from now

I'll still have a mind to," Flintlock said. "I got a story to tell you, O'Hara. It's about Barnabas and me. So one time up on the old Santa Fe Trail when I was still a boy, me, old Barnabas and another mountain man by the name of Lute Hasty came across a whole family that had been murdered, pa, ma, a half-grown boy and a teenage girl. The girl had been ravished—do you know what that means?"

"I know what it means," O'Hara said.

"And after that happened, she was stabbed with a Green River knife like the rest of them. Are you catching my drift?"

The wind whispered around the barn and guttered the flame of the single oil lamp that lit the place so that the shadows danced. The restless ravens still cried out, apparently for no reason.

"Go ahead, I'm listening," O'Hara said.

"Well, the girl lived long enough to tell Barnabas that the murders had been done by their hired hand, a young man named Seth Reid that they'd saved from an orphanage ten years before. With her dying breath she said Reid had escaped on the Arkansas River by canoe. Barnabas listened and then he said we were going after him. Right after that he said something I've never forgotten. 'Sam,' he said, 'the feller who carried out this slaughter is an abomination and an abomination can't be allowed to exist in a civilized society, or any other society, come to that. It cannot be tolerated and must be destroyed. And by God, that's what we're going to do.'" Flintlock patted the buckskin's back. "We have the same thing here, O'Hara. If Jasper Orlov is indeed a cannibal then he's an abomination and we must destroy him. I won't ride away from here and let such a monster live to slaughter more people like meat hogs."

O'Hara nodded. "I'm with you on that, Sam." Then, "You didn't finish the story. What happened to Seth Reid?"

"Oh, him? Well, we tracked him for the best part of a month and then caught up with him a couple of miles south of old Fort Smith," Flintlock said.

"And you killed him?"

"Eventually," Flintlock said. "When it came down to how to treat a hated enemy, mountain men like Barnabas and Lute Hasty had learned a lot from the Indians. They knew how to torture a man and how to keep him alive for a long time, days, before he begged for death." Flintlock's smile was slight. "I was eleven years old when I watched that, way too young. To this day I wish I'd never seen it. Or heard it."

"Maybe that's why Barnabas is where he is," O'Hara said.

"No, killing Reid like that could be justified, I guess. They did far worse, him and Lute. That is, until a brown bear did for Lute up in the Snake River county of the Oregon Territory. Barnabas and me tracked ol' Ephraim for three days and I killed him with the Hawken. Then Barnabas cut him open and buried what little of Lute he found in his belly. That was a sad funeral for everybody and Barnabas never did get over it, made him even meaner than before and from that day forth he was death on brown bears."

"And were you still a younker?" O'Hara said, half amused.

"Nah, by then I'd just turned fourteen and was man grown. The day I killed the bear, on account of how Barnabas's sight was going, he tied a rope around my waist, pinned the end to the ground with an iron tethering stake and gave me three feet of slack. Then he laid a deer at my feet that had been dead for a while and told me to wait for Ephraim, that he'd come around shortly."

"Was he a big bear?" O'Hara said, prodding to get the rest of Flintlock's tale.

"Damn right, he was big. When he stood on his hind legs he was over ten foot tall and as wide as a barn door. I threw the Hawken to my shoulder and fired and that was one lucky shot. The ball took him right in the heart and burst it asunder. When Ephraim fell that day the ground shook."

O'Hara stepped to the barn door and said, "We'd better get back inside." Then, giving Flintlock a long look, "Real nice of Barnabas to stake you out like he did, Sam. He could have got you killed."

Flintlock put down the horse brush and joined O'Hara at the door. "Oh, Barnabas knew I could get killed, all right. I mean, he was well aware of that risk," he said. "But he said later that he didn't want me to take one look at Ephraim and take to my heels, so he staked me down real good to make sure." He smiled. "Barnabas was never what you would call true-blue, and he wasn't much into pampering kids, even his own grandson."

O'Hara slowly shook his head. "Hell, Sam, did he

ever do something nice for you?" he said. "Something a grandfather might do for his daughter's kid?"

"Sure, he did. One time he gave me a piece of honeycomb after I got stung all over when he made me climb a tree and raid a bees' nest." Flintlock pointed to the thunderbird tattoo on his throat. "And he gave me this and a glass of whiskey for my twelfth birthday."

"That was mighty generous of him," O'Hara said.

CHAPTER FIFTEEN

Lucy Cully, looking pretty in a pink silk dress, and Jeptha Spunner sat on either side of the library fire when Sam Flintlock and O'Hara stepped inside.

"Please help yourselves to a drink," Lucy said. "Mr. Spunner has just been regaling me with tales of his time as a first mate on the steamships out of New York."

"Hell ships, they were called in those days, dear lady," Spunner said. "And I guess they still are. Shanghaied crews, sadistic, drunken captains and the billy club and the lash do not make for pleasant voyages."

Flintlock poured himself a glass of Tobias Fynes's excellent bourbon, found a chair and said, "I never took you for a seafaring man," he said.

"I had eight years of it and that was enough," Spunner said.

"I can't imagine you laying a lash on any man's back, Spunner," Flintlock said.

"I never did, but a time or two when there were whispers of mutiny I was forced to enforce discipline with my revolvers. God forgive me, I sent many a lively lad to Davy Jones's locker."

Flintlock grinned, feeling the whiskey. "Somehow I can't imagine that either."

"Really? How interesting." Spunner lowered his dark glasses and Flintlock looked across the room into scarlet eyes . . . and caught a glimpse of hellfire that was there for an instant and then was gone. But that one hellish glance made Flintlock totally reverse his opinion of the man. Whatever the albino had been, whatever he was now, one fact stood out loud and clear—he was a killer.

Lucy, slightly flushed from the whiskey and the heat of the fire, said, "Mr. Spunner, you perform magic. Will you do a trick for us?"

The albino tore his fire-and-ice gaze from Flintlock and said, "Alas, dear lady, I don't do mere conjuring tricks. My magic is of a much more important kind. I am part of the wonder of the age of steam."

Lucy leaned forward in her chair, as eager as a child, "Oh, please, what is it you do? I am so impatient to hear."

Spunner's voice pitched higher, revealing his excitement. "I'm building a great flying machine," he said. "I will soon experience the magic of flight, and so can you if you ever decide to share in that adventure. Think of it, dear lady, you can soar high above the smoky rooftops and grab a handful of stars."

A stunned silence fell on the room like a shadow. The wind rattled the library's lattice windows and with a soft, grating sound a log dropped in the fireplace and sent up a shower of scarlet sparks. Finally, Lucy smiled and said, "A flying machine, Mr. Spunner? How deliciously droll, yet so exciting."

Flintlock refused to be impressed. "You mean a balloon? I saw one of those once, took a couple of men up higher than the trees and then collapsed and hit the ground. A newspaper reporter feller got a broken leg."

"The reporter was in the balloon?" Spunner said.

"No, it fell on him," Flintlock said, and O'Hara, not a laughing man, grinned.

"How unfortunate," Spunner said. His voice was frosty again. He blinked his strange eyes and glared at Flintlock. "You misunderstood me," he said. "I'm building a flying machine, not a hot-air balloon."

"We still have a little time before supper is ready," Lucy said. "Tell us more, Mr. Spunner."

"There's so much more to tell it would take us well beyond suppertime," the albino said. "But I will tell you this . . . steam is the immortal soul of our modern industrial age, and it's that almost supernatural force that will power my airship."

Flintlock, still angry with himself for being intimidated by Spunner's glare, said, "Airship? Hell, for long-distance travel nothing will replace the stagecoach and the steam train. Everybody knows that."

"Sam has a point, Mr. Spunner," Lucy said.

"Yes, perhaps that is true," the albino said. "But I plan to use the flying ship only on a voyage of exploration, not public transportation." Spunner warmed to his subject. "Think of it, Miss Lucy. I will fly westward across the great Pacific Ocean all the way to ancient Cathay. From thence I will visit darkest Africa and fly north again to Europe. Rome, Paris, London,

I will visit them all and then cross the North Atlantic and back to the Americas."

"Huzzah!" Lucy said. "What a wonderful voyage of discovery, and what a honeymoon it would be for my dear Roderick and me. Oh, the poems he could write."

"Then I'll take you both with me, Miss Lucy," Spunner said.

"And you and your poet will break your fool necks somewhere around the first mountain range you hit," Flintlock said.

"Sam, what a wet blanket you are," Lucy said, frowning. "Now I'm feeling quite melancholy."

Flintlock said, "Lucy, Spunner told me that the Jasper Orlov ranny fears his magic. Well, a flying machine ain't magic and never will be and that's how the pickle squirts."

"You're right, Flintlock, it isn't magic, but Orlov fears me nonetheless. The Orlov clan's village is hidden deep in the woods, but a flying machine like mine fitted with Gatling guns fore and aft could find it and attack from the air. Orlov's people believe that the world will end when fierce dragons destroy the nations by fire. Orlov heard the roars when I tested my steam engine and I believe he thinks I keep a fiery dragon in the arroyo close to my cabin."

"I don't want to talk about Orlov, whoever he is, I—" Lucy lifted her head and sniffed. "Oh Lordy, my roast is burning!" She rose from her chair and rushed toward the kitchen.

As soon as the girl was gone, Spunner looked hard at Flintlock and said, "Take a word of advice, bounty hunter—don't push too hard."

Before a surprised Flintlock could answer, Spunner followed Lucy, calling out advice on how to save scorched meat.

During dinner Flintlock was in a black mood and Lucy Cully kept the conversation light, the only cross words uttered when Jeptha Spunner said that the old house was definitely not haunted, unlike his cabin, which was, and by more than one entity. Flintlock, anxious to stretch out Tobias Fynes's task to its full seven days, told the albino that he was full of bull crap and to quit trying to reassure Miss Lucy that there were no ghosts when they'd only just moved into the house and it was too soon to come to that conclusion. "When I say there are no ghosts, only then can Lucy be assured that there are no ghosts," Flintlock said. "And I need a week to investigate the matter."

The wind had shifted direction and now it blustered from the north and the mansion spoke for itself . . . doors banged open and shut, windows shook, hanging iron and brass pots clanged in the kitchen, and to make matters worse a gray wolf pack hunted close and filled the unquiet night with howls. Lucy quickly changed the subject and Spunner did not press the matter about a lack of specters. For his part, Flintlock was very glad to let it go. He'd spent an anxious few moments having visions of his five hundred dollars flying out the front door and now he needed to relax and digest his dinner.

Despite the wild night, Spunner declined Lucy's offer of a bed, saying that he had urgent business the next day and needed to make an early start and that his own cabin was closer to his appointment.

Flintlock wondered what business Spunner could possibly have in this wilderness, unless it was with Jasper Orlov. But he was glad to see the man go and didn't detain him with a bunch of questions.

"Damn, but that feller puts me on edge, like coming face-to-face with a scrub bull in a canebrake," Flintlock whispered as he and O'Hara stood in the dark hallway outside his bedroom.

"How does he know you're a bounty hunter, Sam?" O'Hara said. "He's never met you before."

"With the thunderbird on my throat and my noble demeanor I'm an easy man to describe," Flintlock said. "Spunner has heard of me, that's all."

The candelabra in O'Hara's hand cast a yellow circle of light in the gloom. The echoing grandfather clock struck two and the wind had finally fallen silent, as though holding its breath, waiting for something to happen.

"I think he spooked Lucy with his talk of Orlov," O'Hara said. "She's sleeping with a derringer under her pillow."

"Or I did, talking about ghosts," Flintlock said. "A belly gun isn't much good against a ghost."

O'Hara shrugged. "Is that a fact? I wouldn't know since I've never tried to gun a ghost." Flintlock opened his door a crack. "We'll keep an eye on Spunner," he said. "I don't trust him. The more I talk with him the more I'm sure he's in cahoots with Jasper Orlov."

"Why?" O'Hara said. "You heard the man. He's only interested in visiting Cathay in his flying machine."

"Maybe. But it could be that him and Orlov may want this house because of the treasure map," Flintlock said.

"Remember Shade Pike told us he'd searched the place and there was no trace of a map," O'Hara said. "So maybe there's no Jasper Orlov either. Spunner never came straight out and said that he'd met him."

"Pike was an outlaw," Flintlock said. "Who sets store by anything an outlaw says? But I reckon there is an Orlov, a damned cannibal, and soon I'll rid the earth of his shadow."

"Well, that's a thought to sleep on," O'Hara said. "I'll talk to you in the morning, Sam."

After O'Hara left, Flintlock stepped into the darkness of his room and stumbled around trying to find the candle. But suddenly light flared, banishing darkness and shadow, and old Barnabas squatted in the middle of the floor, a flaming torch raised in his right hand.

Flintlock was not glad to see him. "I don't need you around here, Barnabas. I've got enough ghosts to contend with."

The old mountain man shook his silvery head. "You're an idiot, boy. Didn't I tell you when you were a younker that there's no such things as ghosts?"

"What the hell do you think you are?" Flintlock said.

"I'm not a ghost, boy. I was a live person, then a dead person and now I'm a half-dead person, an ambassador from beyond. Catch my drift?"

"No, I don't," Flintlock said. "How come you staked

me out as bait for a man-killing grizzly bear, you old reprobate?"

"Hell, I gave you the Hawken, best damned shooting rifle ever made."

"Suppose it had misfired? It was raining that day and the powder could have been damp."

Barnabas sighed. "Then you'd be a dead person like me. Or are you too stupid to figger that out for you ownself?"

The old man's torch sputtered and showered bright red sparks on the floor.

"Why are you here, Barnabas?" Flintlock said.

"You-know-who has some advice for you, Sammy."

"I don't want his advice. I don't want his advice now or ever. Understand?"

Barnabas blinked and said, "He says you're to have your wicked way with the girl, then you've to pitch her over the side of the crag and listen to her scream all the way down. Then you and O'Hara are to mount up and continue the search for your ma. He says it ain't Christian for a man to be called for a damned musket."

"What would Beelzebub know what's Christian and what's not?"

"Because he's an expert on every religion in the world, past, present and future. That's his line of work and he takes it real serious, does a heap of studying."

"Go away, Barnabas, and take the torch with you. It smells like a dead skunk."

The old man rose effortlessly, up, up, until his moccasins hovered three feet above the floor.

"Listen to me, boy," he said. His eyes glowed with scarlet fire. "Hell is full of cannibals and any one of them could tear you apart and crunch your bones like soda crackers. Messing with man-eaters is not a job for idiots." Barnabas cupped a hand to his ear. "Hark! The hunting horn sounds and I have to go." He tossed the flaming torch onto Flintlock's bed and vanished in a yellow cloud of sulfurous smoke.

"Damn you, Barnabas!" Flintlock yelled. He threw the torch onto the floor, did the same with the smoldering blankets and stomped out the fire, his boot heels rapidly rapping on the wood floor like a kettledrum.

"Sam, are you all right?"

Lucy Cully's voice at the door.

"Yeah, I'm just fine. I was smoking in bed, fell asleep and dropped the cigarette on my blanket."

Then this from O'Hara, "Do you need help? I can smell smoke."

"No, no, everything is under control," Flintlock said. "You can go back to bed now."

A few red sparks rose as Flintlock stomped out the last smoldering remnants of the fire from a corner of a blanket. He picked up the still-burning torch, opened the window and tossed it as far from him as he could. He watched the torch cartwheel into the night and then drop over the side of the crag.

"Barnabas, you're a scoundrel and low-down," Flintlock said, looking around him through a pall of smoke.

There came a sound like a cackle of mocking laughter . . . but it could have been the cries of the sleepless ravens.

CHAPTER SIXTEEN

Although the transcontinental railroad reached Texas in 1881, stagecoach services in the Arizona Territory connecting settlements and their mining, business and commerce centers were just beginning and would continue for the next forty years. Thus the arrival of a stage in Mansion Creek was a matter of great excitement that always drew a crowd of onlookers.

Tobias Fynes, moodily gazing out his office window into the bright morning, was one of them.

A tall man, a pugilist by the look of his flattened nose and the scars on his battered face, lifted down a wicker wheelchair from the top of the stage and placed it near the open door. A moment later a pale young man with a black patch over his left eye emerged from inside and stepped into the street. He was thin to the point of frailness with the narrow, esthetic features of the artist and dreamer. Strands of lank brown hair fell over his narrow shoulders and a great silk cravat, black to match his frock coat, flounced at his throat. A high-crowned hat with a floppy brim completed his attire and his one good eye was blue and as bright as that of a sparrow.

At first Fynes dismissed the man as just another consumptive invalid come west for the good of his health . . . but then bit by bit it dawned on him. The young man looked like a touring, third-rate actor but there was no theater in Mansion Creek. Then he could only be Lucy Cully's intended, the poet, a city dude, by the look of him. Just then the damned rhymester was prancing around the wheelchair, his pale hands hanging from his coat sleeves as limp as week-old lettuce.

Fynes yelled for one of his junior tellers and when the frightened young man stepped into the office the banker said, "Your eyes are younger than mine. Is that Poke Henry up on the driver's seat?"

The man said it was.

"Then get him over here. I need to talk with him," Fynes said.

Poke Henry was a wiry, buckskinned old coot of an indefinite age. He'd scouted for General George Crook during the winter campaigns of the 1870s that had finally pacified the Apaches, and in 1883, riding with the Texas Rangers, he'd outdrawn and killed the Mexican bandit Ramiro Callaraga. If he was intimidated by Fynes's massive bulk or in awe of his importance, he didn't let it show.

"Good to see you again, Poke," Fynes said. "Have a good trip?"

The driver nodded. "Uneventful, and that's just as well since I got a famous person on board."

Fynes lost his smile. "Is that the man with the eyepatch?"

Henry's eyes moved to the street. "No, it's the older feller being helped out of my stage right now."

Fynes followed the driver's gaze and saw a well-built man with gray hair and beard being helped into the wheelchair. "Is that him?" he said.

"Yup, that's Walt Whitman the poet."

"Never heard of him," Fynes said. "He looks more like a blacksmith than a poet."

"Well now, that don't surprise me none, I mean that you've never heard of him," Henry said. "On account of how he's mostly famous back East and in England. I was told he has friends in high places in Washington, but I don't know about that."

"And the one with the eyepatch?"

"His name is Roderick Chanley. He's a poet too, but he ain't famous. He's here in the territory to wed his intended."

Fynes nodded as though that was something he knew already and said, "And the bruiser?"

Henry grinned. "Dang, Tobias, I never knowed you to be so interested in my passengers afore. You drumming up business for your bank?"

"Yes, that's exactly what I intend to do. Now, who is the tough?"

"His name is Rory O'Neill, a Limerick man and now a bare-knuckle booth fighter out of Boston town. He's a bodyguard for Walt Whitman on account of how the old man gets a lot of threats." Henry smiled. "Ol' Walt ain't exactly what you'd call a ladies' man, if you catch my drift."

"Thank you, Poke," Fynes said. "I'm sure I can drum up some profitable business with those three."

After Henry left, Fynes hurried to the premises of the *Apache County Herald* and he was red-faced and sweating like a hog when he barged into Roland Ives's office.

Without ceremony he said, "Did you see the stage come in?"

"Sure did, Mr. Fynes," Ives said, being civil to a man he hated, but one who held his mortgage. "Walt Whitman was one of the passengers and I was sad to see him look so ill."

"That's who I wanted to talk to you about," Fynes said. "How famous is he back East?"

"Pretty famous. His *Leaves of Grass* collection of poems was well received in certain quarters, especially in New York and London. Why do you ask?"

"If he dies he'll be sorely missed, huh?" Fynes said.

"I imagine so," Ives said. He was puzzled. Why was the fat man so interested in Walt Whitman, of all people? It just didn't add up.

Fynes cut his visit short. "See you later, Ives," he said, heading for the door.

"Yes, see you later Mr. Fynes," Ives said, frowning.

By the time Tobias Fynes reached the Ma's Kitchen restaurant, dark arcs of sweat stained the armpits of his pale blue sack coat, and his celluloid collar chafed his bull neck. As he'd expected, Hogan Lord sat at his favorite table, his back against the wall so he had a view of the door. He had a pot of coffee and a single cup before him and an untasted bacon sandwich, cut into two triangles, lay on a plate.

Fynes flopped into a chair that looked too spindly for his massive weight and without preamble said, "We're in trouble."

Lord said nothing, waiting for Fynes to explain himself.

"Did you see the stage come in?" Fynes said. Then, without waiting for an answer, "Lucy Cully's intended, that poet feller, is here and there's somebody with him. You ever hear of Walt Whitman?"

Like many Western men of that era, Hogan Lord was well read and he always carried a volume in his carpetbag when he traveled. Currently he was reading Carlyle's history of the French Revolution and as yet unread, a book of the philosophical musings of John Stuart Mill.

"Whitman's *Leaves of Grass* is well known as are some of his other works, particularly his essays," Lord said. "He supports his widowed mother and invalid brother so he just scrapes by." Lord shrugged. "Some people, including other poets, call him a genius and I'm not going to argue with that assessment."

"Just answer me one question," Fynes said. "Can we gun the son of a bitch?"

"We can," Lord said. "But his death might have repercussions. He is quite famous, you know."

Fynes slammed a fist onto the table so hard that heads turned in his direction. Lowering his voice, he said, "I was afraid of that." Then, after a few moments' thought, "But he could meet with an unfortunate accident, couldn't he?"

"Anything is possible," Lord said. "But now you've added two more people who must be killed for your plan to work."

"Three. Whitman has a bodyguard with him."

Suddenly Lord showed interest. "A gun?"

Fynes shook his head. "A prizefighter. He's a big man with a broken nose, a real pug."

"All right, then with the pug and Sam Flintlock and O'Hara, Poteet and his boys will have to kill six people, one of them a pretty young woman. And to add to your misery, Tobias, I just remembered that I've heard the name Roderick Chanley before. Roland Ives had an old copy of the *Illustrated London News* that he gave me to read when I was laid up with a broken ankle that time. I remember it because a writer compared Chanley to Shelley and Keats and said he was just as sickly. At the time I thought that was funny."

"Who the hell are Shelley and Keats?" Fynes's left eye twitched, a symptom of his agitation.

"A couple of dead English poets," Lord said. He grinned. "I told you they were sickly."

Fynes was not in the mood for levity. "Hogan, if we gun that many white people it will be noticed. It could be messy, very messy."

Lord's grin widened. "Two well-known poets and a young bride-to-be with stars in her eyes numbered among the slain? I'd say it will be noticed."

"Hogan, I want the Cully house," Fynes said. "I want it real bad. Say something to please me. I need to hear some good news for a change."

"All right, then here's my advice, Mr. Fynes. Don't make a move until Whitman goes back East."

"When will that be?" Fynes's heavy face with its pendulous jowls took on the look of a grotesque, petulant cherub.

"I'll find out for you and we'll go from there," Lord said.

"All right, but in the meantime tell Poteet to stand by," Fynes said. "If I'm pushed to it I'll kill them all and blame it on Jasper Orlov."

"He's a myth," Lord said. "A boogerman made up by a bunch of rubes to scare their children into bed at night."

"Hell, I know that but the folks around town will believe anything I tell them," Fynes said. "It's easy to pin six killings on a fairy-tale monster. Who can ever prove that Orlov didn't do it?"

Lord was about to speak but the words died in his throat as the door burst open and a freckled youth stuck his head inside and yelled, "Fight!"

It was still early in the day and the three Macklin brothers were only half drunk, but intoxicated enough that they figured a duded-up city slicker and an old graybeard in a wheelchair were fair game for some teasing. Why the brothers ignored the significant presence of Rory O'Neill would never be explained. It could be the brothers were too drunk to notice, but it's more likely that their entire attention was fixed on Roderick Chanley and Walt Whitman in the same way that a hunter has eyes for only the antlered buck in the clearing and ignores everything else.

At first the Macklin teasing seemed innocent enough, good-humored play by three high-spirited young men out for a little fun. Bruno, the oldest brother, a man generally considered by those who knew him as an ignorant lout and bully, pushed Chanley away from the wheelchair, grabbed the handles and then, grinning, leaned over and said to Whitman, "Let's go for a ride, pops."

The poet took it all in stride. He smiled, nodded and didn't seem in the least afraid or concerned, an artist prepared to enjoy an experience new to him, perhaps to be put into verse at a later time. Cheered on by his brothers, Tom, at twenty-three the youngest, and Dave, who was just as loutish and bullying as his older brother, Bruno tipped back the wheelchair so that the small front wheels lifted a foot off the ground and Whitman, now looking a little worried, quickly grabbed on to the arms for support. A grinning Bruno then bounced the chair up and down and there was a real possibility he could tip its occupant into the dirt.

Then things started to go wrong, very wrong.

A respectable-looking man among the crowd of onlookers that had gathered yelled to Bruno, "Here, that won't do. That man has friends here."

Roderick Chanley, his sensitive face flushed with anger, also objected to the horseplay. He grabbed Bruno by the shoulder and tried to pull him away from the wheelchair. He got a hard right cross for his pains that slammed into his chin and dropped him like a puppet that just had its strings cut. Bruno watched Chanley fall, laughed and grabbed on to the chair again.

"Let him be."

Bruno turned and saw Rory O'Neill advancing on him, his fisted hands at his side. Confident that his brothers would pitch in, Bruno held his ground and put up his dukes. He'd won too many fist, skull and boot fights against unskilled, flailing cowboys and frightened rubes to be intimidated by O'Neill. But he should have been aware of the man's determined chin and his athletic economy of movement, the hallmarks of the professional pugilist.

Bruno grinned and said, "Well, well, well, slicker. I guess I'm gonna have to take you ap—"

O'Neill moved very fast. He backhanded Bruno across the bridge of his nose with the hard, calloused edge of his hand. The bone broke and immediately the lower part of Bruno's face was covered in streams of blood and mucus. Macklin turned his head, spat scarlet and then threw a left. O'Neill ducked the punch and slammed a right and a left into Bruno's soft belly and then followed through with his head, splitting the man's left eye to the bone. His face a mask of gore, Bruno Macklin knew he was in big trouble, but with his younger brothers and half the town watching he had to win this fight or never show his face in Mansion Creek again.

But O'Neill, coldly professional, almost detached, was merciless.

He moved in on Bruno, brushed aside his increasingly feeble punches, and hammered his rock-knuckled fists into the younger man's face and belly. Pounded into a bleeding pulp, Bruno held on to O'Neill and attempted to pin the fighter's arms to his side. In desperation he tried a head butt, a move his raised shoulders and stiffened neck telegraphed.

O'Neill, his face expressionless, sidestepped Bruno's clumsy attack and landed a roundhouse right to the man's chin. His jaw broken, Bruno Macklin whimpered, staggered back a few steps and then lowered his fists, signaling his defeat.

His experience in the professional ring coming to the fore, it did not enter into O'Neill's thinking to further punish a surrendered opponent. He dropped his hands, stepped back and without a word or a further look at Macklin he wheeled Walt Whitman back to John Tanner's freight wagon that had drawn up behind the stage. Bruno Macklin fell to his knees, sobbing. Perhaps he would have sobbed louder had he known that his days as a fighting man were over. The legacy of his one-sided fight with O'Neill was a glass jaw that could never again take a punch. His brothers wanted no part of Rory O'Neill and, their scared faces ashen, they gave the prizefighter a wide berth as they carried away what was left of brother Bruno. The Macklin boys, who owned a two-by-twice ranch ten miles outside of town, soon left the territory and were never heard from again.

CHAPTER SEVENTEEN

With sullen eyes Tobias Fynes watched the big prizefighter take apart Bruno Macklin, a tough man who was dangerous to cross, or so people said. "The pug is yet another complication," he said.

Hogan Lord nodded. "You pay me to take care of complications."

They stood on the boardwalk outside the bank. Over by the stage blood stained the ground and Poke Henry kicked at it with the toe of his boot.

"I want that house, Hogan," Fynes said. "The sooner we bring this thing to a head the sooner I can tear it apart." He thought for a few moments and then said, "Sam Flintlock is another complication. How about you lure him into town and then take care of him?"

"Gunfight him, you mean?"

"What else?"

"Flintlock is no bargain. I won't draw down on him unless I'm pushed to it."

"Hell, then listen to me—I'm paying your wages and you're pushed to it."

"Not yet. In a few days' time Flintlock will come collect his five hundred dollars and ride on out of here. If he does, I won't stand in his way."

"Well, let's hope that's how it happens," Fyne said. He took out his gold pocket watch, glanced at it and snapped the lid shut. He grinned. "It's ten o'clock, time I went to spend some morning time with Estelle."

Hogan Lord watched the fat man waddle away, once again deeply offended by Fynes's crudity and lack of respect for women, and that included his own dying wife. Raised among Southern gentlemen who held fast to the unwritten rules of the Culture of Honor that demanded people avoid intentionally offending others and maintain a reputation for not tolerating such improper conduct in anyone else, the Culture included the notion that ladies, no matter their position in life, should never be insulted by a gentleman. Southern men were expected to be chivalrous toward women in word and deed and the women of the South showed those same qualities, a reason why a former Georgia belle like Ruth Fynes never openly criticized her abusive husband to anyone.

Tobias Fynes ignored the code of the gentleman and seemed to delight in constantly putting his lack of good breeding on display as though he were proud of it. No wonder then that Lord, raised in the Southern tradition, had grown to hate him.

Out of idle curiosity and nothing more, the gunman walked in the direction of the stage. The prizefighter saw him coming, his eyes dropped to Lord's gun, and he quickly placed himself in front of Whitman and his wheelchair.

Lord stopped, lit a cigar to show that his hands were busy, and from behind a cloud of blue smoke he said, "You must be Mr. Walt Whitman, the poet. I hope I'm not intruding."

Whitman smiled in his gray beard and said, "Stranger, if you in passing meet me and desire to speak to me, why should you not speak to me? And why should I not speak to you?"

"Name's Hogan Lord." He extended his hand. "It's an honor to meet you."

Lord had expected an invalid's limp, four-fingered dead fish but to his surprise there was steel in Whitman's dry grasp, as though the man spent his day arm-wrestling blacksmiths.

The poet waved a hand. "This is Roderick Chanley, my fellow traveler. As a poet he's as I am, as bad as the worst, but, thank God, as good as the best."

Lord shook hands with Chanley. The man was beautiful rather than handsome and the eye patch added a rakish look. His left cheekbone was red from Bruno Macklin's fist but apart from that he seemed fine. But not healthy. There was a gray pallor about Chanley's delicate features and his voice when he said to Lord, "Pleased to meet you," was weak and slightly labored.

Whitman then introduced the rather distant Rory O'Neill as a "pugilist of renown" and then John Tanner as "the young man who will carry us to our destination."

Tanner and Lord exchanged glances, and then the

youngster said, "Are you gentlemen sure you want to do this? Maybe you'd be better staying at the hotel and conducting your business from there."

"Why do you say this?" Roderick Chanley asked.

Tanner said, "The switchback trail up the mesa to the crag where the house sits is difficult." He looked at Whitman, who seemed very weak and slumped in the wheelchair. Then Jasper Orlov shouldered his way into the young man's mind. "And there's always the possibility of . . . outlaws," he said.

Walt Whitman smiled. "My dear young man, the future is no more uncertain than the present. We will proceed as planned."

Hogan Lord said, "How long do you aim on staying, Mr. Whitman?"

That question was information gathering for Tobias Fynes.

"Not long," the poet said. "I've been very ill and Roderick suggested the clean Western air will help me recover."

"Help both of us recover," Chanley said. He spoke directly to Lord. "I too have been sick."

"Sorry to hear it," the gunman said with as much sincerity as a robust man could muster. Then to Whitman, "So you'll be in the territory for at least a couple of months."

"Oh dear, no," Whitman said. "I plan to return to New Jersey by the end of September. When is that? Yes, two weeks from now. I must leave before the weather turns cold and I'm too ill to travel." Whitman read the concern in Chanley's face and said, "I do not expect a cure in two weeks or two years, Roderick. I accept reality and dare not question it." He smiled, his good, open smile. "Besides, nothing can happen to me that is more beautiful than death."

Hogan Lord had most of the information he needed. He touched his hat and said, "Have a safe journey, gentlemen." Then he turned on his heel and walked back to the bank.

"Two weeks for Whitman," Tobias Fynes said. "What about the other one?"

"I don't know, but I'm sure the prizefighter will leave with Whitman," Hogan Lord said. "That's one less complication."

Fynes grunted his agreement as he rose from his chair and poured a couple of drinks. One whiskey he kept for himself and the other he passed to Lord. "We're just a few weeks away from being rich men, Hogan," he said. He raised his glass. "Here's to a speedy conclusion to our glorious enterprise."

"Even if we have to step over a few dead bodies to get there," Lord said.

"Then so be it. What's the saying? You can't make a cake without breaking a few eggs."

"Something like that," Lord said.

"You don't seem yourself today, Hogan. Flintlock preying on your mind? Or is it the Cully girl?"

Lord shook his head. "No, I can take care of Flintlock and the girl if need be. But, damn it, there's something about all this that doesn't feel right."

"Your conscience troubling you?"

"I learned to live with my conscience years ago. It's just a feeling in my gut that we're up against something . . . somebody . . . more cunning and powerful than either of us."

"In this part of the territory there's no one more powerful than me," Fynes said. "And I'm pretty cunning myself, come to that." He gave Lord a sympathetic look. "When did you last have a woman?"

"It's been a while."

"Then that's what you need, man. A woman will make you relax and help you put your fears to rest. Go see Kate Coldwell. She knows a trick or two that will cure what ails you. I guarantee it." The fat banker had been talking in an amiable, joshing tone, but suddenly he became deadly serious. "Hogan, I need your smarts and I need your gun. Don't turn traitor on me now. The stakes are too high." Then a threat. "I don't want to put my trust in an illiterate brute like Nathan Poteet, but by God, Hogan, if I have to, I will."

Lord didn't allow himself to get angry. His voice even, he said, "I never in my life turned quitter. I'll see this thing through to the end, whatever that end might be."

"Hogan, don't think of our enterprise as an ending, consider it a beginning," Fynes said. "Once we find the treasure map we'll be only a few shovelfuls of dirt away from a fortune."

"Are you even sure there is a treasure map?"

"Of course there is and I would have it already had not the Cully woman decided to occupy the house."

"We could have demolished the place and then set whatever was left of it on fire," Lord said. "That was a missed opportunity."

"I thought the bitch would sell," Fynes said. "But you're right, I could have acted earlier and told her the place burned down. But then, the whole town knew Lucy Cully was left the mansion by her uncle and when I sent demolition crews up to the crag questions would have been asked."

Fynes leaned forward in his chair, trying to make his sincerity obvious. "There is a map, Hogan. I was the one who toasted Mechan Cully's feet and I was there when he died. The old man was stubborn and kept his mouth shut but it was pretty clear that he was hiding something."

Lord rose to his feet. "Thanks for the drink," he said.

"Thanks for the drink, Tobias, you mean," the fat man said.

"Of course, Tobias," Lord said.

Fynes stared at the gunman's back as he left. His eyes calculating, he decided that Lord could be trouble and was worth watching for signs of weakness or lack of resolve. Thank God for Nathan Poteet. The outlaw was just as fast on the draw and shoot as Lord and as pitiless a man as he'd ever known. It was a time to watch and wait.

Hogan Lord left the bank and made his way to a frame and tar paper shack about twenty-five yards behind the saloon. Lord rapped his knuckle on the rough timber door and when it opened he said, "Howdy, Kate, I need to spend some time with you."

A slender arm reached out, grabbed Lord by the lapel of his coat and pulled him inside.

CHAPTER EIGHTEEN

Lucy Cully sat naked in an old tapestry wing chair she'd discovered in the topmost room of the mansion, the sharply angled slope of the roof just a few feet above her head. She closed her eyes and listened to the house breathe. The walls creaked with its every intake of breath and she fancied that the house whispered to her, assuring her that all was well. Never, in all of her twenty-two years had she known such tranquillity, serenity, the peace of mind that came with the house's assurance that it would take care of her. Outside, ravens flapped around tall chimneys that were a dizzying height above the crag that bore the mansion's great weight, and the birds, as black as midnight, called out to her constantly, telling her that all was well.

Born and raised in genteel poverty that denied access to the upper levels of Philadelphia society, owning her own home had once been an impossible dream for Lucy Cully. The aunt who raised her after the death of her parents "took rooms" on the less-desirable upper floor of a large terraced building in an unfashionable part of the city. Aunt Phoebe, half German and unapologetically Teutonic, living on a small inheritance from a deceased relative in Berlin, did her best to keep up appearances but her visits to the pawnshops became more and more frequent as Lucy grew to womanhood. Gentlemen callers were discouraged, partly due to the prohibitive cost of tea and cake but mostly because Aunt Phoebe, a lifelong spinster and by her own account still a virgin, distrusted men and their devious ways.

"My child," Aunt Phoebe said on Lucy's thirteenth birthday, "a man will do his utmost to lure you into his bed with his empty, honeyed words. You must resist this temptation with all your heart and soul. Once he has his iniquitous way with you, he'll cast you out into the street and slam the door on your bustle. Men are wicked, wicked creatures that set traps for the unsullied maiden and are to be avoided at all costs."

However, Aunt Phoebe made an exception for Roderick Chanley. A sickly, impoverished poet who had lost his left eye in a childhood accident, he was not a threat and had never revealed the slightest indication of laying siege to Lucy's maidenhood. Nevertheless, Aunt Phoebe made sure the young couple were never left alone for very long and touching was strictly verboten.

Now Lucy had her own home and there was a tantalizing possibility that old Mechan Cully had hidden a treasure map somewhere within its walls. She smiled to herself and settled deeper into the chair. She felt that she and the towering mansion were becoming one . . . but slowly . . . a pair of shy, hesitant lovers taking their first steps along the path to romance.

For the first time in her life Lucy had a home that was hers and hers alone and she made a vow that she would never leave it.

"Hey, Lucy, you got visitors!"

It was Sam Flintlock's stentorian voice calling from the bottom of the stairs.

"I'll be right there, Sam," she said.

Lucy stood and when she reached the foyer she squealed in delight and ran into Roderick Chanley's arms. After a while she freed herself from the young man's embrace and said, somewhat breathlessly, "Roderick, why are you here? And you brought dear Mr. Whitman with you." The girl smiled. "I declare, Roderick, you're such a man of mystery."

Chanley smiled. "No mystery, dear one. I couldn't bear to be parted from you one minute longer. When you left Philadelphia my muse fled with you, but even now I feel it returning to me, filling my head with wondrous words that need only be marshalled together and be born again as an ode to happiness. As for Walt, I convinced him that a spell in the West would restore him to good health and here he is."

Whitman nodded and then smiled. "It was an arduous journey to say the least, but an interesting one and one I'm glad I made. I have learned that to be with those I like is enough and standing here with you, Lucy, and Roderick pleases my soul."

"Then we must retire to the parlor and celebrate with a glass of wine," Lucy said. Her eyes moved to the big man with a broken face who carried in a valise. "And you are?"

"Allow me to introduce Mr. Rory O'Neill, a pugilist and bodyguard courtesy of my friend, the overly protective Mark Twain," Whitman said. "I told him that this old body is hardly worth guarding, but he would not listen and Rory is the result."

Roderick Chanley said, taking Lucy's hand, "Come now, Walt, Mr. Clemens considers you America's greatest living poet and as such you are a national treasure well worth guarding." He lifted the girl's hand in his and gently, one by one, kissed her fingertips. "And now, my dearest, shall we restore ourselves with a glass of wine and recount our adventures?"

"Of course," Lucy said. "Mr. Whitman, please come this way."

A product of the Victorian class system and her aunt's upper-crust pretensions, Lucy did not invite O'Neill into the parlor. As a member of the servant order he would be ignored until needed, as were Flintlock and O'Hara. The arrival of her intended and Walt Whitman, by the nature of their calling both comfortably upper middle class, had awakened a latent snobbishness in Lucy Cully.

Sam Flintlock watched this without understanding any of its implications. All he knew was that he'd not been invited to the party and the big man who looked like a fistfighter probably needed a drink. He asked that very question of O'Neill and the big feller smiled and in a pleasing Irish brogue, said, "Indeed, your honor, that would be most welcome."

"Call me Sam and this here Injun studying on your scalp is O'Hara."

O'Neill shook hands with both men and then followed them to the kitchen.

Once settled at the table with a bottle of whiskey, Flintlock said, "How was your trip, Rory?"

"Tiring but uneventful, until we arrived in Mansion Creek, that is, and then things took a turn for the worse."

"What happened?" Flintlock said.

O'Neill told of his run-in with the Macklin brothers and O'Hara said, "Not exactly a warm welcome to the Arizona Territory, huh?"

"I would say it wasn't," O'Neill said, "and not one I'd expected."

"So how is this Bruno Macklin? He sounds like a bully used to picking on weaker folks," Flintlock said.

"Yes, he was a bully and probably a braggart to boot. As to how he is, I suppose that right now he's not feeling very well."

Flintlock smiled. "Broken jaw. Serves him right."

"A man who can't fight should never put up his dukes, in or out of the ring," O'Neill said. "Besides, Macklin should have known better than to pick on an unhandsome fellow like me." He smiled. "I've got nothing to lose."

That last was greeted with laughter from Flintlock, and even O'Hara grinned.

CHAPTER NINETEEN

Former army scout Clem C. Gilman, a Texan some called the most merciless man-killer on the frontier, was a bounty hunter out of Amarillo with twenty-six kills, a figure he didn't keep track of himself since the awed newspapers were all too happy to do it for him . . .

> We tip our collective hats to a man who has rid our great state of more lawless vermin than all of the Texas Rangers combined.
> —*The Fort Worth Herald*

> A shootist of renown who brings 'em back dead. Go get 'em, Clem.
> —*The Houston Gazette*

> We stand in the heroic shadow of the renowned Clem C. Gilmore, the conquering hero of the Plains.
> —*The Dallas Express* (which didn't even get his name right)

Over the years the list of fawning news stories went on and on, and then this, from the *Amarillo Record* published on the same day Sam Flintlock and O'Hara rode into Mansion Creek:

HAIL THE CONQUERING
HERO COMES

We hear with beating hearts that our renowned native son Clem C. Gilman is once again on the trail of a miscreant. You will remember a year ago that intrepid Texas Ranger Charlie Fairman headed into the Arizona Territory in search of the notorious bandit chief Jasper Orlov and to this date has not

Returned to His Native Soil

The Record is proud to report that, armed with an arrest warrant and the promise of a $5,000 reward, Clem has now taken up the task and he tells us he's resolved to uncover the mystery surrounding Ranger Fairman's disappearance and that he'll bring back Orlov

Dead or Alive

We believe that when the murderous Orlov learns that Clem is on his trail he'll be shaking in his boots, and who can blame him? It is well known that Clem never fails to find his quarry due to his skill with

His Deadly Six-Gun

All the Record can do now is to lift our hearts and wish Clem all the luck in the world and we say in all sincerity

Haste Ye Back!

URGENT: As the Record went to press we learned that before he rode out of town the Rangers presented Clem with a brand-new Winchester rifle and a handsome Smith & Wesson revolver. *Huzzah!*

Clem Gilman did not fit the hero mold. He was a small, thin man with so much bitterness in him he lived with the taste of bile in his mouth. He was a man filled with hate, not for individuals but for all of humanity. The spawn of rape, the unholy union of an illiterate servant girl and a bullwhacker with a Slavic name, he never knew his parents. The day he was born his mother left him on the steps of a mission in Laredo where he was taken in by monks, who gave him a name and then sent him to a foster home as soon as he was able to walk. Beaten, abused and half starved the boy was passed from home to home until his thirteenth birthday, when he stole a revolver and thirty-five dollars from a farmer and ran away. He soon discovered he had a skill with firearms and very soon after that he killed his first man, a Negro drover named Henderson who happened to have a two-hundred-dollar reward on his head. As the local sheriff counted the bills into his hand, young Clem knew he'd found his calling.

It was a measure of Gilman's unprepossessing appearance that he rode into Mansion Creek unnoticed. Who looks at a forty-year-old man with a narrow, sun-wrinkled face, dressed in a threadbare duster and battered hat astride a small brown mustang that couldn't have weighed more than eight hundred pounds? When he dismounted outside the *Apache County Herald* Gilman's five-foot-six height in his boots did nothing to attract attention either. He was an easy man to underestimate.

Gilman stepped into the newspaper office, then stood just inside the doorway for a few moments to let his eyes adjust to the gloom.

"Can I help you?" Roland Ives said. He'd smiled when he said that but now as he looked into his visitor's eyes the smile withered on his lips. Blue eyes, cold as ice, with no spark of any kind of emotion.

"Are you Roland Ives?" the stranger said.

"Yes, I am. And you are?"

Gilman ignored that and said, "Charlie Fairman. Tell me about him."

Ives shook his head. "I don't understand. Tell you what?"

"You brought him here, didn't you?"

"No, he wrote a letter to me and he came of his own accord."

"The letter, was it about Jasper Orlov?"

"Yes, it was. The Texas Rangers had heard reports of people suddenly disappearing around these parts and Charlie Fairman wrote and asked if they were true and if Jasper Orlov was real."

"And what did you tell him?"

"I told him that the reports of missing people were true, but I doubted if Jasper Orlov really existed."

"Then what happened? Speak up now."

Ives felt a twinge of anger. He was being bullied by this insignificant little man who looked like a puff of wind could blow him over. Gilman read the newspaperman's eyes. Whether by accident or design his slicker opened wider and Ives saw a Colt on the man's hip. Ivory handled, nickel plated, worn in an exquisitely carved brown leather holster and gunbelt, it was a Texas rig no working man could afford and the only one Ives had seen that equaled it in quality was worn by Hogan Lord.

"What happened was that Charlie Fairman showed up in town a month later with a leave of absence from the Rangers and orders to bring in Jasper Orlov," Ives said. "For questioning, the Ranger said."

"Describe Fairman," Gilman said.

"Tall man, on the heavy side, with a mustache and full beard. His hair was black as I recall and . . . yeah, I remember, he walked with a limp, favored his left leg."

"What did he do after he got in town?"

"Not much. He loaded up with enough grub to last a couple of weeks then rode away."

"Away where?"

"East. In the direction of the mesa."

"Why east?"

"Because that's where the people go missing."

"What about Orlov? Has anybody seen him and left a description?"

"No. The talk around town is that if you see Orlov you're already as good as dead."

"Not much to go on," Gilman said.

Ives said, "Mister, ride east of the mesa and if Orlov really exists, he'll find you." Then, "Why all this interest?"

"All this interest is because of the five thousand dollars the Rangers are paying for Orlov's scalp."

"Then good luck," Ives said, anxious to rid himself of the little man.

"All the luck I need I carry right here on my hip," Gilman said. "Nobody is immortal and Orlov can die like any other man." He reached into the pocket of his duster and rang a silver dollar onto the counter. "Buy yourself a drink," he said.

When Clem Gilman was halfway up the switchback the sky unrolled like sheets of lead, and thunder rumbled to the north. Rain ticked around him as he reached the top of the mesa, pulled up his mustang and looked around, taking stock of the unpromising landscape. Somewhere in this wilderness of rock and pine was Jasper Orlov, the man he'd come to kill. The man was no myth, no tall tale told by idlers huddled around the potbellied stove in winter, he was real, as real as the lightning that now flashed in the sky. Gilman, the consummate manhunter, sensed his presence as though he could read it written on the wind. The north slope of the mesa dropped to a rise, a wall of rock notched by a narrow valley that rose again to a lofty crag. In heavy rain, the bounty hunter studied the crag through his field glasses and then lowered them again, his eyes alight.

Could the house on the crag be the home of Jasper Orlov?

He raised the glasses again. The house was like no other he'd seen, high and spindly, floor after floor of arched windows with small, diamond-shaped panes held together with lead casings, balconies, spires and a steeply pitched slate roof topped by tall brick chimneys. Lashed by rain, surrounded by sizzling forks of lightning and pounded by blasts of thunder, the house seemed to thumb its nose at nature, defying it to do its worst. Dim orbs of light glowed behind the windows on the ground floor and despite the tempest that splintered apart the day ravens fluttered around the eaves and roosted on the sharp peak of the roof.

Gilman was a cautious man. He could ride up to the house on the crag and ask for shelter for the night. If Jasper Orlov was in residence it would be a simple matter to kill him. Or would it? How many others were in the house? Judging by the number of rooms that were lit, there could be a few, and if they were guns . . . Gilman, a sure-thing killer, couldn't take that chance.

He found the talus slope and rode off the mesa onto the flat and took refuge in a stand of juniper that offered little shelter. His mouse-colored mustang didn't need much, didn't expect much and there was graze enough among the trees for its needs. Oblivious of the rain and shimmering lightning, Gilman squatted under a tree, his back to the trunk. He trained the field glasses on the house again . . . and settled down to watch and wait.

A few minutes passed and then during a lull in the thunder Gilman heard a giggle behind him . . .

CHAPTER TWENTY

As the thunderstorm raged around Lucy Cully's house, the talk was of poetry, art and the delicious bed-hopping scandals of Philadelphia's high society, of which Walt Whitman seemed to have an inexhaustible knowledge. Lucy was in her element, her face radiant with laughter as Whitman recounted his tales and her beloved Roderick added the odd saucy embellishment, especially to the case of the married captain of industry caught in flagrante delicto with a scullery maid.

"The outraged wife, who walked in on this unhappy scene, then chased the husband and the maid all over the house, taking the occasional pot at them with a pepperbox revolver," Roderick Chanley said.

"And then what happened?" Lucy said, sitting forward in her chair, her eyes shining.

"Well, the fracas spilled outside onto the street and as far as I know the maid is still running," Chanley said. "As for the husband, the terrified butler, who'd been grazed by an errant ball, called in the constabulary and the whole affair was written off as a marital spat and no charges were filed." The young man smiled. "But later I did see the wife at a reserved table in Partridge's showing off a new diamond ring and necklace."

Lucy smiled. "So all was well that ended well."

"Except for the poor scullery maid, I guess," Chanley said.

Sam Flintlock had listened with interest to the city talk but when the conversation again turned to poetry and literature he made an excuse and retired to bed. O'Hara had escaped earlier, having no interest in either poetry or the sexual peccadillos of Philadelphia's upper crust.

Several leaks from the roof ticked into Flintlock's tiny room but none fell on his cot, for which he was grateful. He lay on his back staring at the slanted ceiling only a few feet above him. Lightning flashes illuminated every corner of the room and the walls around him stood out in stark, silvery white, and for a moment afterward when he closed his eyes he saw streaks of red and electric blue.

Flintlock was worried. Now that Lucy's intended and Walt Whitman were living in the house and the girl seemed quite settled, his and O'Hara's reason for being there was gone. If they pulled out early, would Tobias Fynes honor his pledge to pay five hundred dollars? If he was in the fat man's shoes, would he? Probably not. The answer then was to stick it out for the whole seven days and then demand their money. If Fynes refused, there was always O'Hara's option of robbing the bank. But that was a last-ditch choice. Flintlock had gone straight for a long spell since he split with Bill Bonney and that hard crowd up Lincoln County way and he didn't want to step over the line again.

He decided to sleep on it and then worry the problem with a clear mind come morning.

But O'Hara had a very different plan.

Flintlock had been sleep for only a couple of hours when he was roughly shaken awake. "Get up," O'Hara said.

Like any man who often puts himself in harm's way and spreads his blankets in the open, Flintlock woke instantly, his hand reaching for the Colt beside his bed. "What the hell, O'Hara?" he said.

"Get dressed. I sense danger."

Flintlock blinked, focusing on O'Hara. The man was a changeling, often appearing more Irishman than Indian. But that night he was all Apache. He'd combed out his hair so that it hung loosely over his shoulders and, a thing he seldom did, he wore the red headband of his mother's tribe. As a concession to the rain, he wore a slicker, but it was unbuttoned so as not to impede his draw. O'Hara's expression was grim and Flintlock realized that he took the present danger seriously, and he did not for one moment doubt him. Apache warriors had the senses of a bronco wolf, the reason a frontiersman hiding from a war party never looked directly at them, not if he wanted to live. An Apache could sense eyes on him like a white man feels the heat of the summer sun on his neck.

Flintlock dressed hurriedly, shoved his Colt into his waistband and like O'Hara shrugged into his slicker. O'Hara handed him his Winchester and said, "Let's go."

Only after Flintlock had safely navigated the stairs and walked out of the sleeping house into the raging storm did he speak, or rather yell into O'Hara's ear. "What's out here?"

"I don't know."

"Where is it?"

"I don't know."

Flintlock looked back at the house, peering through the raking rain. Lightning glimmered on the windows and for brief moments turned them white, as though the building looked down on him and O'Hara with a dozen shining eyes.

"O'Hara!" Flintlock said. "Is this a wild-goose chase?"

"I don't think so," O'Hara called back. "This way."

He had almost disappeared into darkness and rain before Flintlock, limping, went after him. Worried now, he stared at the sky and saw only blackness. The lighting had lessened and the thunder grew quiet but the wind was rising, blowing in sudden gusts that threw the downpour straight into his face and threatened to suck the air from his lungs.

O'Hara in the lead, they made their way off the crag and followed the shingled slope, smoothed out by the passage of wagons, onto the flat and then into a deep gully that gave a little protection from the wind. After a hundred yards the gully opened up onto treed ground that was already muddy from the rain. Flintlock could see only a few yards in front of him and although he heard O'Hara's breathing he was invisible in the murk.

Then, suddenly, a revolver shot shattered into the night. Then a second, followed by a shriek of terror.

"O'Hara?" Flintlock said, making a question of the name.

"I don't know. It's somewhere ahead of us. I can't see a damned thing."

Flintlock's Colt was in his hand but in pitch-darkness, pounded by rain and bullied by the gusting wind, there would be little chance of using it. O'Hara felt the same way. He backtracked a couple of steps and said, "Sam, there's shelter just ahead. We can't do anything in this storm but wait until it passes."

Flintlock wanted to say, *If it ever passes*, but he kept quiet, deciding to save his breath. He followed O'Hara, his boots squelching in mud, and then bumped into the breed when he suddenly stopped. "Over here," O'Hara said. He grabbed Flintlock by the front of his slicker and dragged him into a deep V-shaped depression just wide enough for two men to sit side by side. The break was roofed over by several fallen juniper and on top of those a layer of uprooted brush and other debris. The shelter, damp and muddy as it was, gave good protection from the wind and cut back the downpour to a few fat drops that ticked on the shoulders of their slickers.

Flintlock gave O'Hara a sidelong glance. "Tell me again why we're here, Injun."

"I sensed something. I felt danger."

"I'm crazy to be sitting here in a downpour with a wild half Apache when I should be asleep in bed," Flintlock said. "That's what I feel."

"Sam, I can't shake the feeling that there is evil abroad tonight. Those shots . . . that terrible scream . . ."

"A bobcat screams like that, especially when somebody takes a couple of shots at it."

"Who would be out hunting in this wilderness on a night like this?"

"Only lunatics like us. Barnabas once told me that inside every man there are two wolves, one good, the other evil. O'Hara, your fear is feeding the evil wolf."

"I'm not afraid, Sam."

"Well, good for you, O'Hara, because I am," Flintlock said. "Maybe a boogerman fired those shots, huh. Or maybe it was Jasper Orlov sending us a warning."

"Jasper Orlov couldn't see us in the dark and in this weather," O'Hara said.

"Unless he can see better than we can, like an animal," Flintlock said. "There's just no telling what a boogerman can do." Rainwater ran off the brim of his hat. "Well, I'm about to nod off, so keep watch, O'Hara. If Orlov comes for us with a meat cleaver in his hand, wake me up."

O'Hara made no answer. Strain showed on his face as he listened into the thunderstorm and a night that hissed and roared like an angry dragon.

For the second time that morning O'Hara shook Flintlock awake. "It's light," he said.

Never at his best in the morning, Flintlock blinked, looked around him and said, "What the hell? It's still raining."

"I know," O'Hara said. "And the thunder is back."

"I need coffee. You got any coffee?"

"No, I got none of that. Let's go."

"Damn it, man. Give me a minute." Flintlock fumbled into the pocket of his slicker and O'Hara passed him the makings and a rolled cigarette. "Made this while you were asleep," he said. "I found the tobacco sack in your pocket."

O'Hara thumbed a match into flame and Flintlock said, "You find the lucifer in my pocket as well? I don't recollect putting anything in there."

O'Hara, looking exhausted, managed a smile. "Sam, as long as I've known you, you've kept the makings in every pocket you got."

"Never have to do without that way," Flintlock said, inhaling deeply on his cigarette. "Running out of tobacco is a bad thing for a smoking man who carries a gun. Makes him mean. Pat Garrett, the lawman who done for poor Billy, was like that. He was a dangerous man to be around before he had his first cigar and cup of coffee. 'I like my coffee black as mortal sin and as bitter as wormwood,' he once told me." Flintlock shook his head. "Just as well he knew I could outdraw him so he left me alone."

"You've known all kinds, haven't you, Sam?" O'Hara said, intently watching the cigarette burn away.

"Most kinds," Flintlock said. "You know what? I've never swapped lead with a Frenchman. When I was a boy me and Barnabas met French trappers all the time and we got along with them just fine."

"Got a big hole in your education there, Sam," O'Hara said.

"Or an Englishman either," Flintlock said. He dropped his cigarette butt into the mud and it sizzled as he ground it out under his boot. "All right, O'Hara, let's go find out what spooked you last night." He looked out at the pounding rain. "Glad I didn't bring the Hawken," he said.

CHAPTER TWENTY-ONE

Tobias Fynes looked out at the pounding rain. "A rotten day for business," he said. "A man can't make money on a morning like this."

Hogan Lord nodded, "Seems like that's the case. The street is empty." He poured coffee into his cup and replaced the pot on the silver tray on the banker's desk. "Why did you send for me so early, Tobias?"

"Because I have an idea, a way to end this Cully mansion affair without unnecessary bloodshed," Fynes said. The morning air was still cool, but the fat man was already sweating. He'd nicked his throat shaving and there was a red bloodstain on his white celluloid collar. He took time to light his morning cigar and then said, "The poet is the key to my plan. He's the man who can make it work."

"You mean Walt Whitman?" Lord said.

"No. The other one. What's his name?"

"Roderick Chanley."

"Yes, him. I have to talk with Chanley. I think me and him can work together, sort things out between us."

"In what way?" Lord said. He looked puzzled.

Fynes didn't answer that question. Instead he said, "Did you see him?"

"You know I did. I spoke to him and Whitman at the stage."

"But did you take a good look at him, Hogan?" Fynes said.

"As much as I look at any other man, I guess." The gunman sipped his coffee, then, "Tobias, I'm not catching your drift."

Fynes smiled in the superior way that infuriated Lord. "He's threadbare, Hogan, just a hop, step and jump away from ragged. I studied the man closely. His ankle boots are so scuffed that no gentleman of means would wear them. His linen is yellow with age and the carpetbag he took from the stage is frayed, moth-eaten, so shabby it should have been thrown out years ago. He has neither watch chain nor signet ring, a sure sign of poverty. But in the unlikely event that he ever owned such, the pawn tickets for them will surely be in his pocket."

"You saw all that at a distance?" Lord said, surprised. "You have excellent eyesight, Tobias."

"No, I don't, but I'm a banker and I see enough. It's my job to sum up a man when he steps into this office hat in hand to beg a loan. I wouldn't loan Roderick Chanley a nickel." Fynes's smug smile again stretched his moist, fleshy lips. "But I will give him five thousand dollars."

"I've never known you to talk in riddles, Tobias," Lord said. "Makes it difficult for a man to figure out what you're saying."

"No riddle, Hogan. It's all very simple, really." Fynes exhaled a cloud of blue cigar smoke. Then said, "When I lived back East and worked as a lowly junior banking clerk earning twenty dollars a week I met Chanley's kind and I witnessed their desperation for income enough to live in a big city like Philadelphia or Boston and be thought of as upper middle class, just a step below the Brahmins, don't you know." As he said that last, Fynes's face twisted into a mask of hatred. "I could never become one of them since my poverty was too obvious and because of the Chanleys of this world I was kept down, ignored, never allowed to rise above my station. God damn them, I hate them so, seed, breed and generation of them."

"But you'll give one of them five thousand dollars," Lord said.

"For the house! For the house, Hogan. For the stinking house on the crag."

"It belongs to Lucy Cully, not Chanley."

"Until he marries her and she becomes his chattel. Then as her husband, Chanley can sell the place right out from under her."

Lord smiled. "So Tobias Fynes plans to turn marriage broker?"

"Exactly."

"How will you play it?"

"Play it . . . yes, an excellent choice of words, Hogan. I will visit the mansion and play the concerned friend, like a kindly Dutch uncle if you will, and persuade the so-much-in-love young couple to say their vows right away, on the spot. I will bring food and drink for the wedding feast and the parson . . . what the hell is the pulpit pounder's name?"

"The Reverend Uriah Reedy."

"Yeah, him." Fynes grinned. "I want Reedy ready. Tell him that he's got a marriage to perform tomorrow, once this damn rain clears."

"That soon, Tobias?"

"Yeah, that soon."

"Suppose Lucy Cully says no?"

"Why should she? She was planning to marry her poet anyway. All I'm doing is expediting the matter. Hell, I'm sure she'll jump at the chance to get what Chanley will give her on her wedding night."

"If he's *mucho hombre*," Lord said.

"And if he's not, I'll take care of the young widow myself when the time comes," Fynes said. He saw the surprise on Lord's face at his use of the word *widow* and said, "You don't think I'll let Roderick Chanley leave Mansion Creek with five thousand dollars of my money, do you?"

"You got it all figured, Tobias, huh?" Lord said.

"Damn right, I have," Fynes said. He leaned back in his chair, settled his outspread hands on his great belly and grinned.

After Hogan Lord left, Tobias Fynes grabbed his umbrella and stepped out of his office. He told the bank tellers he was going home to retrieve some papers he'd left on his desk and would be back in fifteen minutes.

Fynes stood on the boardwalk, opened the black umbrella above his head and looked around town. Because of the incessant rain the street was empty of all but a few tradesmen except for one of last night's drunks who'd been tossed from the saloon and promptly fallen on his face in the mud. The man sat up, wiped gore from his eyes and then proceeded to sing a tortuous rendition of "O'er the Hills and Far

Away." Fynes, in a good mood, grinned at him, stepped
along the walk a few paces and spun a silver dollar into
the mud. It pleased him to watch the drunk scrabble
around in the filthy mire searching for the coin, but
after a few moments he grew bored with the spectacle
and headed for home.

Fynes's gingerbread house lay a short distance
behind the bank and was accessed by a nearby alley
he'd spread with a foot of gravel to keep flooding at
bay. He was pleased that his patent leather ankle boots
were barely spattered with mud as he followed another gravel path to his house, shook the umbrella
free of raindrops and stepped inside. But his good
humor evaporated immediately as the smell of sick-
ness assailed his nostrils. Without a word he stepped
into his office, picked up a few papers from his desk
and turned to leave.

Dr. Theodora Weller blocked his way.

"Aren't you going to visit with your wife?" she said.

"Why?" Fynes said. "She was dying this morning
and she's still dying now. Nothing has changed and I
have nothing to say to her."

Fynes saw anger flash in Theodora's eyes and he
was struck by what a fine-looking woman she was, even
in her mannish clothes. The brown skirt that ended
just below the calves to reveal high-heeled ankle boots
and the military-inspired fitted coat of the same color
did nothing for her, nor did the tan derby perched on
top of her piled-up hair.

"Ruth is in a great deal of pain," the doctor said.
"And it grows harder for her to bear with every passing day."

"She hangs on and on and I tell her she should just

roll over and die," Fynes said. "But she doesn't listen. Ruth only hangs on to life to torment me and she is succeeding. Now, if you will excuse me, I have work to do."

Theodora stepped aside and Fynes walked to the door. He stopped and turned as the woman said his name, her voice strangely flat.

"Tobias Fynes," she said, "I never in my life thought I could be capable of hate. I was wrong. I hate you with my heart, my soul, with every fiber of my being. I want to see you in hell where you will suffer like your wife suffers."

Theodora's mouth tightened. "One day I'll kill you, Tobias, and I'll dance on your grave."

"What you need is to open your legs to a man, and then you'll see things differently," Fynes said. "You've already failed as a doctor and now you're failing as a woman. After Mansion Creek there's no place left for you to go and you know it. That's why I will very soon run you out of town."

Fynes opened the door then turned and touched the brim of his bowler. "Have a wonderful morning," he said.

The door slammed shut and Theodora swallowed hard, fighting back the bitter hatred and salt tears she knew to be self-destructive.

"Doctor, who was that?" Ruth said from her bedroom, her voice as fragile as spun crystal.

"It was no one, Ruth," Theodora said. "It was no one at all."

CHAPTER TWENTY-TWO

The same rain that fell on Tobias Fynes as he walked to his bank pelted Sam Flintlock and O'Hara when they left their scant shelter and scouted into the gray morning. Flintlock was less than sociable. He wanted coffee, dry clothes and a considerable amount of git between him and the increasingly irritating O'Hara.

He made his foul mood clear. "O'Hara, there's nothing out here but trees, mud, rain, a man without a name and one crazy Injun." He tripped over an exposed root, caught his balance at the last moment and let out a stream of cusses in English, French and, courtesy of old Barnabas's tutelage, Ojibway.

O'Hara suddenly crouched low and gestured at Flintlock to do the same. Then, after a few moments of silent listening, he made another hand signal for his companion to stay where he was.

Annoyed, Flintlock said in a whisper, "O'Hara, what the hell?"

"Blood," O'Hara said. "Blood in the wind."

There was sufficient urgency in O'Hara's voice to

make Flintlock reach inside his slicker and draw his Colt. "I can't smell it," he said.

"I know you can't," O'Hara said. He moved forward, one slow step at a time, and made no sound. Flintlock followed, gun in hand, his eyes scanning the windtossed trees around him. Thunder, a reminder that it was still the territory's monsoon season, rumbled like a gigantic boulder hurled down a marble hallway, and lighting forked across the sky. It was, Flintlock would recall later, a dismal, dark, dreary and dangerous day, a day when all Christian white men should be safe at home. Drinking coffee.

"Sam, come up here," O'Hara said without turning, his eyes fixed on something ahead of him. When Flintlock got down on one knee beside him, O'Hara said, "Look there, under the tree."

Flintlock looked, looked again and said, "Is that blood?"

O'Hara nodded. "Yeah, it's blood, a lot of it."

"Maybe a wolf or a bear killed a deer there," Flintlock said.

"I don't think so." O'Hara rose to his feet and walked to the tree. He bent and picked up something from the ground that he held out for Flintlock to see. "Unless wolves are using field glasses to hunt."

Flintlock saw blood, a lot of blood. Something or someone had been slaughtered there. "O'Hara, you don't suppose it was Spunner?"

"I don't know who it was," O'Hara said. "The field glasses you're holding are German and expensive. Whoever died here wasn't a poor man." He scouted around the base of the juniper where there were tracks in the mud, sheltered enough that they were not yet washed out by the rain.

"Hard-soled moccasins," O'Hara said.

"Apache?" Flintlock said.

"There are no Apache," O'Hara said. "Not any longer."

"Maybe a few who escaped the roundup?"

O'Hara shook his head. "Women and children, maybe so. But the warriors are all in Florida."

"We saw those same tracks before," Flintlock said.

"When we found what was left of Shade Pike's boys. But this time the body has been taken."

O'Hara kneeled to take a closer look at the ground and rivulets of rain ran down the back of his slicker. Then, after a few moments of frowning concentration, "Sam, look here." He pointed to an indentation in the wet earth. "What do you make of that?"

Flintlock's temper was short and he said, "Hell, I can't see anything."

"Look closer," O'Hara said.

Then Flintlock saw it, an indentation in the ground about three inches long, narrow and not too deep. He thought for a while and then said, "Made by a tomahawk?"

"Or a white man's ax," O'Hara said. "Somebody swung and missed, maybe when the victim was trying to roll away."

"Then who was he and why was he here? And why the field glasses?"

"One of them bird-watchers maybe?" O'Hara offered, but without much enthusiasm.

"Old ladies and retired professors are bird-watchers," Flintlock said. "They wouldn't venture into this wilderness in a thunderstorm to watch a tomtit, especially with Jasper Orlov around."

O'Hara didn't answer. He had the field glasses to his eyes and was intently looking up at the crag. "You get a good view of the house from here," he said. He handed the field glasses to Flintlock. "Take a look."

Flintlock studied the house. O'Hara was right, the glasses gave an excellent view of the front and right side wall. As he watched, Lucy opened the front door a crack, stuck her head outside, watched the rain for few moments and then ducked inside again. Flintlock lowered the glasses and said to O'Hara, "Do you think someone stood under the tree and watched the house?"

"And then was attacked? Yeah, it's possible," O'Hara said.

"But why? I mean, why all of it. Why did he watch the house and why was he killed? There's a lot of blood but we don't know for sure if he was killed."

O'Hara shook his head. "No, we don't, Sam." He kicked at the scarlet ground, now slowly turning pink in the rain. "But I doubt that a man can lose this much blood and live."

A moment later a rifle roared and a bullet chattered through the brittle branches of the juniper.

Flintlock and O'Hara dived for the ground at the same time. A drift of gunsmoke ghosted from a stand of pine to their left and was quickly shredded by the wind. Flintlock estimated the range was about twenty-five yards, too far for revolver work, but beside him

O'Hara cut loose with his Winchester. He sent a bullet into the thinning smoke then bracketed that area with shots, working the lever from his shoulder. Flintlock didn't shoot, his narrowed eyes seeking a target. There was none. O'Hara ceased firing and said, "You see anything?"

"Not a damn thing," Flintlock said. He dashed rain from his eyes with the back of his gun hand. "It's uncivil and low-down to bushwhack a man on a day like this."

Then, like a jack-in-the-box, a figure popped up from the brush, a rifle to his shoulder. Flintlock and O'Hara fired at the same time. A yelp of surprise and pain and the man dropped.

"We got him, Sam," O'Hara said. "Do you think we got him?"

"We winged him at least," Flintlock said. "Or you did. I'm not much of a hand for target shooting with a Colt." Then, his hand cupped to his mouth, he yelled, "Hey, you out there, show yourself." Flintlock baited his trap. "We have coffee."

There was no answer and no sound but the fall of the rain and the grumbling growl of thunder. Lightning flared and for a moment silvered the bleak landscape.

"Unless we know whether or not that ranny is dead, he's got us pinned down here," Flintlock said. "Go take a look, O'Hara."

"You take a look—walk into his rifle your ownself," O'Hara said.

"I got a bum ankle and I can't walk that far," Flintlock said.

O'Hara shook his head. "I'm not going out there."

"Hell, you're half Apache. You can sneak up on him."

"Maybe so, but the Irish half of me is telling me to stay right where I'm at."

His eyes scanning into the distance, Flintlock didn't turn his head as he said, "You're one ungrateful Injun, O'Hara. I mean, after all I've done for you."

"What did you ever do for me, Sam?" O'Hara said.

"Plenty of stuff."

"Name one thing."

"Well, I can't bring anything to mind right now, but—"

A rifle shot, a puff of smoke and then an echoing silence.

After a few moments Flintlock said, "I think somebody just done for the bushwhacker. Seems like we have a friend out there."

O'Hara said nothing, frowning as he thought through this new development.

"Well, I'm damned tired of lying here in mud and rain," Flintlock said. "Let's go take a look-see."

This time O'Hara made no objection. He rose to his feet, his rifle at the ready, and he and Flintlock walked across the open ground between them and the trees. Lightning cracked across the sky and thunder banged directly overhead as they reached the pines. Because of thick undergrowth it took a few minutes before they found a body of a young man. Flintlock saw at a glance that he'd taken his own life. He had two bullet wounds. One in the belly and the other was self-inflicted. The man had lain on his side, shoved the muzzle of a .44-40 Henry rifle in his mouth and pulled the trigger. The back of his head was blown away.

"He done for himself," O'Hara said, stating what was obvious.

Flintlock nodded. "He took one of our bullets in the belly and then killed himself right quick. Now, why would he do a thing like that?"

"He was gut-shot, Sam. You know better than me how long it takes a gut-shot man to die. I guess he couldn't bear the thought of going through all that pain," O'Hara said. Then, "He's a white man but he wore Apache moccasins." He took a knee beside the body. "He's young, Sam, a beardless boy. He can't be any older than fifteen or sixteen."

"He's sure wearing strange duds," Flintlock said.

The body was dressed in a sleeveless tunic made of sackcloth or some other coarse material, and it came down to the middle of his thighs. The waist was gathered tight by a deerskin belt, and a bandolier of ammunition for the rifle crossed his chest.

"Look, he's got a tattoo on his forehead," Flintlock said. "What the hell is that . . . a snake?"

O'Hara nodded, his face like stone. "Yes, it's a serpent, the bringer of chaos, corruption and darkness and all that is evil."

"Then why does this feller have it on his forehead?" Flintlock said.

O'Hara looked up at the dreary sky. "Sam, that I do not know," he said.

CHAPTER TWENTY-THREE

"Do you think the young man you shot is connected in any way to the death of whoever sat under the tree?" Lucy Cully asked Flintlock.

"We don't know for sure if anyone died there," Flintlock said. "We found blood and field glasses and put two and two together."

"Do you think he was watching my house?" Lucy said.

"He had a good view of it from where he was located," O'Hara said. "Yes, my guess is he was watching the house but then somebody attacked and killed him. The attackers wore moccasins and so did the young man who killed himself after we shot him."

"Was that strictly necessary? Shooting him, I mean?" Roderick Chanley said. "Surely there was another way that didn't involve violence."

Flintlock, a towel over his naked shoulders and his back to the warmth of the kitchen fire, looked at the man over the rim of his coffee cup. "Out here when a man bushwhacks you, then yeah, shooting him becomes strictly necessary."

"Sam, you can't leave the body out there unburied," Lucy said.

"Yes, I can," Flintlock said.

"The soul of an unburied man will never rest," Walt Whitman said. "It is our duty to see that he's laid under the earth."

"You know what the northeast Arizona Territory is?" Flintlock said, his irritation growing. "It's bedrock that the good Lord tossed a handful of soil on top of. How the hell do we lay him under the earth? There is no earth."

"I'm sure we can find a way," Chanley said. He adjusted his black eyepatch and smiled. "Where there's a will there's a way. Isn't that how the saying goes?"

"We? There is no we." Flintlock sighed deeply. "All right, me and O'Hara shot him, we'll bury him."

O'Hara looked surprised. "Bury him where?"

"I don't know. Maybe in the holler where we spent the night. There's room for a body in there."

Lucy nodded her approval. "You're true-blue, Sam Flintlock, and you too, O'Hara."

"I didn't say I was going to bury him," O'Hara said. He pointed to Flintlock. "He did."

"I know what I said and I said it for you as well," Flintlock said.

"O'Hara, I'll never sleep a wink knowing there's an unburied body almost on my doorstep," Lucy said. She looked very pretty that morning, her dark hair done up with blue ribbons, rouge highlighting her good cheekbones. "Please do it for me."

Chanley said, "No, not just for you, darling, do it for all of us."

"It's still raining," O'Hara said.

That was met by an unsympathetic silence.

As Flintlock and O'Hara saddled up, Rory O'Neill stepped into the barn. He wore a yellow oilskin that must have belonged to old Mechan Cully because it was a couple of sizes too small for him. "I'd like to go with you gentlemen," he said.

"You'd be welcome, if you had a horse," Flintlock said.

O'Neill smiled. "I can run."

O'Hara said, "You can't run as fast as a horse."

O'Neill nodded. "No, I can't. But I can run longer."

"Suit yourself, Rory," Flintlock said. "But if you can't keep up we're leaving you behind." He looked for a bulge under the oilskin. "You're not wearing a gun?"

O'Neill held up his fists. "I don't need a gun. I've got these."

"It seems to me that when a prizefighter goes up against a man with a Colt, the Colt wins and he loses," Flintlock said.

"No, both of us lose," O'Neill said. "I'll take my hits, keep on coming and kill him in the end."

O'Neill stood there without any hint of brag, an unsmiling, immovable pillar of hard bone and muscle, a man who could take a terrifying, dreadful amount of punishment and still come up to scratch. Looking at him, Flintlock said, "And maybe you could, at that."

* * *

"The body was here," O'Hara said. "Right here in the brush."

"Then what the hell happened to it?" Flintlock said.

"I don't know. Maybe a bear carried it off somewhere."

"Well, if it isn't here, it's buried as far as I'm concerned," Flintlock said. "You shouldn't have let Lucy Cully talk you into burying the body in the first place."

"Talk me into it? You're the one who said—"

"Somebody coming," Flintlock said. He reached inside his slicker and put his hand on his Colt. Then, after a while, "Hell, it's that albino feller."

The rain had stopped but the sky was still black, as though it had forgotten all about the sun. A brisk wind whipped through the trees and the air smelled of moldy vegetation, an acrid odor like shoaling fish.

Jeptha Spunner let his white mule pick its way toward Flintlock and O'Hara and when he was a few yards off he drew rein, looked over Rory O'Neill, then touched his hat brim and said, "Howdy, boys, we meet again. Earlier I heard shooting this way. Thought I'd come see who got shot."

"We did the shooting, Spunner," Flintlock said. "Well, me and O'Hara and the feller who bushwhacked us."

"And he's not with us anymore, huh?" the albino said. Because of the gloom he'd dispensed with his dark glasses and his eyes were pink and unblinking.

"We cut his suspenders, all right, well, us and the dead kid. He was gut-shot and killed himself," Flintlock said. "A man with a bullet in his belly doesn't have much choice in the matter."

O'Hara said to Spunner, "He killed himself right

here. We came back to bury him but his body is gone. We reckon maybe a bear took it."

"And if that ain't enough, we think another man was killed under the tree over yonder," Flintlock said. "All we found of him was his blood and his field glasses."

"Field glasses?" Spunner said.

"Yeah, these," Flintlock said.

Spunner examined the glasses, nodded and said, "Good-quality German work. The best binoculars I've seen since I left the sea. I'd say they belonged to a bounty hunter after the reward for Jasper Orlov. There's been a few of them killed around here. Whoever he is, I'd guess that he's supper by now."

Flintlock and O'Hara exchanged glances as the albino explained, "Some say that if a man tastes human flesh he'll never want to eat any other kind of meat. Jasper Orlov made that choice a long time ago."

"Damn that man. He's a low person and a monster who needs killing," Flintlock said.

"Easy to say, hard to do," Spunner said.

"That might be the case, but I won't leave the Arizona Territory until I put a bullet in him," Flintlock said.

"Many have tried and all have failed," the albino said. "Perhaps you will succeed." Then, "My cabin is close and I have coffee on the stove if you gents would care for a cup." Then, again studying O'Neill, "I haven't met this gentleman before."

"My name's Rory O'Neill."

"By the look of you, I'd say you are a prizefighter, or were," Spunner said.

"If I can get a match with John L. Sullivan I'll fight again," O'Neill said.

Spunner nodded and said, "I'm told that when John L. Sullivan shakes hands he says, 'Shake the hand that shook the world.' Is that true?"

"I don't know, I've never met the gent," O'Neill said. "But he's one to go on the brag. I know that."

"Oh well, let's hope you meet him in the ring. I'd like to see that scrap. Now, about the coffee, do you all care for a cup?"

"Much obliged," Flintlock said. "I could use some."

O'Hara said, "Suits me. I'd like to see that flying machine you're building, Spunner."

"Not much to see yet, I'm afraid," the albino said. "I'm still trying to refine the steam engine." He gathered up the reins of his mule. "Step right this way, gentlemen."

Jeptha Spunner's cabin stood on the bank of a small stream lined by several tall cottonwoods. Behind the shack rose a thirty-foot wall of red sandstone notched by a narrow arroyo. A walking path worn in the grass between the dwelling and the canyon mouth was evidence that Spunner visited it often, and Flintlock guessed that was where he was building his steam-powered flying machine. It was all tomfoolery, of course, but for now Flintlock decided to keep his opinion to himself. You can't make fun of a man whose hospitality you'd just accepted.

The cabin was typical of its time and place, a single room with a dirt floor and wood shingle roof. Its furnishings were few, a stove, a bed, a dresser, a rough wooden table and a few rickety chairs. Several animal skins covered the log walls, and an old Hawken rifle, not unlike his own, hung on the stone fireplace with its powder horn. On the dresser there was a four-masted sailing ship in a bottle that showed exquisite workmanship. The place was clean, the floor swept and strewn with fragrant herbs, and more grew in small clay pots along the sill of the only window. Flintlock guessed, rightly, that Spunner had not built the cabin but had occupied a place abandoned by a settler or prospector years before.

As though reading Flintlock's mind, Spunner said, "The original owner of the cabin lies buried on the other side of the creek. Until recently there was a wooden marker on his grave with the name Les Howie and it said that he was killed by Apaches in 1879. I don't know what happened to it. Either the Indians took it or it blew away in a big wind."

Spunner hung up his guests' dripping slickers on pegs driven into the wall and then ushered them into chairs set around the table. Perhaps to reassure Flintlock that he had no evil intent, the albino hung his holstered Colt and cartridge belt on a hook behind the door. The gutta-percha handle of the revolver was smooth from much use and that stirred something in Flintlock's memory . . . a name . . . a story he'd heard . . . As Spunner laid a scalding-hot cup of coffee in front of him Flintlock tried to bring what he half remembered to mind, but the recollection remained elusive, tantalizingly just out of reach.

Spunner was talking again. "How is Miss Cully settling in?" he said. "Is she still worried about ghosts?"

"Not so long as we three are there," Flintlock said.

"You're staying with her for a full week?" Spunner said.

"Few more days and then she'll decide if she wants to stay in the house or not," Flintlock said. Then, a mean little spike in his belly, "Hell, I've got five hundred dollars at stake and you didn't help none by telling her the place was haunted."

Spunner sipped his coffee and then smiled, "All old houses have some kind of ghost in them, whatever that may be. A lingering bad memory perhaps or the imprint of a strong emotion that hasn't faded with time. They're usually harmless." The albino waved a hand. "Old Les Howie is still here. I feel his presence sometimes, even smell his pipe smoke. But is he a ghost? No, I don't think so. The memory of the man still lingers within these four walls, that's all."

"Well, next time you visit the Cully mansion, tell Lucy that," Flintlock said.

"Yes. Good idea. I most certainly will." Spunner smiled at O'Hara. "Once you finish your coffee I'll show you my creation."

In a fine drizzle, Jeptha Spunner led Flintlock, O'Hara and O'Neill along the worn path to the arroyo. O'Hara didn't know what to expect but he couldn't hide his disappointment when he saw what was lying within the walls of the narrow canyon. What looked like an ordinary rowboat about fifteen feet long lay on its side, and Spunner seemed to be working on patches of its bottom where the wood had rotted. Leaning against one wall was a four-foot wooden object that the albino called a *propeller* and beyond the boat stood an engine of some sort that looked like a rusty iron barrel surrounded by a mass of copper and brass tubes and an attached cylinder.

Spunner pointed to the barrel-shaped object, beaming with pride. "The heat needed for the engine comes from fuel burned in the firebox and it boils water in the pressurized boiler here," he said, touching the barrel-shaped object, "turning it into saturated steam. The steam transfers to the motor, which uses it to push on a piston sliding inside the cylinder, powering the machinery that spins the propeller. The engine is simplicity itself, steam power at its finest."

"The engine goes in the rowboat?" Flintlock said.

"Yes, indeed," Spunner said.

Flintlock shook his head. "It's way too heavy. You'll never get this thing off the ground. Hell, you won't even get it out of the arroyo without an ox team."

"If an ox team is what it takes, then so be it," Spunner said. "But it will fly, and fly well."

O'Hara looked puzzled and was obviously trying to come up with something encouraging to say, but he was spared the effort when a *tick . . . tick . . . tick . . .* sound came from just outside the mouth of the arroyo.

Flintlock turned to see a small rock bounce on the ground, followed by another and then another. "Spunner, is this arroyo going to collapse in on us?" he said.

"No, it won't. This is very strange," Spunner said. He stepped outside, looked up at the rock face and then quickly leaped to the side as a fist-sized rock missed his head by inches.

Flintlock drew his Colt and rushed to the path

leading into the arroyo, O'Hara, levering his rifle, on his heels. O'Neill followed but at a slower pace. They immediately came under a bombardment of rocks of all shapes and sizes. A few of the smaller ones, better aimed, hit Flintlock on the shoulders and others thudded into the ground close to O'Neill's feet. He and O'Hara beat a hasty retreat to the jeers and catcalls of the two dozen women and children who lined the top of the rock wall on either side of the arroyo. Flintlock, limping from his hurting leg, was hit by another rock before he scampered out of range.

O'Hara, who'd been hit above his left eye and was bleeding, was not a forgiving man when others did him harm. He threw the Winchester to his shoulder and dusted half a dozen quick shots just under the rim of the wall to his right, and then did the same to the other side. His fire threw up chips of sandstone and a few rounds whined off the rock like angry hornets, and the ferocious fusillade had the desired effect. After a few more jeers and taunts the women shepherded the children back from the edge and then disappeared from view.

Flintlock shoved his gun back in his waistband and said to Spunner, "What was all that about?"

The albino's pale face appeared even whiter. "It was a warning," he said. "It's one of Jasper Orlov's little jokes, but its message is deadly serious."

"What message?" Flintlock said, irritated.

"That you killed one of his and now he will kill you. Didn't you see that all those woman and children bore Orlov's serpent on their foreheads?"

"No, I was too busy dodging rocks," Flintlock said.

His smile was thin, without humor. "He aims to kill me and I aim to kill him, so we break even on that score."

"Orlov's disciples are not gunmen, Flintlock," Spunner said. "They'll shoot you in the back if they can."

"I guard his back," O'Hara said.

"Now he knows I was with you today, I wonder who will guard mine," Spunner said.

CHAPTER TWENTY-FOUR

Nathan Poteet was done with hiding out in the badlands eating salt pork and beans as he waited for Hogan Lord's summons to ride into town. Dave Sutherland and the others, a restless breed, had quit days before and were probably already back in Texas raising a hundred different kinds of hell.

Poteet threw his saddle on his horse and grinned. It was high time he raised some hell of his own.

"Just put up your hands and step away from the hoss, mister."

Poteet froze as he heard the voice behind him and then slowly raised his hands.

Then a second man spoke. "There's a nice gentleman, now step away from the hoss like Deke here said. It won't bother me none to kill you but I'd surely be sorry to put a bullet in that big American stud."

"You boys are making a big mistake," Poteet said.

"No mistake, mister," Deke said. "We're just going to kill you, take your hoss and traps and then ride on. Where's the mistake in that? Huh? Well, let me tell you there isn't one. Now, move away from the stud like Les told you in the first place."

Poteet moved away from the horse and the man called Deke said, "Don't turn around. Stay right where you're at." Then, "Les, get his gun."

Poteet heard footsteps behind him . . . directly behind him, proving that Les wasn't too smart. For the moment at least the man screened him from Deke's gun. When Les was close enough that Poteet heard his nervous breathing, he turned, drawing from a shoulder holster. Les's eyes opened wide as he suddenly saw himself face-to-face with the muzzle of Poteet's .450 caliber Webley Bulldog revolver. But his horrified surprise lasted only a split second before Poteet's bullet crashed between his eyes and ended his life in an instant. Poteet, a big man and strong, didn't allow Les to drop. He held the thin body in front of him as a shield and Deke's hastily fired bullet thudded into the dead man's back. At a distance of seven feet Poteet fired, a belly shot that made Deke gasp in pain and stagger back, his face stricken. Poteet held his fire as the man threw his gun away and dropped to his knees. "Don't shoot me again, mister, I'm done," he said.

"Damn right, you're done," Poteet said. He crossed the ground and picked up the man's revolver, a rusty cap-and-ball that had seen better days. He looked at the gun and shook his head. "You boys should've chosen another line of work, maybe in the millinery business. You surely don't have a talent for bush-whacking folks."

His teeth gritted as he fought back against the pain in his belly, Deke said, "We were poor folks, Les and me. Born poor, raised poor and stayed poor. We never could catch a break."

"Times are hard all over," Poteet said. He pitched the old revolver into the brush and then cinched up his saddle. The big outlaw stepped into the leather, looked down at the wounded man and said, "How old are you, Deke?"

"Twenty-six, near as I can tell."

"Old enough to know better, huh? Better make your peace with God. Your time is short."

"Mister, I need a doctor," Deke said, his face ashen. "My belly is hurting awful bad, like my guts are on fire."

"Then I got some medicine for you, Deke," Poteet said. "It comes all the way from the British Isles." He raised the Bulldog and fired, abruptly cutting off Deke's scream of terror as a red rose blossomed in the middle of his forehead.

Without another glance at the two dead men Poteet kneed his horse into a walk and rode in the direction of Mansion Creek.

"Right now I have nothing for you, Nathan," Tobias Fynes said. "But something might come up in the next few days."

"Fill me in," Poteet said. He glanced outside at the street, busy now that the rain had ended. "I'm ready for some gun work. Hell, any kind of work."

"I don't have much to tell you at this time, but as you say, there may be gun work to be done a few days down the road," Fynes said. Then, as though the thought had just occurred to him, "Can you take Sam Flintlock? The man is a thorn in my side."

Poteet nodded. "Sure, I can take him, any day of the week."

Hogan Lord looked at the gunman with half-amused eyes but said nothing.

Fynes smiled. "That's exactly what I needed to hear. In the meantime, set yourself up at the hotel and tell them Mr. Fynes said to send the bill to him. Do the same at the saloon, but if you want a woman you're on your own."

"Right now I need some grub," Poteet said. "I killed two men this morning and it gave me an appetite."

Lord was alarmed. A double killing could draw some unwelcome attention to him and Fynes.

Poteet read Lord's face and said, "A couple of rubes in the wrong line of work tried to steal my horse. I done for both of them." Then, to put Lord's mind at rest, "It was a ways out of town, Hogan."

"There's all kinds of poor white trash in this part of the territory," Fynes said. "They won't be missed."

"I reckon not," Poteet said. "They were real raggedy-assed."

Fynes shuffled some papers on his desk and said, "Well, gentlemen, I have work to do. Hogan, perhaps you could accompany Nathan to the restaurant and see that he gets fed. By the way, Nathan, I'm officiating at a wedding tomorrow if you'd care to attend."

"Sure, I like weddings," Poteet said. "I get to kiss the bride, if she ain't ugly."

Fynes smiled at that. "This bride is very pretty. You won't be disappointed."

* * *

Hogan Lord was acutely aware that Nathan Poteet was a powder keg with a very short fuse, ready to blow at any second. The outlaw enjoyed killing and he'd once told Lord that shooting a man was better than lying with a woman, better than the finest whiskey, better than anything.

Although Poteet gave his total attention to the steak and eggs on his plate, Lord was on edge. Three noisy cowboys in from one of the neighboring ranches sat at another table and one of them was a redheaded youngster who called himself the Pima Kid, having been born and raised in the territory's Pima County. The Kid had once sought out Hogan Lord to sit with him in the saloon so he could be seen with a named shootist. At first Lord was flattered by the youngster's adoring attention, but then things took a serious turn when the Kid outdrew and shot down Morgan Fanning, a profane loudmouthed teamster who boasted that he had killed three men in gunfights. That had been a year ago and ever since then the Kid fancied himself a draw fighter to be reckoned with, telling everyone who would listen that he'd killed a named man.

But Lord knew Morgan Fanning to be a coward and a braggart, a bully who picked on the timid, sick or elderly. To the best of his knowledge the man had never been in a gunfight, and old Jamie MacDonald, the mountain man killed by Poteet and his boys, had once put the crawl on him right out there in the street.

As the cowboys grew louder, enjoying the attention they were getting from the other diners, Lord's uneasiness grew. Camped out in the badlands Poteet had been a valuable asset to Tobias Fynes's plans, but now he was in town the moody, volatile gunman was a liability.

Poteet pushed his plate away from him, lounged back in the chair and said, "That was good. I haven't had a beefsteak in an age." His cold gray eyes slid from Lord and settled on the boisterous cowboys. "Noisy, ain't they?"

"They're young, Nathan. Letting off some steam, is all," Lord said.

Then his heart sank. The Pima Kid stared back at Poteet and said, "Hell, mister, I had a picture made of me. Do you want it?"

Poteet just smiled and shook his head. He picked up his coffee cup and drained it to the dregs and Lord felt a flood of relief. "Let's get you a hotel room, Nathan," he said. "Then I'll buy you a drink."

Poteet was almost affable. "Suits me, Hogan," he said. "How's the whiskey in this burg?"

"Middlin'," Lord said.

"Middlin' sounds better than what I've been drinking," Poteet said.

Lord paid their score and then he and Poteet rose from the table and stepped toward the door. Then the Pima Kid did a foolish thing. He stood up and blocked their way. He wore a pearl-handled Colt high on his hip in the horseman's style and he also wore an expression on his face that was part arrogance, part a shining-eyed desire to again prove himself. Maybe he only wanted to frighten Poteet and put the crawl on him, a victory of sorts he could boast about later. In a future time when men spoke of it and argued the matter back and forth they finally agreed that we'll never know the Kid's true intentions. What is certain is that he braced Nathan Poteet, a perfect stranger to him, and paid dearly for it.

"Mister, I asked you if you want my picture," the Kid said. "You didn't answer me and that's not polite." He looked back at his grinning companions and then turned to face Poteet again. "Answer me. Why were you staring at me?"

"Trying to figure out what kind of little animal you were, boy," Poteet said. "Now will you give me the road?"

The Kid looked into Poteet's eyes and realized in that moment that maybe, just maybe, he'd made a mistake. The big man wasn't wearing a gun, but he didn't scare worth a damn. However, the Kid was committed to a course of action and with a dozen townspeople watching him he had to see it through to the end.

"Sure, I'll give you the road . . . after you apologize," the young cowboy said.

"Apologize? Apologize for what?" Poteet said.

His faltering confidence returning, the Kid said, grinning, "For getting in my way."

"Go to hell," Poteet said.

In the dime novels the Kid had read, when harsh words were spoken the time had come for the hero of the piece to draw his trusty revolver. The Pima Kid did just that.

Poteet had been watching the youngster's eyes and he anticipated the draw. As the Kid's hand clawed for the butt of his Colt, Poteet, moving with the speed of a rattlesnake, backhanded the youngster across the face. The crack of the blow sounded like a pistol shot in the confined space of the restaurant. At the same time Poteet's left hand shot out, grabbed the Kid's revolver and wrenched it violently upward, breaking the youngster's trigger finger.

The backhand was powerful enough to drop the Kid. He lay on his back on the floor for a few moments and then sat up, his frightened eyes on Poteet. The big gunman opened the Colt's loading gate and one by one, taking his time, he dropped all five cartridges into the Kid's full coffee cup.

Poteet then stepped toward the Kid. Blood trickled from the corner of the young man's mouth and his right cheekbone and eye were bruised and swollen. Poteet dropped the fancy Colt on the Kid's lap and said, "Come back and see me when you grow up."

Hogan Lord, relieved, said, "Come, let me buy you a drink, Nathan."

And that's where the scrape could and should have ended. But it didn't.

Every eye was on Nathan Poteet as he and Hogan Lord left the restaurant. One grizzled customer, wearing good broadcloth, and more savvy about the ways of gunmen than the rest, looked up at Poteet as he headed for the door and said, "That was well done." Poteet nodded, acknowledging the compliment, and then he and Lord stepped out the door onto the boardwalk.

The Pima Kid, in a desperate attempt to salvage his reputation as a dangerous gun, would not let it go.

He rose to his feet and yelled, "I'm gonna kill that

son of a bitch." He walked toward the door, his left hand feeding shells into his Colt from his cartridge belt.

One of his companions, using the Kid's given name, said, "Cass, don't go out there." He and the other cowboy tried to hold the Kid back, but he cursed them both, broke free and stormed out the door.

Nathan Poteet had stopped to light a cigar, and he and Lord were about thirty feet away, standing under a painted, hanging sign that read:

THE GENERAL STORE

Fudge ~ Candies ~ Groceries

The Pima Kid's gun hand was out of action, his forefinger broken and already swelling, and he fired with his left. He put his first bullet in that sign neatly between *Fudge* and *Groceries* and the hole was still there until the store burned down in 1902. His second splintered timber inches from Poteet's feet and a third grazed the leg of a bartender who was reporting for his shift at the saloon.

The Kid didn't get off a fourth.

Poteet drew the British Bulldog and adopted the duelist position. He turned side-on to the Kid, right arm extended, the inside of the left foot tucked behind the heel of the right. Despite the Bulldog's heavy trigger and rudimentary sights, Poteet needed only one shot . . . the shot that struck the Kid high in the chest and dropped him. After he hit the board-walk the youngster stared at Poteet with stunned, unbelieving eyes, gasped a few times and then died.

Diners spilled out of the restaurant and drinkers from the saloon, and already angry voices, led by the Kid's fellow punchers, were raised against Poteet.

Hogan Lord tried to undo the damage. "Fair fight!" he yelled. "The Kid fired first."

No one in the crowd recognized Poteet as a notorious outlaw but for some it was enough that a local boy had been shot down by an out-of-towner. Lord recognized a few members of the Mansion Creek Peace Commission, a fancy title for vigilantes, and they looked grim. A few of the drunker citizens from the saloon were talking rope and the angry cowboys took up the chorus. A hanging mob is like a savage, mindless animal and Lord feared he may have to go to the gun and shoot Poteet free of its clutches.

The bartender, at a time when mixologists were considered respected members of frontier society right up there with doctors, lawyers and merchants, saved the day. Bleeding from the bullet that had cut across the back of his right thigh, he raised his arms for quiet and said, "The Kid shot first." He showed his bloody pants leg and said, "He could have killed me."

That last calmed the mob a little and then the enormous, reassuring presence of the banker Tobias Fynes did the rest.

He waddled along the boardwalk and said to the crowd, "Mr. Townshend is telling the truth. From my office window I saw him get hit by the young man's deadly bullet and then I saw poor Mr. Poteet forced to fight for his very life."

The crowd became silent and even the cowboys quit yelling for a rope. Then, in touching regard for the fallen youth, Fynes forced his face into a sympathetic expression alien to him and said, "Does the dead lad have family close?"

One of the cowboys said, "I think Cass has kin in Texas, but I don't know where."

"Anyone else know?" Fynes looked solicitous but the question was met with silence. He said, "Then take the poor boy back to his ranch where people who liked him and worked beside Cass can bury him."

In truth, Cass Wilson was arrogant and lazy and not well liked, but the two cowboys who'd ridden into town with him saw no other alternative.

After that the crowd dispersed and the Pima Kid was taken away hanging over his pony's saddle, his long yellow hair almost dragging in the dirt. Fynes took Poteet aside, stood as close to him as his belly would allow and said between gritted teeth, his eyes blazing, "Why the hell did you kill the damned waddie? You've drawn unwelcome attention to yourself."

Hogan Lord said, "He didn't give Nathan any choice, Tobias. The kid came out of the restaurant shooting."

"Come to my office," Fynes said. "Both of you."

If there were people in the street who wondered why the town's most prominent citizen would be seen in the company of a killer like Nathan Poteet, no one voiced that question because Fynes had Mansion Creek by the throat. If the banker ever decided to call in his mortgages the town would wither on the vine and die.

"Mr. Poteet, I don't need you right now, but I'll need you in the future and when that time comes it will be almighty sudden," Tobias Fynes said. "Do you understand?"

"Sure do, boss," Poteet said, taking a sip of the banker's excellent whiskey.

"Good, then we are in perfect accord," Fynes said. "Now that's settled, you will occupy a hotel room and stay there until I send for you. I'll provide you with everything you need so you won't be in want."

Poteet was wary. "How long?"

"Probably no more than a week or two. There is a matter that must be brought to a head very quickly."

"What kind of matter?"

"I'll tell you all you need to know in due course. In the meantime, Hogan will act as my go-between." Fynes smiled. "Patience, Mr. Poteet. You'll soon get all the excitement you need. That concludes our business for now. I have a wedding to arrange."

CHAPTER TWENTY-FIVE

"Mr. Flintlock, both myself and Mr. Whitman have assured Miss Cully that there are no supernatural entities in this house, so we've all agreed that your services are no longer required," Roderick Chanley said.

"If it's all the same to you, O'Hara and me will stay until the end of the week," Flintlock said, his growing dislike of the eye-patched poet apparent in the harsh tone of his voice.

"Suit yourself, but I must ask you to vacate the house immediately," Chanley said. "I find your presence unsettling and so does Lucy."

"Unsettling how?" Flintlock said, on a slow burn.

"Lucy and myself are pacifists, a word you perhaps have never heard and do not understand. To explain, we're nonviolent people and we both find the presence in the house of men with guns unsettling. There has already been killing, men shot to death."

"You know that Lucy has a derringer, don't you?"

"I am aware of that, but she no longer has it. I confiscated the weapon and threw it over the side of the crag." Chanley looked down his long nose at

Flintlock. "You have already brought violence to this house and we don't want any more."

Flintlock decided to be brutally honest. "If me and O'Hara hadn't shot it out with Shade Pike and his boys Lucy would have been raped and probably murdered." He glared at Chanley. "Mister, you weren't there."

"I am here now, and since Lucy will soon be my wife I am the master of this house and I want you to leave it," the poet said. "We will never see eye to eye on guns and violence, Flintlock, so our conversation is over. You and the breed can bed down in the barn if you like, but you must be gone by the end of the week."

"I'd like to hear that from Lucy herself," Flintlock said.

"My fiancée is indisposed," Chanley said.

"I'd still like her to tell me and O'Hara that we have to burn the breeze out of here."

"Very well, I'll get her," Chanley said. He rose from the kitchen table and stepped toward the door. He turned and said, "I would normally not tolerate the presence of Rory O'Neill here, another man of violence, but since he is with Mr. Whitman I agreed to let him remain. You see, I don't play favorites."

O'Hara pushed his cup away from him and said, "Looks like we just got our marching orders, Sam."

"We'll see out the week, even if we have to camp on the mesa," Flintlock said. "We need that five hundred from Tobias Fynes. It's our stake for when we ride away of here and head west."

"A couple of more days," O'Hara said. "I guess we can handle that."

"But I'm not leaving until I bed down Jasper Orlov," Flintlock said.

"Sam, you heard the man, we're not wanted here," O'Hara said. "I say we ride out and leave the poet to deal with Orlov himself."

"I can't leave that monster alive," Flintlock said. "Any one of those rocks his women and children tossed down on us could've killed us."

"Spunner said it was only a warning."

"Maybe so, but I won't let Orlov see me turn tail and run." Flintlock poured himself more coffee and said, "O'Hara, there has to be a reckoning. If you don't want to be a part of it, you're free to light a shuck."

"That's a hell of a thing to say to me, Sam," O'Hara said.

Flintlock grinned. "I know, and if I thought for one minute you'd take me up on it I never would have said it."

O'Hara frowned. "See, you take me for granted, Sam."

"Yup, I do, constantly," Flintlock said.

Just then Lucy stepped into the kitchen. She looked pale and there were dark shadows under her eyes as though she hadn't slept well.

Before Flintlock could say anything she said, "Did Roderick speak to you about leaving, Sam?"

"Yes he did, but—"

"Good," Lucy said. "Then it's all settled."

She turned on her heel and left, her petticoats rustling.

O'Hara stared at Flintlock and then said, "Seems like nobody wants us, Sam, huh?"

"Shapes up that way," Flintlock said. Then, "Get your stuff together, O'Hara, we're leaving. I won't stay where I'm not wanted." He glanced out the kitchen window and managed a smile. "Well, at least it's not raining."

The rain had indeed ended, but a strong wind buffeted the house and it creaked and groaned like a storm-tossed sailing ship. Outside around its tallest spires the ravens cawed a warning about dangers only they knew of and then joined together in a ragged flock and fluttered into the restless sky.

"Fixing for a big blow, Sam," O'Hara said.

"Seems like," Flintlock said, his face bleak.

Suddenly, he had a strange feeling of hard times a-coming, of bad happenings, that he could not shake.

CHAPTER TWENTY-SIX

On the morning of what was destined to be Lucy Cully's wedding day and Nathan Poteet's last day on earth, the outlaw was wakened from sound sleep when the door of his hotel room was kicked in and damaged so badly that it hung askew on its one remaining hinge.

The shattering crash of the splintering door jarred Poteet to action. He reached for the Colt on his bedside table but didn't make it. Strong hands pinned him down and then dragged him kicking and cussing from the bed.

Grim old Hawk Collins, owner of the Rafter-H ranch, waited until Poteet was punched into submission by several of his hands and then said, "Put on your duds, Poteet. I will not hang a man in his underwear. It ain't decent."

"What the hell is this about?" Poteet yelled, his face black with anger.

"You know what it's about, Poteet," Collins said. "Now dress like I said or by God we'll do it for you."

"That youngster, the one who tried to kill me.

You're here about him, ain't you?" Poteet said. His mouth was bloody and his left eye was swollen shut from the beating he'd taken. "It was a fair fight and he fired first."

"Fired first, fired last, didn't fire at all, I don't give a damn," Collins said. "He rode for my brand and I won't let his death go unanswered and unpunished."

Hawk Collins, a hard, unforgiving man, was a stern product of his time and place. He'd once counted Jesse Chisholm a friend and still kept up a cordial correspondence with old Charlie Goodnight. Collins was seventy years old that fall and in his lifetime he'd killed four men in gunfights and had hanged eighteen more. His first wife had died of the cholera in 1880 and he married his second a year later, a lass of seventeen who doted on him. He had no children from either marriage, a disappointment to him.

Poteet knew nothing of this but when he looked into Collins's green eyes he saw no mercy there. But damn the man, he would not beg for his life like a common coward. He pulled free of the punchers who held him and said, "Boys, let me dress by myself."

The hands looked at their boss and Collins nodded and said, "He can put on his own clothes."

Poteet dressed meticulously in a clean shirt and collar and then brushed his frock coat. He settled his hat on his head and polished the toes of his boots on the back of his pants leg. "I'm ready. But if it ain't too much of an inconvenience, I'd admire to know the name of the man who's fixing to hang me."

"My name is Hawk Collins," the rancher said.

"You're named for a bird of prey," Poteet said.

"My pa said a hawk flew around our cabin as I was

being born, or maybe it was his idea of a joke, I don't know," Collins said.

Poteet stared intently into the older man's face. "You look like a hawk, like a mad old falcon."

Collins said, "Best you don't make comments on a man's appearance and instead make your peace with God, son. Your time is short." Then, to the dozen punchers who'd crowded into the room. "Take him down to the street, boys."

Tobias Fynes always arrived at the bank early, eager to leave what he called the Death House. And, as was his habit, he stood at his office window to smoke his first cigar and watch the comings and goings of the wakening town. But that morning the procession he saw leaving the hotel made his eyes nearly pop out of his head and he squeezed his cigar in sudden a stab of panic.

Nathan Poteet was surrounded by the tough punchers of Hawk Collins's Rafter-H, and old Hawk himself carried a noosed rope and led a saddled paint cow pony. It looked like the rancher was making a beeline for the livery stable with its sturdy rafters.

Fynes's breath came in quick little gasps and he felt a cramping pain in his chest. This situation was bad, very bad. Then, unreasonably angry, where the hell was Hogan Lord? Probably still abed with that Kate Coldwell whore. Fynes's hands trembled when he thought about Hawk Collins. Damn his eyes, the man owed him nothing, not a penny. The old rancher bought everything he needed with cash on the barrel-head and owed money to no man and never had.

With a trembling hand Fynes mopped the sudden beads of sweat off his brow. He must intercede on Poteet's behalf. Collins was a tough, relentless and pitiless man but surely he'd listen to reason from a wealthy and respected citizen like Tobias Fynes.

Fynes hustled out of his office and waddled to the livery at the edge of town. He arrived just as Collins tossed his rope over a rafter.

"Hawk Collins, you must stop this," Fynes said, desperately keeping hold of his fading courage. "Mr. Poteet has friends in this town."

"That he has friends in this town doesn't surprise me, Fynes," Collins said. "Mansion Creek has been a lawless cesspit for long enough and it took the murder of one of my boys to push me to do something about it."

"Hawk, listen to reason, the kid ran out onto the boardwalk and cut loose on Mr. Poteet, who had to fight for his life," Fynes said. "It was a fair fight, anybody in town will tell you that. Let them speak up and you'll change your mind about taking this terrible course of action."

"My mind is made up, Fynes, and empty words won't change it. If young Cass Wilson hadn't ridden into this damned town he'd be alive today and there's the bottom line," Collins said. He looked up at Poteet, who'd been hoisted onto the horse. "And there's the man who killed him. That's all I need to know. I've read to him from the Book and it's his time to die."

Desperately, Fynes tried a different tack. "Collins, if you hang Mr. Poteet I'll bring the full force of the law down on you and you'll swing yourself. That I swear."

Contempt showed in Collins's chiseled, rough-hewn

face. "You, Fynes, you damned scoundrel, you dare to talk about bringing in the law? If there was law in this town you'd have been strung up years ago. Now get the hell away from me before I do something I might regret and hang you next to Poteet."

Hawk Collins was a known man-killer, unrelenting when it came to his narrow view of justice, and Fynes was suddenly scared enough that he could almost feel the coarse hemp noose around his fat neck. He backed away, and then to save face he said, "Hawk Collins, you'll be sorry for what you're doing this day."

The rancher glared at Fynes, dismissed him and said to Poteet, "Do you have any last words, son? I can pray with you and ask for God's forgiveness."

"Yeah, I have last words," Poteet said. "You go to hell."

Collins nodded and a puncher slapped the horse out from under Poteet. The gunman dangled in the noose, kicking and gasping for long, agonized minutes before he died.

Fynes beat a hasty retreat back to his office, his heart hammering in his chest, fear clutching at his belly. My God, it could be him dangling at the end of a rope.

For five long minutes the rope creaked as Poteet's corpse swung in the rising wind that sighed mournfully through the open door of the barn. The owner, an army veteran named Cordell, finally stepped out of his tiny office and stared at the dead man, his face expressionless.

"Did you know this man?" Collins said.

"I only spoke with him when he left his horse here,"

Cordell said. "Since he was a customer, if no one else claims the body I guess I can sell the horse and bury him."

"I bury my own dead," Collins said. He spun Cordell a coin that the livery owner caught deftly. "Plant him decent."

But Hawk Collins still had an important task to complete.

"Cut him down, boys," he said. "Lay him out. Slim, come with me."

Slim Hart was forty years old, a tall drink of water with the long, lugubrious face of a suffering saint in a Renaissance painting. But his ability with a gun belied his appearance. He'd been a cowtown lawman, Texas Ranger and a Butterfield stagecoach guard and in his younger years had dabbled in train robberies with Jesse and Frank and them, but he quit the profession when he decided that he wanted to stay on the right side of the law. Hart was twenty years past it for cowboying but Hawk Collins kept him around because of his gun skills. He was fast with the Colt on the draw and shoot and a crack shot with a Winchester. His widowed mother was still alive and he sent her ten dollars out of his pay every month.

Hart followed his boss to the bank and then stepped inside with him. "I'm here to see Fynes," Collins said.

"Mr. Fynes is busy and can't be disturbed," a teller said, blocking the rancher's path. Collins roughly pushed the man aside and charged into Fynes's office.

The fat man, still visibly shaken, sat with John Tanner, the wagon driver. He glared at the rancher and said, "I'm busy, Collins."

"You're not too busy to hear this," Collins said. "This here is Slim Hart, one of my punchers. He's worked as a lawman afore and that's why I'm making him the town marshal of Mansion Creek."

"By what authority?" Fynes said. He was outraged, his flabby face brick red.

Collins drew his Colt and slammed it on the desk. "By this authority, Fynes. And I've got two dozen men backing me who also carry authority in their holsters."

Fynes got to his feet and retreated into bluster. "Now, see here—"

"No, you see here, Fynes. Slim Hart is now the law in Mansion Creek," Collins said. "He'll answer to no one but me. Understand?"

"About time we had some law around here," Tanner said, earning himself an angry glance from the fat man.

"Well, son, you got the right of it," Collins said to Tanner. "And Fynes, if anything should happen to Marshal Hart, an accident of some kind—his fault, somebody else's fault, nobody's fault—I'll blame you and by God I'll hang you."

Fynes said, "It's hardly my fault if—"

"You heard me, Fynes. If Marshal Hart even comes down with the croup or has to lie abed because of the rheumatisms I'm blaming you." Hawk Collins holstered his revolver. "I'd say that it's in your interest to see that he stays alive and well. Slim will set up at the hotel until the town builds him an office with a couple of jail cells in back. Get it done, Fynes. And make sure Marshal Hart gets a star. I'm sure there's one gathering dust around this town somewhere."

Collins turned and walked out of the office, but

Slim Hart stopped at the door and said, "Been a right pleasure making your acquaintance, Mr. Fynes."

Go to hell. Fynes thought that, but didn't say it. Then to Tanner, "The wedding must go ahead as planned." He glanced at his watch. "It's almost ten o'clock. Be ready to leave in an hour."

CHAPTER TWENTY-SEVEN

Flintlock and O'Hara spent an uncomfortable night in the stable behind the house and they were surprised when Lucy Cully stepped inside at first light bearing a tray loaded with coffee and a pile of bacon sandwiches.

She handed the tray to Flintlock and said, "I'm so sorry about yesterday. Mr. Whitman said I should apologize for Roderick's behavior."

Flintlock smiled. "I've been thrown out of worse places."

"Me too," O'Hara said.

Flintlock set the tray on an upturned crate and poured coffee for him and O'Hara.

"What will you and O'Hara do, Sam?" Lucy said. She smiled. "I do worry about you two."

"Well, tomorrow I'll go get the five hundred dollars Tobias Fynes owes us," Flintlock said. "I don't reckon you're going to run screaming out of the house with a ghost at your heels."

Lucy smiled slightly. Flintlock thought she didn't

seem happy. She said, "No, this is my home now, Sam. Haunted or not, I'll never leave here."

Flintlock chewed on bread and bacon and then said, "I'm glad to hear you say that. A woman should have a home she calls her own. What about Roderick? How does he feel about the old house?"

"I don't know. I thought he would write poems here but he says the place doesn't inspire his muse but does intimidate him. I even told him about the hidden treasure map, hoping that it would motivate him to put pen to paper but he dismissed the story as nonsense."

"Sorry to hear that," Flintlock said. It was lame but he couldn't think of anything better to say.

"When you get your money will you ride on, Sam, and find your mother?" Lucy said.

"Yeah, that's the plan," Flintlock said. He decided not to mention his intentions regarding Jasper Orlov.

"I wish you and O'Hara would stay around for a while, maybe in Mansion Creek," Lucy said. "For just a couple of weeks, Sam."

"You've got Roderick now, Lucy, you don't need us," O'Hara said. He talked over the steaming rim of his cup, his blue eyes reading the girl's reaction.

She barely reacted and then, her voice faint, she said only, "Yes, I have Roderick. Still, I'm scared, O'Hara. But of what I don't know."

"It's not ghosts, is it?" Flintlock said.

"No, not ghosts. Something else . . . something that's coming toward me and I'm afraid I won't be able to step out of its way."

Flintlock reached out and took Lucy's hand. "We'll stick around for a while, depend on it."

The girl got up on tiptoe and kissed Flintlock's stubbled cheek. "Thank you, Sam," she said. "I feel much better already."

After the girl left, O'Hara said, "All right, what do we do now?"

"Finish the coffee and sandwiches," Flintlock said.

O'Hara saddled up and left the barn, saying he wanted to scout around to see if he could find a reason for Lucy's fear. Flintlock poured the last of the coffee into his cup, lit a cigarette and scowled at old Barnabas, who sat in a stall polishing a black iron helmet with a bright yellow cloth.

"What the hell are you doing here, you old coot?" Flintlock said.

Barnabas stared at the helmet, saw a spot he didn't like, breathed on it and then polished it again. "For your information, I'm shining up a helmet," he said.

"I can see that," Flintlock said.

"It belongs to the Black Knight of Augsburg, a disagreeable feller who spent all his mortal life a-killin' and a-rapin' and a-cuttin' off of maidens' heads." The old mountain man leaned closer, put a hand to the side of his mouth and whispered, "You-know-who says he's true-blue and should be a fine example to all of us."

"Go away, Barnabas," Flintlock said. "I've a lot on my mind."

"Don't tell me you're still sore about me staking you down to face the grizz that time?"

"Yes, I am. That and other things that left scars on me, both mental and physical."

"Sure hold a grudge, don't you, boy? No, don't answer that. I'm not going to bandy words with an idiot. Now listen up, and this is my last advice on the subject: Get yourself back into that house they threw you out of, gun them two scribblers and the pug and then have your villainous way with the girl. After you're done with her, toss her over the side of the crag. Then you and the crazy Injun go find your ma." Barnabas held up the helmet. "Ain't that purty, shining like a new coin."

"I'm sure the Black Knight of Whatever-the-hell-you-said will be real pleased with it. Now beat it."

"Nobody's ever pleased with anything in hell," Barnabas said. He shook his head. "What an idiot you are, boy. Now go right away and do what I told you to do."

Then Barnabas was gone and the barn smelled of fire and brimstone.

O'Hara sat his horse outside the barn and sniffed. "Barnabas was here?"

"Sure was," Flintlock said. "Giving me Old Scratch's advice again."

"Well, saddle up. You'll want to see this."

"See what?"

"I think it's a wedding party," O'Hara said. "I saw Tobias Fynes up on the seat of a wagon and Hogan Lord riding point, both of them dressed in their best. They got all kinds of stuff in the back, including a right pretty gal, a preacher and a fiddler who was playing 'Fire on the Mountain' when I first saw him and then 'Cluck Old Hen.'" He nodded. "Plays real good, that fiddler feller."

"You sure it's a wedding party?" Flintlock said.

"What else could it be?" O'Hara said. "I don't think a man as fat as Tobias Fynes would climb the mesa for a picnic."

"'Cluck Old Hen,'" Flintlock said. "Yeah, that's a hitching tune, right enough." He made up his mind. "All right, we'll go meet them."

Flintlock had both his Winchester and the Hawken booted on either side of the saddle. If he encountered Jasper Orlov he planned to be as well armed as possible.

He and O'Hara met Fynes and his wedding party just as they reached the top of the mesa. Hogan Lord, riding up front, drew rein and said, "This is a friendly visit, Sam. We're not here to do harm."

"And I'm taking it as sich," Flintlock said. He looked over the approaching wagon and the fat, sweating form of Tobias Fynes and said, "Looks like a wedding. Sounds like a wedding."

"And it is a wedding," Lord said.

"Who's getting hitched?"

"Lucy Cully and her intended. At least that's what Tobias Fynes intends it to be."

"Suppose she don't want to get hitched?" Flintlock said.

"Then I guess we'll cart everything back, the champagne, the wedding cake and ourselves," Lord said. "That's a mighty discouraging prospect, Sam."

"Hogan, if this turns out to be a shotgun wedding I'll take it hard," Flintlock said. "Lucy has to say, 'I do,' of her own accord. You catch my drift?"

"Sam, I don't have a shotgun and I won't draw my gun today," Lord said. "You have my word on that."

"Your word on it is good enough for me," Flintlock said. "Just make sure you keep it."

And then, as though he'd just remembered, Lord said, "Nathan Poteet is dead, hung for a murderer."

Flintlock was shocked. "Who hung him?"

"Rancher by the name of Hawk Collins. Rousted ol' Nathan out of bed, dragged him to the livery and strung him up. Nathan was a tough man and it took him a long time to die. He kicked and strangled for quite a spell, so I was told."

"Poteet murdered a lot of folks in his time. What done for him in the end?"

Lord told Flintlock about the shooting of Cass Wilson and said, "Seems to me that Nathan got hung for the only killing he ever done that wasn't his fault. He got a raw deal, that's my take on the situation."

Flintlock shook his head. "Well, well, doesn't that beat all. Nathan Poteet hung by a bunch of waddies. It's hard to believe."

"Believe it, Sam. Hawk Collins is a hard old man and he doesn't take any sass. And now thanks to him we got a new town marshal in town."

Lord didn't explain any further as Fynes hailed Flintlock from the wagon.

"Well met, Mr. Flintlock," he said. "Will you join us for the feast?"

"I wouldn't miss it, and that's a natural fact," Flintlock said. "By the way, me and O'Hara will come see you tomorrow."

"Yes, yes, we'll discuss that later," Fynes said. "Right now my mind is on the forthcoming nuptials. Now, will you give us the road?"

Flintlock backed his horse away and the wagon rumbled past, a grinning John Tanner at the reins. The fiddler struck up with "Golden Slippers" and beside him preacher Uriah Reedy clapped to the beat and looked as though he was already half drunk. The pretty girl at the back of the jolting wagon seemed both sad and miserably uncomfortable.

CHAPTER TWENTY-EIGHT

"But this is too sudden," Lucy Cully said. "I . . . I need a few days, Roderick."

"Nonsense, dear one," Chanley said. His one good eye shined. "Our return to Philadelphia will be our honeymoon."

"An excellent plan, Roderick," Walt Whitman said. "The grand old city will welcome such a lovely married couple with open arms, myself included."

"I don't want to return to Philadelphia," Lucy said. "This house is now my home. I'll never leave it."

Chanley's smile slipped and gave way to a frown. "Lucy, we will talk about that after the wedding," he said. "Ah, and right on cue here is Mr. Fynes come to give away the bride."

The fat man, perspiring heavily, stepped into the parlor and said, "Your guests are assembled in the library." He hoped his smile was sincere. "Now all we need are the bride and groom."

Lucy had the eyes of a startled deer. "But I wanted a wedding dress, a white wedding gown," she said. "I can't get married in this old house dress."

"Of course you can, my dear," Chanley said. "You look quite ravishing. Does she not, Mr. Fynes?"

"Yes, a vision of loveliness." Fynes reached into a pocket and came up with a plain gold band. "Look, my dear Lucy," he said, "I even have your wedding ring."

Chanley looked stern. "A noble gesture, Mr. Fynes," he said. "Lucy, you look just fine, pretty as a picture. After all the trouble your guardian Mr. Fynes has gone to, you will marry me now or not at all."

"Fynes is not my guardian and I need some time to think, Roderick," Lucy said.

"Think about what?" Chanley said. "There's nothing to think about. We love each other and we're going to get married, that's all. It's very simple."

"Think about whether or not I want to marry you," Lucy said.

Chanley looked as though the girl had just slapped his face. He said, "That is an insulting thing to say to me, Lucy. The impression you give is that I'm no longer good enough for you and such a sentiment makes my heart turn cold toward you. Who is the man? Is he the ruffian who calls himself Flintlock, or is it the breed or perhaps Rory O'Neill?"

"Roderick, I won't dignify that question with an answer," Lucy said.

Tobias Fynes had been listening to this exchange with growing impatience. He felt the Cully mansion and the treasure map slipping through his fingers— and all because of a headstrong, stubborn girl.

He decided to take matters into his own hands and solve this problem the way he always did, by charging straight at it like a maddened bull.

"You two stay here and talk things over while I go

and tell the guests there will be a short delay," Fynes said.

"There's nothing more to talk about," Lucy said. "And tell the guests to go home because there will be a long delay."

"Stay here nonetheless," Fynes said, his piggy little eyes vicious.

The fat man left the room and crossed the hall to the library. When he stepped inside Flintlock and the others looked at him expectantly.

"There will be a short delay," Fynes said. "The bride and groom wish to join in prayer for a while before the ceremony. At the moment they wish only to take spiritual counsel with the Reverend Reedy."

Uriah Reedy, now more than half drunk, bowed his head and said, "The Lord be praised."

"Yes, indeed and so he should," Fynes said. He grabbed his mistress Estelle Redway by the arm and said, "I'll wait outside the parlor door until I'm needed and you will come along too, Estelle. A bride should have another woman close on this, her happiest day. Fiddler, give us a tune while we wait."

As Fynes and the others left the room, Flintlock and O'Hara exchanged puzzled glances and Walt Whitman seemed concerned. Rory O'Neill stood behind the old man's chair and laid a comforting hand on his shoulder. Hogan Lord stood with his back against a wall, his face like stone. Only the fiddler and young John Tanner, who had stayed for the festivities, seemed to be enjoying themselves, helped by a plentiful supply of Fynes's bourbon.

"It seems the bride is shy," Tanner said. "I guess that's to be expected."

The fiddler, a red-nosed man named Slattery, grinned and said, "Let's drink to that." He downed three fingers of Old Crow and then picked up his fiddle, launched into "Old Joe Clark" and while Flintlock and O'Hara stood silent, young Tanner applauded and tapped his toes.

"Well, have we reconciled our differences?" Tobias Fynes said. He'd given up trying to look like a benign uncle. Now his face was flushed and angry.

"The only difference we have is a matter of timing," Lucy said.

"And you've made it clear that you don't want to marry me," Chanley said. He looked like he'd just sucked on a lemon.

"Roderick, I didn't say that I wouldn't marry you," Lucy said. Tears started in her eyes. "I just need a little more time to think about it."

The Reverend Reedy, swaying a little, blinked like an owl and said, "Dearly beloved, shall we now proceed with the marriage?"

Fynes said, "Of course you need time, Lucy." He stepped toward her and held out his arms. "You're very distraught, my child. Here, let me give you a hug."

Estelle gave a little gasp of alarm as Lucy hesitantly let Fynes embrace her. It was the easiest thing in the world for him to grab her left arm, twist it behind her back and push up hard until her hand was between her shoulder blades and she cried out in pain.

Fynes whispered into Lucy's ear, "All you have to do say is 'I do' and the pain will stop."

"This is for your own good, Lucy," Roderick Chanley said. "This cursed house has done something terrible to you. It's turned you into a madwoman."

Fynes said, "Now, Lucy, will you say those two little words? Think of it, my dear, soon you'll be married to Roderick and live happily ever after."

"Let me go," Lucy said. "You're hurting me."

Fynes forced the arm higher up the girl's back and she cried out in pain. Estelle ran to the fat man and attempted to pull his hand away from Lucy's arm. Roderick dragged her away and said, "Don't interfere. Lucy will thank Mr. Fynes for this later."

Beside Fynes's great bulk Lucy looked tiny and fragile, as though the fat man could break her to pieces in his arms. "Listen to me," he said, his florid face close to hers, "if you cry out again, Flintlock and the breed will come to your rescue. Hogan Lord will not allow that to happen. He'll kill them both. Do you understand me?"

Tears of pain and anger in her eyes, Lucy nodded. "Yes, I understand."

"Will you say the words?" Fynes said.

Defeated, Lucy went as limp as a rag doll. She would not allow herself to be responsible for the deaths of two men she liked, and she'd no fight left in her.

* * *

Lucy's cry troubled Flintlock and O'Hara and they both headed for the library door. Hogan Lord got to the door before they did. He'd cleared his frock coat from his gun. "What's going on in the parlor is no business of you boys," he said.

In deference to the wedding, O'Hara had earlier unbuckled his gunbelt and laid it aside on a chair. Now he crossed the floor, drew his revolver and held it by his side. "Hogan, I'm making it my business," he said.

Flintlock kept his voice calm, level. "No, O'Hara. He'll kill you."

Lord and O'Hara locked eyes. The chime of the clock in the hallway was loud in the silence. "I don't want to kill you, O'Hara," Lord said. "But if it comes down to it, I will."

"Hogan, go find out what's happening and come back and tell us," Flintlock said. Then, his eyes accusing, "You gave me your word not to draw your gun."

Lord stared hard at Flintlock and thought that through. Like O'Hara, Flintlock had laid his gun aside, figuring that no one cares to be around a gun-toting wedding guest. As he faced Lord he knew the gunman would not draw down on an unarmed man.

Finally, Lord said, "Yes, I did give my word and I haven't drawn my gun yet. I'll go take a look. But what you heard was a little yelp of happiness from Lucy, nothing else. You two stay right where you're at, and O'Hara, put that hogleg away—doesn't exactly make the place feel homey."

Slattery the fiddler, aware of the tension in the room, launched into a spirited rendition of "Bile 'Em Cabbage Down" and the moment passed.

Lord stepped out of the room and O'Hara said to Flintlock, "I had my gun in my hand, Sam. He knew I could shade him."

Flintlock said, "No, O'Hara, he would have killed you. One way or another, he would have killed you."

Raising his voice over the lilting strains of the music, O'Hara said, "I can't believe he's that fast. I had my Colt in my hand and I put the crawl on him."

Flintlock shook his head. "You didn't put the crawl on him, O'Hara. Hogan Lord is fast. Maybe he's the fastest that's ever been."

CHAPTER TWENTY-NINE

As the tipsy preacher prepared to marry Lucy Cully and her intended, two things happened that spoiled his introductory speech on the joys of marriage. The first was that Hogan Lord stepped into the room and obviously didn't like what he saw, the second was the fusillade of bullets that crashed into the front of the mansion.

Western men, Lord, Fynes and the Reverend Reedy, hit the floor immediately but Lucy and Roderick Chanley stood in the middle of the floor, bewildered.

"Get down!" Lord yelled. From the library he heard the fiddle squawk to a frightened stop.

As a bullet crashed through the parlor window scattering shards of glass, Chanley hit the floor and Lucy followed. She crawled to Lord and said, "Who is out there?"

The gunman shook his head and said nothing. He made his way to the window and crouched behind it, gun in hand. After a couple more shots thudded into the front of the house near him, he slowly raised his head and looked outside. Less than a hundred yards away a stand of juniper was threaded by strands of gunsmoke. Lord ducked down again as a bullet shattered through the window a few inches above his head. During his brief glance outside he'd counted fire from at least six rifles, but there could be twice that number hidden among the trees.

"Hogan, do you see them?" Fynes said. The fat man was sweating heavily but game enough, grasping a Sharps .22 caliber four-shot derringer in his fist.

Without turning his head Lord said, "I see their smoke, but that's all I see."

"How many?" Fynes said.

"I don't know. I'd say at least six."

"Who the hell are they?" Fynes said.

"Beats me," Lord said. "But they're an unfriendly bunch."

He jumped up, thumbed off five fast shots and as answering bullets broke windowpanes, ducked down again. As he reloaded from his cartridge belt Lord looked at Chanley and said, "Hey, poet, crawl across the floor and open the door."

To Lord's surprise Chanley's face was gray, his eyes wide and staring. The man looking back at Lord seemed paralyzed, immobilized by fear. Without taking his eyes from Chanley's face, Lord said, "Tobias, go open the door."

But before the fat man could move, Lucy said, "I'll do it." She crawled across the floor, reached up for the handle and pulled the door open.

"Wide," Lord said.

Bullets buzzed through the parlor like angry hornets.

Lucy pulled the door wide and Lord yelled, "Sam! Sam Flintlock!"

"I hear you!" Flintlock yelled.

"Are you and O'Hara still alive?"

"So far!"

"Who the hell is out there?"

"I think it could be Jasper Orlov and his bunch," Flintlock said.

Lord didn't answer for a few moments and then he yelled, "There's no such person!"

"Stick your head out the front door and then tell me that," Flintlock said. "There is such a person and he means to kill us." Then, "Hogan, can you hear me?"

"Yeah."

"I'm going out back to the barn for rifles. Keep 'em busy, huh?"

"I'll do that," Lord said. "But don't be long. Those boys out there might take it into their heads to rush us."

Flintlock didn't answer. He was already making his limping way to the back door of the house.

A wind always soared across the high crest of the crag and it tugged at the brim of Flintlock's hat as he stepped out the door and crossed ten yards of open ground to the stable. His buckskin nickered a greeting as Flintlock entered and slid his rifle and O'Hara's from their scabbards. He also pulled the Hawken. It was loaded and seemed to be in good shape. Flintlock had a plan for the old smoke pole. He picked up half a box of .44-40 shells from his saddlebags and then made his way back into the house.

Bullets still ripped through the mansion and he heard the flat statements of O'Hara and Lord's Colts as they maintained a slow but steady fire.

"O'Hara," Flintlock said before he entered the library door. There was a good possibility that O'Hara would shoot first and identify his silent intruder later. "It's me."

"You got my rifle?" O'Hara said.

"Yeah." Flintlock took up a crouching position and duckwalked across the floor. O'Hara holstered his Colt and grabbed the rifle. He raised an eyebrow at the Hawken but said nothing. Flintlock hunkered down behind the window and shoved the barrel of the Hawken through a broken pane. He pulled back the hammer as beside him O'Hara levered a stream of shots from his Winchester, empty brass shells chiming on the floor around him.

Thanks to the day-in, day-out tuition of old Barnabas and his mountain men cronies, when a serious shot had to be made Flintlock relied on the Hawken. The rifle was not nearly as good a weapon as a Winchester repeater. In a shooting scrape you got one shot with the Hawken and then you were pretty much done, and sometimes dead. But Flintlock was amazingly accurate with the old rifle and Barnabas, not prone to giving compliments, had once told him he could shoot the tail feathers off a hummingbird at a hundred yards.

Now that skill would be put to the test.

As Hogan Lord kept up a steady fire from the other

room, Flintlock turned to O'Hara and said, "Dust them trees good. Maybe you can flush one of them out of there and I can nail him."

O'Hara nodded, stood and levered the Winchester from his shoulder, laying down a withering fire. Flintlock looked over the barrel of the Hawken and waited. His heartbeat was slow, his breathing normal, and after a few moments his patience was rewarded. A man wearing a brown tunic and knee-high moccasins broke cover and moved toward either a hiding place or a better spot from where to shoot. His mistake. And a fatal one.

Flintlock drew a bead, triggered the Hawken and through the smoke he saw the man stop, stand on his tiptoes and then slowly drop to his knees. A well-aimed shot from O'Hara finished him. The man fell on his face and lay still.

Hogan Lord saw the hit and let rip with a cheer, soon overshadowed by the almost inhuman cacophony of wails that erupted from the tree line. All firing ceased as a lamenting chorus of half a dozen women dragged the body into the brush and out of sight.

"What the hell?" Flintlock said. Then, yelling, "Hogan, what do you make of that?"

"Beats me," Lord said. "It seems that they've all given up and gone home."

Flintlock wondered at that. A similar reaction had taken place during the rock-throwing incident. As soon as O'Hara dusted the ridge with rifle fire Orlov's people had quickly retreated. Now after one of their number went down they withdrew. For some reason they would not stand in the face of determined opposition. It was a thing to remember.

* * *

The moment had passed for Tobias Fynes. That damned little witch Lucy Cully was now with Sam Flintlock and O'Hara and there was no possibility of forcing her into a marriage. Maybe Hogan Lord could shoot them both but that was asking a lot of the gunman. And uppermost in Fynes's mind was the unwelcome fact that during the fight Flintlock had inflicted the only casualty on Orlov's people, if that's what they were. The man was better than he seemed and bore watching.

CHAPTER THIRTY

A wary Flintlock and O'Hara stepped among the trees, Winchesters in hand.

"You bedded him down all right, Sam," O'Hara said. "Looks like he bled out before they moved him."

Flintlock nodded. "He's dead, all right. A man doesn't lose that much blood and keep kicking. They dragged him back that way," he said, using his rifle to point out what looked like a scarlet snail track across the grass between the trees. "You've scouted around, O'Hara. How many were we facing?"

"Judging by the ejected cartridge cases, I count five using Winchesters and three using pistols. A couple of the revolver shooters reloaded several times."

"Eight? Is that all there was?" Flintlock said.

"No, Sam, there was more than that. Judging by the tracks I'd say at least two score people were here, not all of them shooting, because half of them were women and children."

"I'm glad I didn't know what the odds were," Flintlock said. "They might have spooked me."

"We killed one of Orlov's men," O'Hara said. "I say

we've punished him enough. What we do, Sam, is follow Fynes back to town and get our money."

"And leave Lucy here alone with Chanley? I think a couple of vultures are in cahoots. Fyne wants the house and Chanley wants money."

All of a sudden O'Hara looked frustrated and angry. "Sam, listen to me. When we spoke with the preacher he told us the wedding ceremony was going real nice until the shooting started."

"The preacher was drunk and why has Lucy locked herself in her room and refused to come out, huh? And what about that cry of pain we heard? I think she changed her mind about marrying Chanley and he and Fynes tried to force her into it."

"You mean by torture?" O'Hara said.

"Yeah, somebody hurt that girl, hurt her bad enough that she screamed."

O'Hara said. "Sam, I know we heard a cry, but after talking to the preacher and Lord it was probably a shout of happiness. You don't like Fynes and you're real sore about Chanley ordering you out of the house and that's why you're coming up with these wild ideas."

"They're not wild ideas, O'Hara," Flintlock said. "I think Fynes was trying to force Lucy into saying, 'I do.' But the danger has passed and I reckon first things should come first. Fynes has already left, so we'll head back to the house, saddle up and meet him in Mansion Creek. I'll see things clearer once we get our five hundred." He smiled. "Maybe we'll help Lucy get new glass panes for her broken windows."

O'Hara did not answer. His eyes were on the ravens flapping around the tallest reaches of the house, borne upward by a whirling wind. The cries of the birds were lost in distance but their agitation was such that O'Hara knew they were sending him a warning from the cosmos. Too late he heard the shuffle of feet behind him. He saw Flintlock go down under a pile of bodies and then something hard crashed into his head and O'Hara saw nothing at all.

Sam Flintlock woke to darkness stained by the orange glow of firelight. He tried to move but groaned and quickly closed his eyes again. He remained perfectly still, after finding out the hard way that his slightest movement would set the pain in his head to spiking. But then he realized he was cruelly bound hand and foot and couldn't move a muscle anyway.

Flintlock opened his eyes again. His brain quickly registered two things: the glow of a campfire a short distance away and the grinning decapitated head that had been placed between his legs. It was a man's head with a bullet hole in the middle of the forehead. Flintlock giggled. Good shooting!

"Sam, come back." O'Hara's voice from somewhere in the gloom.

"O'Hara, where are you?" Flintlock said. He giggled. "Are you in Timbuktu?"

"Sam, I'm not ten feet from you. Now come back. You've been raving for the last . . . I don't know how long."

"Why . . . why have I been crazy?" Flintlock said.

"Because you were struggling and they forced you to drink something, a potion of some kind. It made you nuts."

Only then did Flintlock realize that his brain was fuzzy and he couldn't concentrate. "O'Hara," he said.

"Yeah?"

"I'm going to be sick."

"Good, get that stuff out of your belly. Only be sick to your right, not in my direction."

In the silence the crackle of the fire was a small sound. But when Flintlock began violently retching the quiet was ripped apart. After a while he stopped, gasped and then groaned.

"Sam, have you stopped puking?" O'Hara said.

"Yeah . . . I . . . I think so."

"Good. It was disgusting."

"What the hell did I drink?"

"I don't know, but I'd guess something to knock you out for a spell. I didn't struggle so I didn't have to drink the stuff."

"My head hurts."

"Mine too."

"What happened?"

"A whole bunch of people jumped on you," O'Hara said. "That's all I remember."

"Orlov?" Flintlock said.

"That would be my guess."

Flintlock groaned, a long, drawn-out paroxysm of agony. "Damn, my belly's on fire. What the hell did they make me drink?"

A tall figure emerged from the yellow dome of the firelight. As the person stepped closer, Flintlock saw a slender woman, with high, arrogant breasts and shapely legs that showed under her short tunic. The woman wrinkled her nose as she caught a whiff of the soiled ground around Flintlock and he said, irritated, "I puked up that stuff you made me drink."

The woman said nothing, but she pinched her nose and she tested Flintlock's bonds. It was only then that he realized that he was roped to a stake driven into the ground. The woman left him, moved into the gloom to do the same to O'Hara, and then she stepped back to the fire, her hips swaying under the thin stuff of her tunic.

Long minutes passed and the coyotes yipped in the shadowed night. "Sam," O'Hara said.

"What?" Flintlock said.

"Are we done for at last, you and me?"

Flintlock fought back against the spasm of pain in his belly and said, "Don't sing your death song just yet, O'Hara. We've gotten ourselves out of worse scrapes than this."

"When?" O'Hara said.

After a while Flintlock said, "I don't remember." Then, "Do you have a skull between your legs like I have?"

"Yeah. It's split wide open and looks like the feller was killed by a tomahawk."

"Why did they do that?" Flintlock said. "I mean, put skulls between our legs?"

"Too make us feel right at home," O'Hara said. "Why else would they do it?"

CHAPTER THIRTY-ONE

"Lucy, my darling, you can come out now," Roderick Chanley said. "Mr. Fynes and the others have gone."

"Go away, Roderick. I don't want to talk to you right now," Lucy said. "I may not want to talk to you ever again."

Chanley pounded on the door with his fist. "Lucy, you're making a terrible fool of yourself," he said. "Walt is very upset."

"Walt is upset! Roderick, I'm the one that's upset. You and that beast Fynes tried to force me into marriage. I'll never forgive either of you."

"It was for your own good, Lucy. I must get you out of this terrible house and we'll return together to Philadelphia. Walt says houses have souls and he says the soul of this one is evil . . . evil, Lucy, and it's destroying you."

"This is my home, Roderick," Lucy said. She stood behind the door, her derringer in her hand. "Here I am and here I'll stay."

Roderick had lied to her about the derringer. He said he'd thrown it away, but she found it on the dresser in his room. If he lied about the little gun what else might he lie about? Was his pledge of undying love for her a falsehood? After what had happened, his excusing, no, encouraging Tobias Fynes's brutal treatment of her, an assault that was almost akin to rape, she guessed that it was. And then there was Roderick's terrified paralysis during the attack on the house. She didn't want to think about that.

"Lucy, dear one, Philadelphia is your home," Chanley said. "I wasn't going to tell you this until after the wedding, but Mr. Fynes has made us a most handsome offer on the house. Lucy, he'll pay five thousand dollars, think of that. What a tidy sum it is to start our married life."

"My home is not for sale, Roderick. Not for sale at any price," Lucy said.

Chanley kicked the door in anger and said, "You can't stay in there forever, Lucy. When you get hungry enough you'll come to your senses. Then we'll talk some more."

Lucy pressed her ear to the door and only when she heard the sound of Chanley's footsteps on the stairs did she sit on the corner of her bed and allow the tears to come.

"I could've twisted her arm clean off and she still wouldn't have said 'I do,'" Tobias Fynes said. "She no longer wants to wed the damned pansy poet and there's the long and the short of it."

"Five thousand dollars is a big inducement," Hogan Lord said. "Maybe Chanley can change her mind."

"She won't change her mind, and damn it, Hogan,

I might have been killed up there yesterday," Fynes said. "Was that Jasper Orlov and his clan?"

"That's what Sam Flintlock believes," Lord said. "He's pretty certain it was Orlov who was behind the attack on the house."

"I used to think it was all a big story, that there's no such person," Fynes said. "But now I'm not so sure."

"I don't know." Lord shrugged. "Maybe there is such a person. It's a big country, plenty of room for all kinds, sane and insane."

Fynes stared out his office window frowning, deep in thought. Finally, he turned to Lord and said, "Hogan, if all else fails, and it will, we may need to go to the gun."

"Tobias, we have a new sheriff in town and I don't want to brace him. The last thing we want is to make an enemy of Hawk Collins," Lord said.

"Collins already hates my guts," Fynes said. "He threatened to hang me, damn his eyes." He locked on Lord's face. "Earn your money, Hogan, tell me, what should I do?"

"I think our best hope lies with Roderick Chanley. Maybe he can convince the girl to sell."

"No! I don't want to hear maybes. What I want is for you to tell me that going to the gun is the best plan. The damn house, and my treasure map, is situated in a wilderness. We hire some men who'll kill for fifty dollars and wipe out everybody, the girl, the pansy poets, Flintlock, O'Hara and the prizefighter. Toss their bodies over the side of the crag and who's to know? Their bodies will never be found."

Lord said, "The men you hired for fifty dollars will know."

"And they'll keep their mouths shut. They know they'd swing themselves if they uttered a word about what happened," Fynes said.

"Tobias, I told you before, you can't murder Walt Whitman," Lord said.

"Yes, I can. So the old coot went west and disappeared. It's happened to hundreds, maybe thousands of people." Fynes leaned back in his chair and smiled. "Hire the men, as many as you can find, and we'll visit the Cully mansion again. But this time we won't be a wedding party."

"Suppose the treasure map isn't in the house," Lord said. "It could be a myth, like Jasper Orlov."

"After the attack on the mansion I think Jasper Orlov is real and so is the treasure map," Fynes said. "Old Mechan Cully struck it rich and buried a fortune because he didn't put stock in banks. Depend on it, Hogan, the map is there and now I'm beginning to suspect the reason Lucy Cully is suddenly so uppity is because she's already found it and doesn't want to share it with anybody."

"I guess it could explain her change of heart toward Roderick," Lord said.

"Damn right it does, and soon we'll know for sure," Fynes said. Then, as though he'd just remembered something, "Before you go, Hogan, I've a question to ask."

"Ask away," Lord said.

"Do you want Estelle?"

Lord was surprised. "I'm not catching your drift."

"You can have Estelle if you want her. Secondhand goods, I know, but then she was secondhand when I got her."

"I'd have to think about it," Lord said.

"Don't think too long. Good heavens but she bores me. I mean, the first time you taste a lamb chop you say to yourself, *Well, that was real good.* But if you eat a lamb chop for dinner every goddamned night pretty soon you get bored and want something else. Well, I want something else so she's yours if you want her."

"And what if I don't?" Lord said.

Fynes raised his head and scratched his fat throat. "Then I'll throw her into the street. That's where the hussy belongs."

"I'll talk to Estelle," Lord said. "See what she thinks."

Fynes waved a dismissive hand and said without interest, "Yeah, you do that." Then, pointing a chubby forefinger, "Hire those men we need, Hogan. Things are coming to a head and there's no time to waste."

CHAPTER THIRTY-TWO

When the long night shaded into dawn, Sam Flintlock looked around him at what at first glance looked like a Chiricahua Apache rancheria with a dozen dome-shaped wickiups made from poles of oak and willow covered with brush. But unlike an Apache encampment there were no horses and no evidence of pottery and baskets. In their stead store-bought iron and brass pots and pans littered the ground around the fire that burned at the center of the village. In front of each dwelling a human skull spiked on a stake looked out on the camp and grinned. The place smelled rank, a vile mix of stenches that Flintlock couldn't identify, nor did he want to. Beside him O'Hara said, "This isn't a village. It's a pigsty." And Flintlock heartily agreed with him.

The settlement was well hidden, established in the middle of a natural rock amphitheater that protected the inhabitants on three sides, the open end hidden by a stand of mixed wild oak and juniper. Scattered outside the dwellings Flintlock saw evidence of bones that had been cracked open to get at the marrow. He had no doubt that some of them were human. But the real horror of the place didn't hit him until later when the gates of hell opened.

A slatternly woman holding ribbons of different colors appeared and a big man with a meat cleaver accompanied her. A crowd soon gathered, close to a hundred men, women and children, all dressed alike in homespun short tunics and knee-high moccasins. With them a thin fiddler in a tattered frock coat danced and played, and like the rest of them he was dirty with matted, stringy hair and his clothing was stained, apparently never washed. With him was a boy wearing rags; for some reason, he was not allowed the same tunic as the others.

Flintlock's eyes searched the crowd for an attractive female or handsome man. There was none in evidence, just pale faces and dead eyes. Even the appearance of last night's slender woman was an illusion. She'd been made beautiful by darkness.

As the fiddler played "The Devil's Reel" an old, wrinkled crone stepped out of the crowd, a yard of thin blue ribbon in her hand.

She stopped in front of O'Hara, studied him for a few moments and then bent over and with both hands felt him all over, chest, arms, legs and back. Apparently unsatisfied she frowned, kicked O'Hara in the leg and then moved to Flintlock. Behind her, the crowd watched with close interest and the women with other colored ribbons seemed impatient.

The crone, one of her eyes milky white, reached out with skeletal hands and felt Flintlock's heavy shoulders and arms. "Get the hell away from me," he said. The woman ignored him, did the same to his legs and smiled. She bent lower and tied her blue ribbon around Flintlock's left leg.

The man with the meat cleaver, a dull-eyed brute with a massive hairy chest and shoulders, grinned at the crone and said, "A good cut, Sister Hortence."

"He's a big one," the old woman said. "A lot of good chewing meat on his bones."

"Next!" Cleaver Man yelled.

A younger woman went through the same procedure and then tied her red ribbon around O'Hara's left arm. "Just enough for you and Brother Cornelius, eh, Sister Sophronia?" Cleaver Man said.

"We're not big eaters," the woman said, smiling shyly.

"Next!" Cleaver Man said.

Sister Eleanora tied her yellow ribbon around Flintlock's right arm and was complimented by Cleaver Man for her good taste. Sister Clara, whose pink ribbon circled Flintlock's head, said, "It's the best there is for soup." And so it went on, woman after woman making her choice until Flintlock and O'Hara were covered with colored ribbons, including the pink band tied around Flintlock's head and another in a delicate shade of green around O'Hara's.

By this time Flintlock was turning the air blue with curses, but he and O'Hara were totally ignored, as though they were animals waiting for slaughter . . . which they were.

More humiliation and fear was to follow.

The big man laid his cleaver aside, untied Flintlock and O'Hara's ankles, ignored Flintlock's attempts to kick him, and pulled off both Flintlock and O'Hara's boots. Working deftly, he stripped Flintlock of his belt and O'Hara of his suspenders and pulled off their pants and long johns. He then replaced the colored ribbons, tying them loosely. Satisfied, Cleaver Man roped their ankles again and picked up his heavy chopper.

"Sister Hortence, this way if you please!" he yelled.

The old crone stepped forward, a blood-crusted cloth the size of a bathhouse towel held between her arms. She held it up. "Just put it in here, Brother Cyrus," she said.

"I'll be ready to serve in just a moment," Cleaver Man, now Brother Cyrus, said. He removed the red ribbon and then stomped hard on Flintlock's knee with his booted foot, pinning the limb to the ground. He could chop down with the cleaver and sever the leg at the top of the thigh without having to make too many cuts.

Flintlock, his eyes huge, watched the rise of the gleaming, sharp-edged cleaver and braced himself for the inhuman agony that would follow. In the background the fiddler played "Polly Put the Kettle On" at a frantic pace.

As befitted the surroundings, the result of the shot that came from somewhere behind Flintlock and O'Hara was both horrific and spectacular. Cleaver Man's mouth was open in a snarl as he lifted the chopper. The bullet hit him between the teeth, traveled through the base of his skull and exited an inch above the top vertebra of his neck. The big man dropped like a sack of rocks. The crone called Hortence watched Cleaver Man fall and screamed, but a bullet to the chest abruptly cut off her terrified screech and she fell on top of the dead man.

As the racketing echo of the shots died away two

events happened very quickly: Like a wave receding from a dangerous shore, Jasper Orlov's people drew back in horror as they saw two of their number die . . . and Jeptha Spunner came from Flintlock's left and stepped into his line of sight.

The albino wore an ankle-length duster and a battered Stetson replaced his usual top hat. Low on his hips he wore two Colts in crossed cartridge belts, a thing Flintlock had never seen before. But the unusual gun rig jogged his memory and he suddenly recalled what he'd once heard about an almost legendary albino draw fighter. Spunner wasn't the handle he'd once gone by. His real name was Whitey Carson and he was out of Galveston, where he'd began his career as a hired gun in the savage Sutton-Taylor feud. From there he'd quickly climbed to the top tier of the shootist hierarchy and for a couple of years had been considered one of the Lone Star State's elite guns. Then Whitey just vanished. It was rumored that he'd been killed by Apaches in the New Mexico Territory, but the truth was he'd outrun an Arkansas hanging posse and somehow ended up in New York where he'd served as a taskmaster, some called it slave master, on the hell ships.

And now Carson had saved Flintlock's and O'Hara's lives and they were beholden to him. Flintlock decided he would continue to call the man Spunner, unless he said otherwise.

"Untie me," Flintlock said. "And give me a gun."

Spunner briefly glanced at Flintlock but then he was shooting again. A tall man with yellow hair had run into a wickiup and then emerged levering a Winchester. Spunner thumbed off a shot, dropped the man and then killed another rifleman who was coming to his aid.

Then Flintlock again saw that strange phenomenon, the panicked flight of Orlov's clan when some of their number was killed. They'd lost three men and a woman to Spunner's guns and they'd no belly for a fight. Wailing, moaning, men, woman and children, melted into the trees and soon the sounds of their mourning were lost in distance.

"Spunner, cut me free," Flintlock said. "Hell, man, I'm suffering here."

"Stay where you are for now," the gunman said. "I have work to do."

Without another word he searched through the rickety dwellings one by one and when he returned he had Flintlock's revolver in his hand and O'Hara's gunbelt over his shoulder.

"There are a few rifles and pistols in the shacks," he said. "We'll save those before we set everything on fire."

As Spunner used a Barlow knife to cut him free, Flintlock said, "No sign of Orlov? I want to kill that son of a bitch."

"You can't kill him because there is no Jasper Orlov," Spunner said. "At least not any longer."

When Flintlock stood he staggered a little as blood rushed into his numbed legs. He rubbed his raw wrists and said, "I'm not catching your drift."

"I'll explain it to you later, at least as far as I can figure it," Spunner said. He helped O'Hara to his feet. "Now we burn this hellhole."

Spunner led the way.

He dragged the bodies of the man and woman

he'd killed into the largest wickiup and then grabbed a burning brand from the fire and shoved it into the bottom of the dwelling. The dry brush ignited immediately and in a moment the place turned into a roaring pyramid of fire. Flintlock and O'Hara joined in the torching of the shelters and soon all of them were blazing and a thick column of acrid black smoke rose into the blue morning sky.

The three men stood and watched the wickiups burn. Smiling slightly Spunner waited until Flintlock and O'Hara cut the colored ribbons from their bodies before he said, "There was once an unfrocked Russian Orthodox priest by the name of Jasper Orlov, but he died a year ago."

"Sorry to hear that," Flintlock said. He ground fragments of a red ribbon under his boot heel. "I wanted to kill him real bad."

"Who were all those people?" O'Hara said.

"His followers. I guess you could call them his disciples. He set himself up as a holy man and led them here, told them it was a promised land, flowing with milk and honey, the gateway to Heaven. But all the pilgrims found were hostile Apaches and starvation. The only way they could survive that first winter was to eat the flesh off the bodies of the Chiricahua they'd killed or captured. They starved again the second winter and the third, but when good times came again and there was fine weather and plenty of game, they continued to eat human flesh. The people had acquired a taste for it, you see, preferred it, and Orlov preached that eating human meat would give them great strength and endurance. It didn't. The cannibals are very aggressive, as you know, but timid. They won't stand and fight if they think there's a chance they can't win. The Chiricahua taught them that, to never buck the odds, and along with that lesson the Apache defeated them many times. Over a period of four years scores of pilgrims were killed. Of the three hundred men, women and children that Orlov led into the Territory the ones you saw today are all that are left."

Flintlock was unyielding. "They're lawless trash," he said. "A bunch of low-life scum that needs to be wiped off the face of the earth. I can't blame the children, they're too young to know any better. Maybe they can be saved."

Spunner said, "For a few years the cannibals who lived in this hidden village were feared by white men and even the army avoided the place, but since Jasper Orlov died they've become leaderless and weak. I think that after today they'll scatter and move on or they won't survive."

After the village had burned to embers, Jeptha Spunner said, "You boys look as though you could use a drink. My cabin is still within walking distance."

"Best offer I've had today," Flintlock said. "You saved our lives, Spunner. I won't forget that."

"Glad I was passing by," the albino said.

"How come you were? Passing by, I mean?" the always suspicious O'Hara said.

Spunner smiled. "First I heard all the shooting yesterday and that made me curious. I rode to the Cully house this morning and found nothing to see, so I scouted around and then I heard the fiddle music in the distance."

"You knew the cannibals were here?" Flintlock said.

"I visited Jasper Orlov here once, a few weeks before he died. I vowed I'd never go back or tell anyone else where to find the village. But then I saw you two trussed up like Thanksgiving turkeys and changed my mind."

"How come Orlov didn't eat you like a Thanksgiving turkey?" Flintlock said.

"My flying machine fascinated him and he let me live, at least for a while."

"And then he died," O'Hara said.

"Yes, he did and after that I stayed away from the place. That is until this morning."

"Glad you stopped by, Spunner. Ain't we, O'Hara?" Flintlock said.

"We are that. And I could use a drink and some breakfast," O'Hara said. "Almost getting chopped up for a cannibal stew gives a man an appetite."

"Spoken like a true Irish Injun," Flintlock said. "Lead the way, Spunner. You got two hungry and thirsty men here."

CHAPTER THIRTY-THREE

The newly minted marshal of Mansion Creek knew a hired gun when he saw one. The fellow at the restaurant table eating breakfast could have been a prosperous businessman in his expensive broadcloth and snowy white linen, but the ivory-handled Colt on his hip and the self-assured way he wore it gave the game away. He was a gun, and by the look of him his services would not come cheap.

Slim Hart spooned sugar into his coffee and then looked down at the silver and gold star on his vest. Yup, he looked like a bona fide law dog, all right. Time to act like one. He rose to his feet and crossed the restaurant floor. The gunman looked up at him with cold eyes and said, "What can I do for you, Marshal?"

"Mind if I sit?" Hart said. He lowered himself into a chair before the shootist could answer. "Nice morning, huh?" he said. "But it's a little nippy, the first hint of fall in the air, I suppose."

"Marshal, I doubt that you came over here to talk about the weather. Name's Hogan Lord, originally out of Brazos River country, and you're Slim Hart out of Hawk Collins's bunkhouse."

It was a slight, and Hart knew it, but he didn't let his annoyance show. "Passing through, Mr. Lord?" he said.

"You could say that, but I've lingered around here for a while."

"Don't let me interrupt your breakfast," Hart said. "Your eggs will get cold. We can talk while you eat."

"Marshal, we have nothing to talk about," Lord said. He forked some scrambled egg into his mouth and chewed, his ice blue eyes locked on Hart's.

The marshal didn't wilt. "Hard times coming down for some folks," he said. "And I think if you're not very careful you might be one of them, Mr. Lord."

"There's men lying in bone orchards across the country who told me that," Lord said. "Take my advice, Marshal Hart, from now on step around me."

"I can't do that," the lawman said. "I've got a job to do. What's your relationship with Tobias Fynes?"

"I'm his business advisor."

"What kind of business?"

"The banking business."

"And maybe some gun business?"

"If it's needed."

"There won't be any call for that kind of business while I'm marshal of Mansion Creek. If there's any shooting to be done, I'll do it." Lord didn't answer and Hart stepped into the silence. "Hawk Collins wants to hang Fynes, says he's rode roughshod over Apache County long enough. He says Fynes has robbed more people of their farms, homes or their life savings than any outlaw."

"And he abuses women and kicks dogs," Lord said.

Hart was surprised. "And yet you work for him."

Lord rang some coins onto the table and rose to his feet. "I ride for the brand, Hart. You should know all about that."

"Some brands just ain't worth riding for. I quit a laboring job one time, good job paying fifty cents a day, because the foreman beat his Chinese woman. A few days later I shot and killed him, but that's a different story."

"You must tell me about it sometime when I've got nothing better to do," Lord said.

Hart stood and before Lord opened the door he said, "I don't want to hang you, Mr. Lord, but if Hawk Collins gives me the word, I will." As hushed diners stared at the two men, the marshal said, "You've been notified."

Without another glance at Hart, Hogan Lord nodded, stepped outside and closed the door behind him.

Hogan Lord rapped on the door of Estelle Redway's cabin. As cabins went in Mansion Creek it was small, smaller than Kate Coldwell's place, and not as well built. Tobias Fynes kept his mistresses on the cheap. There was no answer to Lord's knock so he tried again, this time harder.

A long minute passed and then a woman's tear-stained voice said, "Who is it?"

"Estelle, this is Hogan Lord. We need to talk."

"I don't want to see anyone right now," the woman said.

"You'll want to see me," Lord said. "I'm taking you away from this place."

"Hold on. I'm not decent."

After a few moments the door opened a crack and Estelle said, "Come in."

Lord stepped inside and looked around. The main item of furniture in the one-room cabin and its focal point was a large brass bed. Lord smelled the warm, musky scent of a woman just risen from sleep and the faint but unmistakable odor of Tobias Fynes's sweat.

"Did he do that to you?" Lord said.

Estelle's fingers strayed to the purple bruise on her cheekbone. "Tobias was angry that Lucy Cully wouldn't marry her intended. He took it out on me"

Lord's anger flared. "He won't strike you again, Estelle. You're coming with me. Get your things together."

The girl was shocked. "Are you a crazy man? I can't leave Tobias. He needs me and I need him. I won't leave him, now or ever."

Lord found himself in uncharted waters as he tried to understand the mental state of this young, pretty woman who steadfastly refused to leave her abuser. He decided to be brutally honest. "Fynes doesn't want you anymore, Estelle. He said you bored him and he gave you to me. Well, he can't trade away a human being as though she was a slave girl, so I'm asking you to come with me. I'll try my best to do right by you."

As Lord spoke, Estelle's expression had grown more and more horrified with every word. Now she said, "You're lying. You want me for yourself and that's why you're making up these terrible things about

Tobias." Her eyes flashed. "Get out! Get out, Hogan Lord, and never come back here again."

"Estelle, listen to me—"

"Tobias loves me and he takes care of me," the woman said. "He will never leave me. He's told me that many times."

"Fynes is a liar," Lord said. "He uses people and when he's finished with them he just wrinkles his nose and throws them away like yesterday's trash. Now he's doing that to you."

"Damn you!" Estelle said. She ran to the dresser, opened a drawer and came up with a nickel-plated .32 caliber Forehand & Wadsworth revolver, a cheap suicide special that was probably a gift from Fynes. She pointed the gun at Lord and yelled, "Get out or I'll shoot you in the belly, you damned liar."

Lord would rather have faced a Texas gunslinger, all horns and rattles, than an armed, angry woman. He turned around and stepped outside. The door slammed shut behind him.

"I thought maybe you could talk to her," Hogan Lord said.

"Why me? There are other women in town," Dr. Theodora Weller said.

"I know, but there are none as smart as you," Lord said.

Dr. Weller smiled. "Thank you for the compliment, sincere or not." She sat down and bade Lord to do the same. "And what about you, Mr. Lord? Are your intentions toward the fair Estelle honorable, or does your hypocrisy only go as far as her brass bed?"

Lord took no offense and smiled. "She's an attractive woman, but not one I'd care to spend time with." He smiled. "Estelle doesn't need me, she's suffered enough."

"How honorable of you, Mr. Lord."

"Not really. I take my women only when I need one, and that's not often."

"Thank heaven for whores, huh?"

"It's a business transaction and never pretends to be anything else. Love and marriage don't come into it."

Lord looked at the pictures around the walls of Dr. Weller's cramped parlor. "Joan of Arc, Eleanor of Aquitaine, Lucy Stone, Julia Ward Howe . . . it seems you admire warrior women and women who are fighting for the vote."

"I'm surprised you recognize them, Mr. Lord," Dr. Weller said. "Indeed, I am more than surprised, I'm astonished."

"You shouldn't be," Lord said. "I've always read history books and I try to keep up with what's happening in the newspapers." He thought Theodora Weller an attractive woman but her mode of dress, a black velvet hip-length jacket cut in the military style, white open-necked shirt with a high collar, narrow skirt and ankle boots was mannish, as was her habit of ceaselessly smoking the cigarettes she built, as well, if not better, than any Texas waddie.

The woman used her thumb and middle finger to delicately pick a shred of tobacco from her tongue and then said, "Some women refuse to leave the man who beats them for many reasons but some of the more common I've heard are, *I'm nothing and I don't deserve any better* or *I'm used to my life being this way.* At one time or another, Estelle Redway has told me both."

"Tobias Fynes will throw her out of the cabin to make room for another woman," Lord said. "When that time comes can she stay here?" He saw the hesitancy in Theodora Weller and said, "Only for a spell until she can catch the next stage out of town."

"Fynes would throw his dying wife out of the house if he could," the doctor said. "But he's afraid of what a public outcry could do to his bank business." Theodora's beautiful black eyes stared at Lord. "Yes, Estelle can come here for, as you say, a spell."

"Until the next stage," Lord said.

"Yes, but only until then, and that is if she wants to."

"When Tobias throws her out into the street she'll want to, I'm sure," Lord said.

"We'll see, won't we?" Dr. Weller said.

CHAPTER THIRTY-FOUR

"You've made progress on your flying machine, Spunner," Sam Flintlock said. "At least you got it out of the arroyo."

Jeptha Spunner handed Flintlock a cup of coffee and said, "My mule dragged it out of there. I've installed the steam engine and the envelope is over there between the junipers."

"Will it fly?" O'Hara said, looking out the window at the huge swath of bright yellow silk among the trees.

"I don't see why not," Spunner said. "I'll take it for a test flight soon and then make preparations for a trip around the world." He smiled. "You want to come with me, O'Hara?"

"Not a chance," O'Hara said. "I like my two feet on the ground or my ass on a paint horse."

"Same with me," Flintlock said. "Spunner, trust me, you'll break your neck in that thing."

"All things considered, a broken neck is not such a bad way to go," Spunner said. "But there's no danger. Unlike Icarus, I won't fly too close to the sun."

"Icarus. Here, O'Hara, didn't we watch a feller by the name of Icarus get hung down Laredo way that time?"

"No, you're thinking of the Dutch blacksmith, went by the name Ignatius van Somebody-or-other. Caught his wife in bed with the mayor and the town marshal at the same time and gunned all three of them."

Flintlock nodded. "Yeah, I remember now. I recollect there were some who said he should've got a medal instead of a noose."

"Including you, Sam, as I recall." O'Hara turned his attention to Spunner. "Let us know when you take up the flying machine," O'Hara said. "I'd like to see that."

"If you're still around, it will be my pleasure," Spunner said. He picked up the fry pan from the stove and said, "Anyone for more salt pork?"

The morning had brightened into afternoon when Sam Flintlock and O'Hara left the Spunner cabin.

"Real nice feller," O'Hara said. "Cooks good too."

"You know who he is, don't you?" Flintlock said. Without waiting for an answer he said, "He's Whitey Carson."

O'Hara stopped in his tracks, absorbed that statement, and then his black eyes lit up. "Damn, I thought he looked familiar. Whitey Carson, the albino draw fighter, of course. I saw him one time when he was riding shotgun for the Butterfield stage and Jim Davis was the whip. I thought I'd never forget the man with the pink eyes, but I guess after a while I did."

"Well, Spunner is Carson, all right," Flintlock said. "I'd say he's killed more than his fair share."

"Seems like," O'Hara said. "And he added four today. I reckon—"

But Flintlock never heard what O'Hara reckoned because a rattle of gunfire shattered the afternoon quiet . . . and it came from the direction of the Spunner cabin.

Keeping low, using every scrap of cover they could find, Sam Flintlock and O'Hara made their careful way toward Jeptha Spunner's cabin and then stopped in the shadow of some juniper. Ahead of them at least a half a dozen shooters kept up a steady barrage of gunfire.

O'Hara leaned close to Flintlock and whispered, "I thought the cannibals were done."

"So did I," Flintlock said. Then, stating the obvious, "I reckon they're not. Seems like we're in a war with those people."

"I have them spotted," O'Hara said. "Over there by the wild oaks among the pile of rocks, six, maybe seven rifles."

"There's a stream running over there," Flintlock said. "It will slow down anybody coming at them from the front." He heard a tinkle of broken glass as a bullet smashed through a cabin window. "Best thing we can do is wait."

"Wait?" O'Hara said.

"Yeah, wait right here. If the cannibals don't take a hit and run away, they'll charge the cabin. I don't think they're the patient kind, so they won't hold off until sundown and risk Spunner making a break for it in the dark. Now down on your belly and keep out of sight."

Flintlock did the same and then his eyes moved between the shot-up cabin and the rocks. A lot of fire was being exchanged but as far as he could tell there had been no execution on either side. The sun still splashed bright yellow paint on the rock walls on either side of the arroyo and the sky was blue and cloudless. Flintlock calculated another five hours of daylight. He and O'Hara were in for a long, hot and uncomfortable wait . . .

However, Flintlock had badly underestimated, not Jeptha Spunner, the maker of magic flying machines, but Whitey Carson, the famed Texas draw fighter and man-killer.

After fifteen minutes, as the firing died away to a few desultory shots from the rocks, the cabin door swung open and Carson, wearing dark eyeglasses, stepped outside, a Colt revolver in each hand.

A man skilled in arms, fast and accurate with the pistol, willing to kill and not afraid to die, can be a devastating force. Such expertise, the masterful coordination between hand and eye, is a rare gift that is given to few men, perhaps one in a thousand. No wonder then that on the frontier, the arrival in a town of a named shootist was an occasion for great wonder and admiration not unmixed with dread.

Now Carson would prove that he was such a man.

He walked almost casually toward the rocks, and the reaction from the cannibal clansmen was immediate. Four of them left cover and stood, rifles coming up to their shoulders. Carson shot with both hands, so fast the roars of his bucking Colts sounded like one. Three men went down. The fourth fired and missed. He attempted to work the lever of his Winchester but the effort seemed too much for him. The chest of his homespun tunic stained bright scarlet, he dropped to his knees and then fell flat on his face. Now for the surviving cannibals anger, raw hatred and the desire to smash, destroy and kill, substituted for courage. Spurred on by their blind rage they left the cover of the rocks and charged Carson, firing from the hip. The three men died knowing that they'd scored no hits and one of them, a gray-haired old-ster with shaggy eyebrows, screamed in frustrated fury before Carson shot him a second time and finally bedded him down.

For a while the gunman stood still as a marble statue in the clearing, gray gunsmoke drifting around him, and surveyed the slaughter he'd just perpe-trated. Then his shoulders slumped and he stared at the ground, like a weary warrior after a battle won.

"Spunner!" Flintlock called out, using what he con-sidered the less pugnacious form of address, "It's Sam Flintlock and O'Hara. Don't shoot, we're coming in."

The gunman's body remained still as he turned his lowered head. "I see you, Flintlock. Come on ahead."

When Flintlock stepped beside the man, he said, "You hit?"

"No, not a scratch. There was a lot of them but they weren't much."

"I thought they'd gone," Flintlock said. "I reckoned it was all over."

"They wanted a taste of revenge first, damned fools." Spunner saw Flintlock's eyes move to the scattered bodies, already stiff in death. "The women will come back for them tonight and then they'll leave."

"Where will people like that go?" O'Hara said. "When a town finds out what they are, or have been, it will not allow them to settle."

"In the old days the Apache would have killed them off," Spunner said. "It would have been a mercy. But now they're pariahs, and they'll wander and starve and perhaps a few of the children will survive. But that's not likely."

"A hard fate," O'Hara said. "Even for people such as these."

Spunner nodded. "Yes, the dead among them are the luckiest."

Then from among the trees the sound of a fiddle, a spirited rendition of "Black Them Boots" as a piping, boy's voice sang the words:

> *Black them boots and make them shine,*
> *A good-bye and a good-bye.*
> *Black them boots and make them shine,*
> *and good-bye, Liza Jane.*
> *Oh, how I love her,*
> *it's a scandal and shame.*
> *Oh, how I love her,*
> *And it's good-bye, Liza Jane.*

Flintlock drew the Colt from his waistband and said, "Come in real slow, fiddle player. We're well-armed men here and in a mighty cantankerous frame of mind."

The playing stopped and a man's voice came from the wild oaks, "Don't shoot, mister. It's only poor Joe

Grimes who's been so close to hell this five years he's smelled the smoke. I got my boy with me."

"Then let's take a look at you," Flintlock said. "And when you come out of them trees all I want to see in your hands is a fiddle."

A few moments passed and a tall, skinny man dressed in the ragged remains of a frock coat emerged from the oaks. Beside him a boy no older than twelve or thirteen wore ragged overalls, an old, collared shirt with a dirty inside neck, and had bare feet. Both man and boy were hollow eyed and hungry and looked as though they'd been up the trail and back again.

"We fiddled and sang because we figgered you wouldn't shoot us," Grimes said. "You knowing we was white men an' all."

"You figgered right . . . for now," Flintlock said. "Tell us your story, fiddle man, and then state your intentions."

"And after that?"

"After that you'll be notified," Flintlock said.

"You gents wouldn't have a bit o' cheese about your person," Grimes said.

"Or a hen's egg," his son said.

Spunner said, "Maybe later. Now tell us what you've been asked to tell us and do it quickly."

Grimes ran a nervous hand over his mouth and beard and said, "You heard me say I've been close to hell this last five years, well, it's the truth. It was that time ago I came into the Arizona Territory with a pack mule and a black serving man by the name of Sable Starling. We were headed for a town west of here where I have huggin' kin, another fiddle player by the name of Dick Slattery. You boys ever heard of him?"

Flintlock nodded. "That name is familiar to me. So you were headed for the town of Mansion Creek but fell in with cannibals."

"Yes, fell in with a man called Jasper Orlov. Sweet Jesus! He and his tribe captured me and my boy, then ate the mule and the black man. He spared me and my son because I could play the fiddle and Orlov loved to dance, and so did his people. Orlov told me that if I ever tried to escape he'd dine on my son." Grimes's haunted eyes lifted to Flintlock's face. "That was five years ago, mister, five long years of hell on earth. Orlov kept me alive so long as I played for him and when he died I had the same arrangement with his folks. I fiddled when they killed, I fiddled when they butchered and ate people and I fiddled when they danced around the fire like the demons they were. And God help me, I was one of them."

Flintlock looked stern. "Did you and your son eat human flesh, Grimes? Come now, don't lie to me. I'll know if you're lying."

"Never," Grimes said. "Not once did me or my son partake of human flesh. We were fed scraps of game and pieces of stale bread and we were always hungry."

"But you never, not even one time, became cannibals?" O'Hara said. "Is that what you're telling us?"

"Yes, and it's the truth. We were never even asked to eat human flesh," Grimes said. "Orlov always told me and my son that we were not worthy. He said, 'Only my disciples can eat man meat and live for a hundred and three score years.'

"Thank God he never forced such a hellish food down our throats."

Flintlock looked at O'Hara. "What do you think?"

"He's telling the truth," O'Hara said.

"Spunner?"

"A man doesn't make up a lie like that." Spunner glanced back at his shot-up cabin and said, "Mr. Grimes, I have cheese and eggs from my own chickens. You are welcome to eat with me."

"Coffee? Do you have coffee?"

Spunner nodded. "That too."

"Orlov didn't hold with coffee. He said it was the devil's drink, a strange thing to say, coming from him."

Spunner looked at Grimes's son and said, "What's your name, boy?"

"Billy, sir."

"You look pale. The sight of the dead men lying around here trouble you?"

"No, sir. I've seen many dead men," Billy said. "The sight of you troubles me. I've never seen a man as white as you before."

Grimes frowned and said, "Billy, watch your tongue."

But Spunner laughed, then said, "The boy speaks his mind. I like that. It means he'll make his mark one day." He looked at Flintlock. "I never did thank you for coming back when the shooting started."

"We didn't do much except watch," Flintlock said.

"I think that you and O'Hara would have done more than watch if the fight had gone against me."

Flintlock said, "Maybe so. But before we leave, I need to tell you that I know you're Whitey Carson and you proved it to me today. I've never seen a man shoot that well, and I've seen some of the best."

Spunner nodded. "I was Whitey Carson but I am not he any longer. That man belongs buried in my past and that's where he'll stay."

"Pity about today," O'Hara said. "Kind of ruined it for you having to resurrect Whitey for a spell, huh?"

"The fight was brought to me. It was none of my doing and I can live with that."

"Well, as far as I'm concerned you're Jeptha Spunner, the crazy man who builds flying machines," Flintlock said.

"Thank you, Flintlock," Spunner said. "I appreciate it." Then, "Mr. Grimes, please be my guest for lunch. You and your son can spend the night in my cabin and tomorrow, after a five-year interruption, resume your journey to Mansion Creek and your loved ones." He read the concern in Grimes's face and said, "This was the last attack Orlov's clan will ever make. Tonight the women will come for their dead and then they'll be gone."

"Is that how it will be, Mr. Spunner?" Grimes said.

"Yes. I'm sure of it."

"Then we'll accept your kind invitation," Grimes said.

CHAPTER THIRTY-FIVE

"He was sure of things before, and look what happened," O'Hara said.

"This time I think he's right," Sam Flintlock said. "The cannibals have taken a beating, lost a lot of fighting men, and their village is burned to ashes. They won't stick around this neck of the woods any longer, not if they have any smarts."

Flintlock and O'Hara followed a dim trail up the talus slope, losing their footing a few times as they picked their way across broken rock and pushed through patches of heavy brush.

Under a sky that had lost its brightness they crossed the mesa to the crag. The house was silhouetted in the afternoon light, an ominous, towering black shape that looked more hunchbacked vulture than eagle. As Flintlock and O'Hara walked closer the white windows revealed no lamp glow but stared at them blankly, like old eyes with cataracts.

"Seems like there's nobody to home," Flintlock said.

O'Hara with his long-seeing eyes said, "At the side

of the house, Sam. See them? Looks like the poet feller in his wheelchair and the prizefighter."

"Where's Lucy and Chanley?" Flintlock said.

"I don't see them."

"Maybe Walt Whitman is taking the air," Flintlock said. "Looks like he's mighty close to the edge."

O'Hara's eyes lifted to the sinister bulk of the mansion and he shook his head. "I don't know what's happening, but Whitman isn't taking the air."

"But something has happened. Is that what you're saying?" Flintlock said.

"Could be. It's just a feeling I got," O'Hara said.

"Then let's go find out. Maybe them damned cannibals attacked the place out of spite."

Walt Whitman and Rory O'Neill watched Flintlock and O'Hara until they were within hailing distance and then the big prizefighter pushed Whitman's wheelchair in their direction. O'Neill stopped in front of the house and then Whitman said, "There's been a terrible tragedy." He paused for a while, tears welled in his eyes and he said, "I am heartbroken. I am devastated."

"What's happened?" Flintlock said. He saw no danger but kept his hand close to his gun.

O'Neill answered that question. "Roderick Chanley is dead. His body lies among the rocks at the bottom of the crag."

The sky had darkened and thunder rumbled in the distance and the ravens flapped and fluttered around the house and uttered distressed cries of *kraa-kraa*. O'Hara heard the birds call out to him and it chilled him to the bone. His hand moved to the medicine bag that hung on a rawhide string around his neck. Death and terror had come to the Cully mansion and the ravens were telling him so.

"You'd better come inside," Walt Whitman said. "There is much beauty in a thunderstorm but it's better admired from inside."

"Where is Lucy?" Flintlock said.

Thunder banged closer and Whitman said, "You'd better come inside."

"Lucy is in the parlor," O'Neill said. "You can talk to her there."

Flintlock had questions but he decided to hold off on them until he saw Lucy. But he decided to try one. "How did Roderick fall?" he said. "Did he lose his footing?"

"Lucy is in the parlor," Whitman said. His face was white as chalk, even his lips. "What happened here today is better told from her lips, Mr. Flintlock."

The wind was picking up and Flintlock felt it blowing stronger. It was going to be a bad night around the Cully mansion.

Lucy Cully sat in a red leather wing chair in the parlor, so large that it almost swallowed the girl's small, slender body. She held a glass of brandy on her lap, clutching the glass with both hands as she gazed into its amber depths. She was very pale, but her eyes were dry. Lucy looked up when Flintlock and the others walked in. She smiled. "How nice to see you, Sam," she said. "You too, O'Hara. Please, take a seat, both of you. Brandy?"

"Not right now, Lucy," Flintlock said. He drew up a chair and sat opposite her. Then, easing into what had to be asked, he smiled and said, "What happened, Lucy?"

Silence. The quiet stretched . . . taut as a fiddle string. Walt Whitman coughed twice behind his fisted hand and Flintlock heard the *hiss* . . . *hiss* of O'Neill's steady breathing through the ruptured bone and cartilage of his broken nose. Thunder blasted and the wind flung rain against the parlor window like a handful of gravel.

"Lucy?" Flintlock prompted. "Will you speak to me and tell me what happened to Roderick?"

The girl lifted her eyes to his and her lashes fluttered. "Roderick tried to kill me and I shot him," she said. That statement should have dropped like a bomb into the parlor, but instead it hovered like a feather in a solemn silence.

Flintlock and O'Hara exchanged a stunned glance and then Flintlock finally found his voice. "Tell me about it, Lucy," he said.

"Roderick tried to kill me and I shot him. There is nothing more to tell."

"Why did Roderick try to kill you?" Flintlock said.

"I wouldn't agree to sell my house to Tobias Fynes and it made him angry, very angry," Lucy said. "I told him I no longer wanted to marry him and that made him angrier still."

"Lucy, how did it happen?" Flintlock said.

The girl looked confused. "How did what happen?"

Talking as softly as he could, a stretch for the normally gruff Flintlock, he said, "You and Roderick were around the side of the house, isn't that right?"

"Yes, we were," Lucy said. "We'd quarreled, you see, right here in the parlor, and I ran out of the house to get away from him. He followed me, Sam."

"And then what happened?"

"We quarreled some more and then Roderick grabbed me by my shoulders and tried to throw me off the crag," Lucy said. She buried her face in her hands and said, "Oh, Sam, it was horrible . . . just so horrible."

"When he laid hands on you that's when you shot him?" Flintlock said.

"Yes. He didn't know I'd retrieved my derringer from his room and I shot him. He staggered back from me and lost his footing. And then he fell over the side. Sam, he screamed all the way down . . . a long time . . . a long time to fall and a long time to scream. And then the screaming suddenly stopped and I knew Roderick was dead, dead, dead." Lucy's pretty face brightened. "Are you sure I can't interest you in a brandy, Sam? Anyone? It's very good, you know. I recommend it."

Walt Whitman looked horrified. "Oh my God," he said, and hung his gray head.

CHAPTER THIRTY-SIX

"Do you think there's a single bone in his body that ain't broke?" Sam Flintlock said.

"Sure doesn't look like it," O'Hara said. "I don't think he suffered much. He must have hit the rocks like a runaway freight train."

"Well, God rest him," Flintlock said. "He was a good poet."

"Was he?" O'Hara said.

"I don't know if he was or not," Flintlock said. "It was the only nice thing I could think to say about him."

Roderick Chanley had hit the rocks headfirst with outstretched arms to break his fall and both skull and arm bones were shattered beyond recognition.

Flintlock and O'Hara agreed that this was not a corpse to be displayed for grieving loved ones, but one to be nailed up in a pine coffin right away.

The huge rocks at the bottom of the crag were large and jagged, not rounded with the weather of millennia. They had fallen from the side of the crag during some violent earthshake just a few centuries before and they'd broken Chanley to pieces.

Flintlock and O'Hara lifted the smashed body from the rocks, akin to hoisting a man-sized flour sack full of shattered pumpkins, and dragged it to a patch of open ground covered in fine sandstone gravel and patches of wild thyme. Because of the bloody state of the body it took several minutes of searching before they noticed two .41 caliber holes an inch to the left of the second button of Chanley's shirt.

"She shot him twice," Flintlock said. "I guess once wasn't enough."

"Lucy was fast on the trigger, Sam. The bullet holes are close together."

"Bang-bang," Flintlock said. "Two bullets into a moving target is good shooting."

O'Hara looked troubled. "If Chanley was moving. Maybe he was standing still, talking to her."

"You heard what Lucy told us, O'Hara," Flintlock said. "He grabbed her shoulders and tried to throw her off the crag, so he was moving, all right."

"I didn't see bruises on Lucy," O'Hara said.

"They were covered by her dress," Flintlock said.

"When a small woman like Lucy is attacked by a man and fights back she gets bruises, and that's a natural fact," O'Hara said. "I didn't see any."

Flintlock frowned in thought for a moment and then said, "O'Hara, are you saying Lucy murdered Roderick Chanley?"

"Chanley wanted to marry her, but she didn't want to marry him. He wanted to sell the house to Tobias Fynes and she didn't. He planned to take Lucy back

East but she wanted to live here in the West. Sam, a passel of men have been gunned for less."

Flintlock looked over O'Hara's shoulder. "Rory O'Neill is here," he said.

The big prizefighter stopped beside Flintlock and looked at Chanley's body. "He's dead?" he said.

"As hell in a preacher's backyard," Flintlock said.

O'Neill shook his head. "No man can survive a fall like that."

"It's not the fall that killed him," Flintlock said. "It was hitting the rocks that done for him."

"He might have been dead before he fell," O'Hara said. "He took two bullets to his chest."

"That's strange, Mr. Whitman and me heard only one shot," O'Neill said.

"There were two," O'Hara said. Then, his face expressionless, "Lucy Cully is fast with a gun."

"I'll help you bury him," O'Neill said. "And afterward we must keep this quiet. The law must not be involved."

"The death of a well-known Yankee poet is hard to explain away," Flintlock said. "Folks back in Philadelphia are bound to ask questions."

"A letter from the Arizona Territory will tell how promising young poet Roderick Chanley got tipsy and fell off a crag to his death," O'Neill said. "'He'll be sadly missed,' says poet Walt Whitman. That's what folks in Philadelphia will read and that's what they will believe."

"O'Hara thinks Chanley was murdered," Flintlock said.

O'Neill had a good smile, an ear-to-ear grin that lit up his battered face. He said, "Sam, at heart you and O'Hara are just a couple of gullible country boys. Of course Lucy killed Roderick Chanley. She had no other recourse."

Flintlock and O'Hara exchanged glances, too shocked to answer.

"One way or another Roderick was going to sell the house to Tobias Fynes and, believe it or not, marrying Lucy by force was still an option," O'Neill said. "In any case, all Fynes had to do was wait. Sam, you and O'Hara will ride on soon and Mr. Whitman and me are hopefully leaving today or tomorrow, so there would be nothing to stop Fynes and Chanley from taking possession of the Cully mansion and selling it out from under Lucy."

"I reckon Chanley would force Lucy to marry him to keep things nice and legal," O'Hara said.

"Yes, or if that failed, they would kill her," O'Neill said. "Chanley told Mr. Whitman that Fynes was offering ten thousand dollars for the house. With that kind of money he could return to Philadelphia and live comfortably while he wrote his poems and became famous."

Flintlock said, "So Lucy took care of Chanley, but that leaves Tobias Fynes. She'd find him harder to kill."

"Lucy will do anything to keep this house," O'Neill said. "If that means inviting Fynes into her bed and while he's in the throes of passion using her derringer to blow his brains out, then so be it."

"She told you this?" Flintlock said.

"No, she didn't. But she knows what Fynes wants and she'll use that to destroy him. Lucy is not the wide-eyed innocent she appears, Sam. Behind that pretty face is a cold, calculating mind."

O'Neill took a knee beside Chanley's broken body and then looked up at Flintlock. "We keep it quiet, Sam, because there's no good reason for Lucy Cully to hang. What's done is done and we forget about it."

"Sam, there's no law in Mansion Creek," O'Hara said. "No law anywhere in this part of the Territory, unless we can find us a U.S. Marshal."

"And that ain't likely," Flintlock said.

"Let it go, Sam," O'Neill said. "Ride away from it and don't look back."

His face like stone, Flintlock said, "Will Lucy Cully attend the funeral?"

O'Neill shook his head. "No, she won't."

"She should bury her own dead," Flintlock said.

Rory O'Neill made no comment on that and O'Hara looked disturbed.

"Then we'll lay Chanley close to her, over there in the open space at the foot of the crag," Flintlock said.

"I think there's a couple of shovels in the house," O'Neill said.

"We can't dig through rock," Flintlock said. "But we can lay rocks on top of him." His face unsmiling he said, "I've recently become quite the expert at that."

It took three hours of hard labor to bury Roderick Chanley under a rock cairn. And when they were done, three exhausted men admired their handiwork.

"God rest him, he'll sleep well there," O'Neill said. "And may Jesus, Mary and Joseph watch over him."

Flintlock nodded and then said, "You feel like saying any more words?"

"I don't have many words to say," O'Neill said. "But I'll try." He removed his plug hat, bowed his head and said, "Dear Lord, in your infinite mercy please grant this young poet Roderick Chanley eternal rest. He never should have come west of the Mississippi. Amen."

"Amen," Flintlock said. "That was real purty, Rory."

"Thank you," O'Neill said. "And now I have to beg a favor."

"Name it," Flintlock said. "You did good work on the rock tomb today."

O'Neill looked apologetic as he said, "As you know I can't ride a horse, so I need either you or O'Hara to ride to town and ask John Tanner to drive up here today or tomorrow and pick up Mr. Whitman and myself." Then, by way of explanation, "We'll take rooms at the hotel until the stage arrives."

"Does the old man know that Lucy shot Chanley?" O'Hara said.

"Yes, of course he does. And that's why he wants to go." O'Neill looked up the dizzying height of the crag to the house. "Mr. Whitman locked himself in his room and won't come out until it's time to leave. He thought of Roderick as a son and he's heartbroken over his death and the fact that Lucy was his killer."

"Then I'll ride into Mansion Creek for you," Flintlock said. "I want to talk with Tobias Fynes anyway."

"Want me to come with you, Sam, and see that you get fair play?" O'Hara said. He looked worried.

"No, you better stay here," Flintlock said.

"Why?"

"That I do not know. I just have a feeling that you should stay at the house."

"Then be careful, Sam," O'Hara said. "Watch your back in that town."

"If I don't return by nightfall, you'll know I've fallen afoul of Tobias Fynes," Flintlock said. "If that happens, tomorrow you'll ride into town and gun him."

O'Hara nodded. "Consider it done, Sam."

Fifteen minutes later under a gray sky Flintlock rode away from the crag. He hadn't seen Lucy Cully.

CHAPTER THIRTY-SEVEN

The day was hot enough that Sam Flintlock had worked up a thirst by the time he rode into Mansion Creek. What to take care of first? A beer or a banker? The day was still young and Tobias Fynes could wait . . . but not the beer.

Flintlock looped the buckskin's reins around the hitching rail and stepped into the saloon. The day was not bright but by force of habit Flintlock stopped just inside the door to let his eyes adjust to the gloom. There were five men in the saloon, two at the bar and three sitting at a table playing penny-ante poker with an obvious lack of enthusiasm, men with nowhere to go and nothing to do just slowly killing time. The two at the bar were of a different breed, a couple of frontier toughs who looked at this new arrival with belligerent eyes and saw in him an object of fun. Both of them had killed before and were confident of their gun skills.

The Mansion Creek Saloon was owned by Bob Pike, a man with sad blue eyes who for thirty years behind a bar had seen humanity at its worst in drinking dives that stretched from the Oregon Territory to Galveston, Texas. In his time, he'd witnessed every one of the seven deadly sins and a couple the Bible missed. Pike had no illusions, no loyalties, and he'd seen it all . . . but nothing had prepared him for Sam Flintlock.

A man who'd spent his life polishing liquor glasses but had never drank from one, Pike's busy hands stilled when Flintlock stepped into the saloon. He thought he'd never be surprised again, but the fellow in the buckskin shirt with a thunderbird tattooed on his throat surprised the hell out of him. The man who'd come through the door was of medium height, broad in the chest and thick in the wide shoulders. He looked to be about forty but he could be younger or older. His lean, brown face was dominated by a great beak of a nose and the dragoon mustache that hung under it. The lines in his face were cut deep and they talked loudly of dangerous trails and hard times. But his eyes when he bellied up to the bar were good-humored and looked directly at a man and the wrinkles at the corners of his eyes were those of remembered laughter. Pike, who could read a man as easily as a menu, saw that the Colt in his waistband was well worn and not there for show. Withal, the tattooed man seemed relaxed, affable . . . and as dangerous as a teased rattler.

Pike would later say, "It was a real pity the hard cases standing at the bar didn't see what I saw."

"What's your pleasure, stranger?" the bartender asked.

"Beer, on account of I'm just off a dusty trail and thirsty," Flintlock said.

A snort of laughter, and Mustang Dave Miner said, "You mean an owl-hoot trail."

Flintlock drained his mug, laid it on the bar, smiled and said, "I'll have another." He turned to the big, unshaven man at the bar and said, "I rode a few of them back in the day. Never cared for night riding much."

"Yeah, I knew I was right on the money," Miner said. "I took you fer some kind of low-life chicken thief."

Flintlock picked up his refilled glass and said, "No, you're wrong, I never stole a chicken in my life."

"Are you calling me a liar, mister?" Miner said, pushing off the bar. He turned and faced Flintlock, his hand close to his gun. "I don't like to be called a liar in front of other men."

"No, not calling you a liar, just saying you're mistaken, is all," Flintlock said.

That should have defused a tense situation but Miner, who in the past had killed his man, would not let it rest. A man of violence certainly, and as game as he needed to be, Miner had a reputation of being hard to handle. But he was not a draw fighter. Trying for speed on a draw and shoot was alien to him. He believed Flintlock was of the same breed, big and tough but unhandy with the Colt stuck in his waistband. Miner had sized up the opposition and come to the decision that he could take the tattooed man any hour of the day, any day of the week.

"Mister, I say you called me a liar, and I take that from no man," Miner said. The small man standing behind him, a weasel named Chad Lawson, said, "That's right, Dave, you take that from no man, right enough."

Flintlock finished his beer and said, "How much do

I owe you, bartender? I'm down to my last dime so I hope it covers it."

Bob Pike looked worried and glanced at Miner out of the corner of his eye. "Five cents a beer, so a dime covers it," he said.

Flintlock laid the coin on the bar. "I'm obliged," he said.

He stepped away from the bar and headed for the door.

"Hey, you! You leave when I say you can leave."

Miner was in the middle of the floor and ready, eager to make the kill.

Beside him the weasel said, "Leave when Dave says you can leave."

"Damn you, draw," Miner said, "Or by God, I'll shoot you in the back."

By times Sam Flintlock could be an irritable man and on any given day he'd only be pushed so far. It annoyed him that this hombre wanted to kill him for no other reason than to put another notch on his gun. Only the lowest piece of trash would do such a thing.

Flintlock sighed. He was trapped. If he tried to walk out the door he'd get shot in the back, there was no doubt of that. He faced Miner and said, "I'm at your service."

Miner, ignorant and brutish though he was, recognized that as duel talk, more likely to be uttered by a gentleman facing an opponent on a Louisiana meadow than a two-bottle bar in the Arizona Territory. He heard the wind rise and a rattle of rain on the saloon's tin roof. It was going to be an inclement afternoon in Mansion Creek.

Miner looked into Flintlock's steady eyes, at the

confident, relaxed way he waited on him to make his move. *"I'm at your service."* This man was no bargain and suddenly Miner knew it. He was aware of the puzzled look on Lawson's rodent face, the intent, expectant stare of the card players. If he backed down now he was finished in this town, this territory.

Knowing he might be only seconds away from death, Miner roared his desperation and made his draw.

"Hell, Sam, did you have to gun both of them?" Hogan Lord said. "I'd just hired those two. The big one is Dave Miner, the other is Chad Lawson, and they came highly recommended." Lord peered at the sprawled bodies. "Two each in the center of the chest. By any standard, that's good shooting, Sam."

"They didn't need to die today," Flintlock said. "They brought it on themselves."

Lord nodded. "Looks like they sure made a big mistake."

"Yeah," Flintlock said. "From the git-go mistakes were made." He watched the undertaker measure Miner for a pine box. "Hogan, you said you'd hired these men? Why?"

"Tobias Fynes wanted them and more like them," Lord said. "If Chanley can't make Lucy Cully see reason, he says he'll go to the gun." Hogan looked into Flintlock's eyes. "Where do you stand on this, Sam?"

"Chanley is dead," Flintlock said.

Lord was shocked. "Dead? But how?"

"We'll go outside. I don't want to talk in here," Flintlock said.

Lord nodded and then said to the undertaker, "Send your bill to Tobias Fynes."

"Then I'll just plant them, no frills," the man said. "Fynes doesn't like bills."

Flintlock and Lord stepped onto the sidewalk. "I have to speak with John Tanner," Flintlock said. "Walt Whitman and his bodyguard want to leave the Cully house today if they can."

"I saw him walk into the restaurant a little time ago," Lord said. "Come, I'll buy you a cup of coffee."

CHAPTER THIRTY-EIGHT

John Tanner, sensing the urgency of Flintlock's request, quickly finished his lunch and agreed to pick up Walt Whitman and Rory O'Neill.

"You don't need to worry about Jasper Orlov any longer," Flintlock said. "He's dead."

Tanner's face lit up. "Do tell, Mr. Flintlock. What happened?"

"It's a long story," Flintlock said. "I'll tell you about it later."

A delighted Tanner had a spring in his step and he walked to the restaurant door and passed Marshal Slim Hart on the way in. Hart's long face bore a sad expression, like a bloodhound that had lost its bone.

He stood at the table and said, "Sam Flintlock, isn't it?"

"Yes, Marshal, that's my name."

"I got it from one of Tobias Fynes's clerks," the lawman said. He paused and then said, "Bob Pike and three other men say it was self-defense, Flintlock. What do you say?"

"They pushed it, Marshal. I had to defend myself."

Hart nodded. "That's the way Pike and the others see it." He looked at Lord. "Did you witness the scrape?"

"Only the aftermath, Marshal, gunsmoke and perforated bodies," Lord said.

Hart turned his attention to Flintlock again and put a hand on his shoulder. "I'd lock you up until I completed my inquiries, if I had a lockup," Hart said. "So stay in town until I tell you it's all right to leave."

"When will that be?" Flintlock said.

"Once I have studied on the shooting scrape and ascertained to my satisfaction that the witnesses are telling the truth," Hart said.

"How long will that take?" Lord said.

"As long as it takes, Mr. Lord," Hart said. He touched his hat. "Now I will bid you gentlemen good day until later."

After the marshal left, Lord said, "Roderick Chanley is dead? How did it happen?"

"Lucy killed him," Flintlock said. Then, talking into the stunned silence that followed, "Put two bullets into his chest and he either fell or was pushed off the crag. Me and O'Hara buried what was left of him earlier."

Lord's handsome face revealed his confusion. "I just can't believe it. Why? Is it because she didn't want to marry him?"

"No, because she didn't want him to sell her house to Tobias Fynes," Flintlock said.

Hogan Lord bowed his head in thought, staring into the inky depths of his coffee cup. Finally, he looked up and said, "Walt Whitman and his bodyguard are leaving. You and O'Hara will ride on and then Lucy will be left alone in that huge house."

"I think she wants it that way, Hogan. What about Fynes? What will he do? Gun her and take the house by force?"

"No. Now that Chanley is dead Tobias will try to charm the girl. He won't use force unless he has to." Lord looked into Flintlock's eyes and held them. "Sam, you'll ride away from this? You'll leave Lucy alone and defenseless?"

"Hogan, she's a murderer, no better than Fynes himself. Yeah, I'm calling it quits and I'll do some long-riding and put some git between me and here."

"What about O'Hara?"

"I don't know what O'Hara will do. I have no idea what part of him will make his decision, the Irish or the Apache half. O'Hara has some fierce loyalties and maybe Lucy Cully is one of them." Flintlock got to his feet. "Thanks for the coffee, Hogan. Now I got to speak to Tobias Fynes and get my five hundred dollars from him."

Lord nodded and said, "Sam, just remember that I work for Fynes and I ride for the brand."

"I may twist his arm a little, Hogan, but I won't kill him. I promise."

Lord smiled and said nothing. Then as Flintlock reached the door he said, "Sam, you did well today."

Flintlock raised a hand, acknowledging the compliment, and stepped outside.

"Mr. Fynes is in conference and he can't be disturbed," the clerk said, barring Flintlock's path. He wore a bow tie and an eyeshade.

The deaths of two men and the cold calculation of Lucy Cully weighing on him, Flintlock's temper was short. "He'll see me," he said. He brushed past the man and stepped into Tobias Fynes's office. The fat man was in conference, all right, talking pretties into the ear of a young girl sitting on his lap while his ringed right hand busily kneaded her breasts.

When Flintlock entered, Fynes pushed the girl off his knee and she stood beside his chair. She was obviously in from the country, possibly a part payment on a loan, a pretty brunette with vacant brown eyes, dumbly accepting her fate.

"Don't you knock before you enter a man's office?" Fynes said.

"Sometimes, but not today," Flintlock said.

Fynes scowled. "You were only in town for a couple of minutes and you killed two men."

"New travels fast in Mansion Creek," Flintlock said.

"It's a small town," Fynes said. He waved a hand. "This is Violet. She's a new friend."

Flintlock touched his hat brim and the girl said, "Pleased to meet you, I'm sure."

"What can I do for you, Flintlock?" the fat banker said.

"I can see you're busy, so I'll come right to the point," Flintlock said. "I'm here for my five hundred dollars."

"I'll have to think about that," Fynes said. "Nothing worked out the way I hoped it would. All that ghost stuff just went away and Lucy Cully is still in the house."

"And here's some more good news, Fynes. Roderick Chanley is dead. Lucy shot him."

Fynes slammed back in his chair, his face ashen. "My God, is this true?" he said.

"Would I lie to you about something like that, Fynes?" Flintlock said, his eyes hard.

Fynes grabbed Violet's arm so hard she winced. "Get out," he said. "Go to the hat shop for a while. I'll meet you there."

The girl pouted, glared at Flintlock, walked out of the office rubbing her arm and slammed the door behind her.

"Now what's this about Chanley being killed?" Fynes said.

"Lucy shot him. She didn't want Chanley to sell her house to you, Fynes."

The banker said, "We'd better keep the law out of this. I'll deal with Lucy myself."

"Deal with her, how?" Flintlock said.

Fynes's smile was an unpleasant leer. "In life there are always choices to be made. Lucy's choice is to be nice to Uncle Tobias or face the noose when he reports her to the authorities. I'm sure she'll agree that me in her bed is a better alternative than facing a United States Marshal in a hanging frame of mind."

"Didn't take you long to get it all figured, Fynes," Flintlock said.

"I can foresee things going well for me," Fynes said. "Hard times are always good times for Tobias. And make no mistake, Lucy Cully will face hard times. She's penniless, you know."

"And that brings us back to my five hundred, Fynes. You hired me and O'Hara to do a job, now pay our wages."

"You brought me good news today, Flintlock, and I'm in a mood to be generous," Fynes said. "I'll pay the five hundred and I'll put another five hundred on top of it if you'll kill Lucy Cully."

It was Flintlock's turn to be taken aback. "You just told me you wanted to play kindly uncle," he said.

"I know, I know, but damn it all, that takes time. I'd need to win her trust first. The little witch will be suspicious and God knows how long I'd have to court her. No, the more I consider it the more I'm convinced the . . . shall we say sudden death of Lucy Cully is the answer. That way the house will be mine in short order." Fynes looked at Flintlock, his anger flaring. "I've been stalled long enough by that little whore. I want the treasure map and I want it now."

Flintlock shook his head. "Just pay me what you owe, Fynes. For fifty dollars you can hire a thug like the two I gunned today to do your dirty work."

"And if I refuse, since the services I paid for were not really needed at the Cully mansion?"

Flintlock smiled, a dangerous sign when he was on a slow burn. "Fynes, as you said, in life there are always choices to be made and this one is simple: You pay me what you owe or you'll end your life right now in that chair."

"You threaten me, with Hogan Lord in town?"

Flintlock ignored that and drew his Colt. "You have a choice to make, Fynes, and not much time to make it in. Speak up now. What's your decision?"

When he looked into Flintlock's eyes the fat banker realized that this man would do as he threatened. Fynes faced a stacked deck, and he knew it. Under the shadow of Flintlock's gun he opened a drawer in his desk and took out a tin petty cash box. Fynes counted out five hundred dollars in bills and said, "Take it, and be damned to you, Flintlock."

Flintlock picked up the money and shoved his Colt back in the waistband. "I'm obliged, Fynes," he said. "It's been a pleasure doing business with you."

"Go to hell," the fat man said.

He needed to find Hogan Lord and even some scores.

CHAPTER THIRTY-NINE

Walt Whitman sat in the back of John Tanner's wagon propped up by a couple of carpetbags and his wheelchair. An oilskin tarp covered his head against the rain as he stared at the house and the ever-present ravens.

The house seemed taller and slenderer than it did when he first arrived. He fancied the roof was hidden in a cloud but knew it was only the gray mist that had surrounded the old place since morning. Level after level soared upward, spires, arches, miniature towers, diamond-paned windows, galleries that went nowhere and served no useful purpose, and everywhere black tiles reflecting the gray sky. Whitman stared and stared and shivered as though he was cold. The house looked like a thin widow dressed all in black, mourning at the graveside of some dear departed, her tears falling like rain. And always he heard the warning cries of the midnight-colored ravens that never slept.

"Mr. Whitman, are you quite comfortable back there?"

"Huh?" the poet said, an old man wakening from a bad dream.

"Are you comfortable enough?" John Tanner said.

"Yes, yes, I'm fine," Whitman said.

"Well, let's hope the rain doesn't get any heavier," Tanner said.

"Amen to that," Whitman said.

The wagon lurched and creaked as Rory O'Neill, wearing an oilskin, climbed into the seat beside the driver. "We ready to go?" Tanner said.

He slapped the reins and the Morgan team stepped forward, but were halted a moment later as Lucy Cully, wearing a slicker, ran out of the house and called out, "Mr. Whitman! Stop!"

"No, drive on, Mr. Tanner," Whitman said.

The wagon moved forward again and Lucy walked alongside. "Mr. Whitman, come back to the house," she said. "Please stay a few days longer."

Whitman shook his head. "I must go. I can't stay in your house a minute longer, Lucy. It's an evil place and it changed you."

The wagon drove on toward the end of the crag and Lucy's voice grew in desperation. "I can't stay by myself, Mr. Whitman. Come back. Mr. O'Neill, make him come back."

Rory O'Neill said, "Miss Lucy, you made your bed and now you must lie in it."

"Mr. Whitman, don't leave me alone with Roderick's ghost. Mr. Whitman, come back. Come back, Mr. Whitman . . ."

The wagon drove on, leaving Lucy Cully behind.

For a long time, she stood in the rain, a lonely, forlorn figure, and watched it go. Then she returned to the echoing house.

The girl went to her room, unbuttoned the dripping slicker and let it drop to the floor. She sat in the wing chair, closed her eyes and let the creaking, groaning house embrace her, protecting her.

O'Hara saddled his horse and led it along the side of the house. He mounted only when he was sure that Lucy Cully would not come out again. The ravens had been warning him all morning of a coming disaster and he wanted to get far away from there. From a place of concealment behind a stack of firewood he'd seen Lucy try to get Walt Whitman to come back to the mansion. But the old man had refused and looked deeply troubled. The murder of Roderick Chanley had changed everything, and Whitman couldn't wait to get away from Chanley's killer. Lucy was alone now, alone with the ravens. O'Hara had no idea what the coming cataclysm might be, but like Whitman he wanted to get as far away from the old place as he could. Despite everything, had he grown to love Lucy Cully? Was that even possible? He'd never loved a woman in his life. And if he loved her should he try to save her? Finding within himself no answers to those questions he rode from the house at a canter and didn't look back.

He needed time to think.

* * *

Despite the rain, Jeptha Spunner, formerly Whitey Carson, was pleased.

He'd mounted the steam engine in the stripped-down old rowboat that would serve as the gondola and the burner and nitrogen cylinder had performed perfectly. Already hot air had inflated the yellow silk envelope to half its size and by tomorrow morning he'd be ready to take a short test flight. Spunner had written off the propeller as unworkable, at least for now, but he had high hopes for its future. He'd prove to the doubters that the modern steam engine could be used to power a balloon, operating the main components, the burner, nitrogen cylinder and propeller. Of course since he lacked the propeller, for now he'd have to depend on the vagaries of the wind. But if it was still holding from the north he would fly the distance between his cabin and Mansion Creek and anchor in a suitable landing place just outside of town. Then he would wait for a south wind to take him home again. Oblivious to the rain, Spunner almost danced with joy as he tested the anchors, listened to the steady pound of the engine and watched the envelope slowly swell with hot air. There would be no sleep for him that night—he was too excited. Come morning he'd rise into the air and fly on the wings of the wind.

CHAPTER FORTY

Hogan Lord's loyalty to the brand had its limits and Tobias Fynes was pushing him to the edge. The fat man's order was straightforward enough: Wait until Sam Flintlock rode out of town and then gun him and get back the five hundred dollars of Fynes's money he carried.

But Flintlock hadn't left town, not yet. He was eating his lunch in the restaurant while he waited for O'Hara and that was where Lord found him.

He sat opposite Flintlock, who was busily wolfing down slices of ham and boiled potatoes. Without looking up from his plate Flintlock said, "Hogan, it seems like we keep running into one another, huh?"

Lord nodded and said, "Yup, seems like. Mansion Creek is a small town and people are forever bumping into each other and giving one another bruises."

Flintlock smiled. "Is that how it is?"

"Most of the time," Lord said. Then, "We go back a ways, don't we, Sam?"

"A fair piece," Flintlock said, chewing. "Ten years off and on, I'd guess."

"I've forgotten about how you made off with the whole bounty that time in Chihuahua and left me flat broke," Lord said. "It's gone clean out of my mind."

Flintlock laid down his fork. It made a clinking sound on the plate. "And I don't recollect that time when we were on opposite sides of the fence up on the Canadian and you shot my hoss. He was only a paint mustang but I set store by that little feller."

"I was aiming for you, Sam, and shot low. But I've forgotten all about that," Lord said.

"Good times, Hogan," Flintlock said. "Do you recall Elena Casales, the Mexican Passion Flower?"

"Yeah, the whore with a heart of stone down Laredo way. You got drunk and wanted to marry her and I talked you out of it," Lord said.

"That was a true-blue thing you did, Hogan. That, I haven't forgotten."

"Good times, Sam," Lord said.

"Good times," Flintlock said. He forked up the last morsel of potato left on his plate and popped it into his mouth. Without looking up he said, "Tobias Fynes wants his money back, huh?"

Lord nodded. "Yes, that's why I'm here. Any chance you'd give it back voluntarily, Sam?"

"Not a chance, Hogan."

"He wants me to gun you and take the money."

"Where? Here?"

"No. Out of town somewhere, but not too far. Tobias wants me close because our new marshal has him spooked. He's terrified that Hawk Collins will come after him with a dozen tough riders and a rope."

"Well, I plan to wait here for O'Hara," Flintlock said. "So I won't be going out of town anytime soon."

"When it comes to money it's easy come, easy go with you, Sam," Lord said. "It's a pity you lost the whole five hundred on the turn of a card in the saloon."

Flintlock smiled. "Is that how you want to play it, Hogan?"

"You drew a trey of hearts against the queen of diamonds, Sam, and the gambling man who took your roll left town in a hurry." Lord nodded. "Yeah, that's the way we'll play it."

Lord rose to his feet and said, "Sam, you and O'Hara ride out of here. There's nothing in Mansion Creek for you. Tobias Fynes has turned this town into a cesspit."

"And what about you, Hogan?" Flintlock said. "Will you stay and wallow in the mud with him?"

"No, no, I won't. But I've got some chores to do before I leave," Lord said.

Flintlock extended his hand and Lord took it. "Well, good luck, Hogan."

"And you too, Sam. Good luck."

The rain followed O'Hara into Mansion Creek. He saw no sign of Flintlock's buckskin and he swung his horse toward the livery. O'Hara dismounted just inside the open doors, looked around and was greeted by the owner. Before the man could speak, O'Hara said, "I'm looking for a man, name's Sam Flintlock." He nodded in the direction of the stalls. "That's his buckskin over there."

Boots thumped on the floor of the hayloft and Flintlock called out, "Is that you, O'Hara?"

"It ain't nobody else."

"I'll come down."

Flintlock stepped down the ladder and said, "I was sleeping off my lunch." He smiled, "Glad to see you, O'Hara, and I've got much to tell."

"First, did Walt Whitman come in yet with O'Neill?"

"No, I haven't seen them. Why?"

"Because we left Lucy's house around the same time. I didn't want to talk to them about Lucy so I found an old game trail that took me the long way around the mesa. They should have been here by now."

Gate Cordell, the livery owner, said, "You want me to put up your horse?"

O'Hara said to Flintlock, "Did you get our five hundred?"

"Sure did."

"Then rub him down and give him a scoop of oats," O'Hara said. "I'm rich."

"Coffeepot is on the stove in my office," Cordell said. "He'p yourself if you have a mind to."

O'Hara availed himself of the offer and he followed Flintlock to the back of the barn, a steaming cup in his hand. He sat on an upturned crate and said, "What's happened, Sam? I see a blackness around you. To the Apache that aura always means death."

Using as few words as possible Flintlock described his shooting scrape in the saloon and then his trouble with Tobias Fynes. He briefly mentioned his conversation with Hogan Lord but did not elaborate.

O'Hara had listened intently, placed his coffee cup carefully at his feet and said, "You have to find your ma, Sam, so where do you go from here?"

"We buy supplies and ride," Flintlock said. "Barnabas said my ma is west of the Painted Desert and that takes in a lot of territory but it's the only lead I have."

"Can we trust Barnabas?" O'Hara said.

"No. But when it comes to Ma, his daughter, he's usually straight enough."

O'Hara picked up his cup, drained it and then said, "Sam, what about Lucy?"

"We're done with Lucy," Flintlock said, his face stiff.

"She's all alone in that big house, Sam. We can't just ride away and leave her."

"O'Hara, she's a murderer, and a cold-blooded one at that. Now that's a natural fact that you can't step around. You can't pretend the killing of Roderick Chanley never happened."

"Sam, you killed two men today. Does that make you a murderer?" O'Hara said.

"They drew down on me and I killed them in a fair fight. No, it wasn't murder and I'd nothing to gain by it," Flintlock said. "And neither of them two rannies was a Yankee poet, if that makes a difference."

"Sam, Lucy changed. The house changed her quite quickly, as though it was impatient and couldn't wait to make her a darker person and a murderer. Yes, maybe she can be blamed for the death of Roderick Chanley but I don't think so. It was the house to blame."

"She pumped two bullets into him, O'Hara. I don't think that blaming the house will hold up in court. No, if you want someone to blame try Tobias Fynes, the greedy banker. A jury of his peers would hate him on sight."

O'Hara rose to his feet. "Sam, I'm going back for her. Lucy needs to get far away from that house and find help."

"What kind of help?"

"Nowadays there are doctors who can treat illnesses of the mind. That's the kind of help Lucy needs."

"Are you prepared to drag her out of the house by force?" Flintlock said.

"Yes, if I have to."

"And take her where? There's a lawman in this town who'll either hang her or turn her over to a U.S. Marshal if he ever discovers that she hauled out a sneaky gun and killed her lover."

"I'll take Lucy to Texas where no one knows her," O'Hara said. "I can get her help there. And Chanley was not Lucy's lover. He never was her lover."

"You could have fooled me. What was he, then?"

"Lucy had always kept Chanley at arm's length, as though there was something about him she didn't trust, something false and devious."

Flintlock let that go. He had lost control of the situation and it troubled him.

"O'Hara," he said, "I have to ask you a question—are you in love with Lucy Cully?"

It took a few moments of thought before O'Hara answered, and finally he said, "Yes, I think maybe I am."

"You're either in love or you're not. There are no maybes about it."

"Have you ever been in love, Sam Flintlock?"

"No. I haven't. I never saw my way clear to make that kind of commitment. Of course, I've loved a whore a time or two but only for an hour or an evening."

"Then you're in no position to tell me what love is," O'Hara said.

"No, I guess I'm not," Flintlock said. "But I'm still qualified to offer you advice as a friend."

The tall, loose-geared form of Marshal Slim Hart walking into the stable ended any further conversation. "I've been looking all over for you, Flintlock," he said. "I thought maybe you'd skedaddled and I would have taken that hard."

"No, I've been right here, Marshal," Flintlock said. Then, a little spike of meanness in him, "I wanted to see your big happy smile just one more time."

"Well, that's mighty strange because I never smile and I ain't never happy."

"Sorry to hear that," Flintlock said. "Was it a woman?"

"No, it's the croup," Hart said. "Now stand up and hear this." Flintlock got to his feet and the marshal said, "I've been studying on things, Flintlock, and I decided you acted in self-defense this morning."

"Glad to hear that, Marshal," Flintlock said.

"If I'd thought otherwise I'd have hung you. Tobias Fynes told me he wanted you hung, said you stole money from him at gunpoint. Is that true?"

"No, it's a lie. Fynes owed me five hundred dollars in wages and refused to pay. I stated my case and convinced him otherwise."

"I figured it was something like that," Hart said. "I don't like that Fynes ranny and when I don't like a man bad things tend to happen to him. But only when I'm wearing a badge, you understand."

Flintlock smiled. "I'm glad you like me."

"No, I don't like you either. I want you out of my town, Flintlock, like now, this very minute. Instanter. *Compre?*"

"I catch your drift, Marshal. I'll be riding."

"And take the Apache with you. Hell, he's gonna murder us all in our beds."

"His name is O'Hara and he's only half Apache," Flintlock said.

"What's the other half?"

"Irish."

"One's as bad as the other," Hart said.

CHAPTER FORTY-ONE

"Sam, I don't need you to come with me," O'Hara said. "You've got to head for the Painted Desert country and find you ma."

"Seems like the natural thing to do is ride with you a spell longer," Flintlock said. "We'll get this love thing out of the way and then point our horses west again."

"Sam, I may not be riding with you ever," O'Hara said. "I meant what I said about taking Lucy to Texas. Don't try to stop me."

"Stop you? Hell, I'm only along for the ride." Flintlock glanced at the sky. "Rain's gone but it will be dark in a couple of hours. We'd best cross the mesa while it's still light enough to see."

"Sam, I won't change my mind about Lucy," O'Hara said.

"And I wouldn't dream of changing it for you," Flintlock said. "Trust me."

O'Hara's scowl signaled that the last man on earth he'd trust that day was Sam Flintlock.

A mile before they reached the mesa a wagon drove toward them and O'Hara with his excellent eyesight said, "Tanner's coming, Sam. Looks like he's got Walt Whitman and Rory O'Neill with him."

"Do you see Lucy?" Flintlock said.

O'Hara shook his head. "No, I don't. She isn't with them."

"I thought there was a chance she might come into town and fess up to the murder of Roderick Chanley," Flintlock said.

O'Hara turned in the saddle and said, "Did you really think that, Sam?"

Flintlock smiled. "No, I guess I didn't."

"Lucy is fessing up to nothing, not now, not later," O'Hara said. "At the moment she is not in her right mind and there's an end to it."

Flintlock said, "Whatever you say, O'Hara." He frowned, his thoughts dark. "Whatever you say."

John Tanner reined in his team and waited until Flintlock and O'Hara rode alongside the wagon. "Howdy, boys," he said. "Fancy meeting you here."

O'Neill, smiled, raised his bowler hat but said nothing. Whitman sat in the back of the wagon and he too was silent, as though what had happened had robbed him and O'Neill of speech.

"Tanner, I saw you leave the house," O'Hara said. "You should be in Mansion Creek by now."

"I didn't see you," Tanner said.

"No, you didn't," O'Hara said.

Tanner smiled. "I bet you can move through this country like an Apache when you need to, you being a breed an' all."

"Yes, I can," O'Hara said.

Tanner waited to see if there was more talk forthcoming from O'Hara and when no words came he said, "We're making poor time because as we reached the mesa Mr. Whitman took real poorly. We had to stop for a spell until he felt he could go on." Tanner managed to look sympathetic. "A man gets thrown around pretty bad in the back of a wagon, especially in this country. Where are you boys headed?"

O'Hara held back, but Flintlock said, "We want to talk with Lucy Cully."

Suddenly Whitman became animated. Turning his head he said, "What will you say to her, Flintlock?"

Flintlock kneed the buckskin closer to Whitman. "I don't rightly know," he said. "Have you any suggestions?"

"No, I have none. The ravens have all gone," Whitman said. "Did you know that?"

"No, I didn't," Flintlock said.

"The ravens were afraid and they flew away," Whitman said. "I think they know something terrible is coming . . . fire, death, the end of everything. I think Lucy knows it's the end. I looked into her eyes and they expressed more than all the print I have read in my life."

O'Hara heard this and said, louder than he usually talked, "I'm taking Lucy away from here, old man. I'm taking her to Texas where she will get well again."

Whitman slowly shook his head and said, "Texas won't cure what ails her. Destroy the house, burn it to the ground, and perhaps she'll get well again." He turned and said, "Please drive on, Mr. Tanner. The hour is getting late and we must reach the town before dark."

As the wagon lurched into motion, O'Neill said,

"Good luck, O'Hara. Do what you have to do." The big prizefighter looked straight ahead and said no more.

Flintlock and O'Hara's route across the mesa was uneventful except for a bobcat that snarled as they passed and then watched them for a few moments before it turned tail and bounded into the brush.

In the fading daylight the house at the narrow point of the crag still looked the same, but the ravens were gone and in their place was a blazing sky, ribboned with bands of scarlet and jade. Up there on the crag the wind drove hard from the north and this late in the fall it had a knife edge.

Flintlock drew rein and said, "O'Hara, it looks like there's nobody to home."

"It's still early," O'Hara said. "Lucy hasn't lit the lamps yet."

Flintlock swung out of the saddle and stepped to the front door. He tried the handle. "Locked," he said. "Do we know she's in there?"

"Of course she's in there," O'Hara said. "Where else would she be?"

Flintlock wanted to say, *Hopefully smashed on the rocks at the foot of the crag*, but held his tongue.

"We'll go round the back and try the door there," O'Hara said. "She usually leaves it open to cool the kitchen."

But it too was locked, probably bolted, and its thick oak presented a formidable barrier.

After taking a step back, Flintlock looked up at the house—in the waning light it looked like a black mountain set to fall on him. Suddenly dizzy, he looked

down at his feet and rubbed the crick out of the back
of his neck.

"We'll go round the front and pound on the door,"
O'Hara said. "Maybe Lucy is taking a nap."

"Poor thing," Flintlock said. O'Hara looked at him
sharply but his face was expressionless.

Banging on the door brought no response, nor did
O'Hara's shouts of, "Lucy, let us in!" But Flintlock
thought he caught a fleeting glimpse of a pale face at
one of the higher windows. He told this to O'Hara,
who said, "Yes, she's in there, all right. We may have to
break down the front door."

"With what?" Flintlock said. "That's a Yankee door,
three inches of solid oak with a cast-iron lock and
behind it a steel bolt that's near as big as a cannon
barrel. And I'd guess the back door is the same only
stronger. The place is a fortress."

O'Hara looked up at the house, his mind working.
"We'll wait, Sam. She'll come down soon."

"Suppose she comes down never," Flintlock said.
"What then?"

"Sooner or later she'll run out of grub," O'Hara
said.

"How sooner or later?"

"I don't know."

"We can't camp here until then."

"It won't be too long, Sam."

"I'm going to try the windows," Flintlock said.
"There's got to be a way to get in there."

But all the ground-floor windows were securely
locked from the inside and Flintlock, irritated, looked
around for a rock.

Horrified, O'Hara saw him heft a baseball-sized rock in his hand and ready himself for a throw. "Wait, stop!" he said. "What are you doing?"

"I'm gonna chuck this rock through a window," Flintlock said. "It's the only way I can get one open enough for us to climb through."

"No, not yet," O'Hara said. "Lucy knows we're here. Wait a spell."

Flintlock looked around at the crowding darkness. "Until first light, O'Hara," he said. "If she ain't down by then I'm riding."

O'Hara laid his hand on Flintlock's shoulder, a thing he'd never done before. "Then so be it, my old friend," he said.

CHAPTER FORTY-TWO

Jeptha Spunner had not slept all night, excitement about his maiden flight in the steam balloon keeping him wide awake, counting the minutes and hours until daybreak. The yellow envelope was fully inflated and tugged on its anchoring ropes like a spirited steed fighting the bit. The burner was performing well, as was the nitrogen cylinder, and the experimental small steam engine, a wonder of modern engineering, had proved itself stable and reliable and when the time came would be ready to turn a propeller shaft. Adding to Spunner's elation was that the wind still blew strong from the north. His intention, hatched in the small hours of the morning, was to fly as low as he could over Mansion Creek and let the folks see for themselves the miracle in the sky. Although the engine did not drive anything at present, it would prove to the doubters steam could be used to power flying machines.

Just before dawn, Spunner cast off the anchors and added more fuel to the burner. The yellow balloon

lifted slowly, just a few feet at a time, still well below
the strong upper air currents. When the long night
began to gray into morning the balloon soared above
the trees, and higher still until it met the concen-
trated force of the north wind and became its willing
slave.

But then a crisis, and one that Spunner had not
expected.

The gondola was proving to be unstable and
rocked like a rowboat in a choppy sea. Maybe because
it was a rowboat! Jeptha Spunner felt a spike of panic
as he realized that he'd made a mistake. Without a
propeller to drive it forward and add stability, the
lightened ten-foot boat hanging underneath the envelope was completely at the mercy of a capricious
wind. Spunner held on for grim life as the bucking
gondola scudded across the sky at what seemed break-
neck speed . . . and then disaster. Fire!

The steam engine's bolts had ripped free of their
timber platform and tumbled across the bottom of
the boat, spilling the glowing coals of the furnace
everywhere. At first it looked to Spunner that the
contents of the furnace would harmlessly burn away
to cinders, but that proved not to be the case. The
dry wood at the bottom of the boat smoldered and
then, fanned by the wind, burst into flame in a
dozen different places. Within minutes the yellow
balloon went into a shallow death dive and dragged
a plume of purple smoke across the fair face of the
morning sky . . .

* * *

Flintlock and O'Hara spent an uncomfortable night in the stable behind the house. As the dawn began to banish the shadows of the night there was still no sign of Lucy Cully.

Irritated as all hell, Flintlock saddled both horses, led them to a patch of grass and then followed O'Hara to the front of the house.

O'Hara stepped back far enough so he could take in the building from its ground floor to the peak of the roof and then, cupped hands to his mouth, he yelled, "Luuucy!"

Long moments passed, grew into several minutes. The house was silhouetted against a lemon sky and stood alone, a lost, doomed structure out of place and time. Its tall, thin Gothic lines harkened back hundreds of years, drawing its inspiration from the age of cathedrals that ended with the Black Death, after which the surviving peoples of Europe just didn't give a damn for the churches that had failed them. Perhaps, as some said, the Cully house was cursed from its very beginnings.

"O'Hara," Flintlock said. He pointed. "Look up there."

Lucy Cully was at the topmost level of the house where a few attic rooms opened up onto narrow galleries that were constructed of black iron and served no useful purpose. Lucy, precariously perched between earth and sky, stood on one of those frail galleries and gazed down at Flintlock and O'Hara. Her face was very pale and she wore a nightdress of some gauzy material that the rude north wind shaped to her slim body.

"Lucy, let us in," O'Hara yelled, his head bent back about as far as it could go. "We need to talk, Lucy. Open the door."

The girl's voice came back very faint, "Go away. I don't want to talk with anybody. You can talk with my fiancé. His name is Roderick and he's downstairs somewhere writing a poem."

"Lucy, open the door," O'Hara yelled. "I have something to tell you."

"Leave me and leave my house," the girl said. "Go away. I don't know you."

"Lucy . . . please . . ." O'Hara said in a normal tone of voice but one that was filled with despair.

"O'Hara, let's go," Flintlock said. "There's nothing we can do here."

Then, looking beyond O'Hara, his eyes grew wide. "Oh my God," he said.

The envelope was burning, the gondola in flames, and the balloon, like a runaway horse, was out of control. The north wind hurtled Spunner's creation toward the crag where the tall house stood and with no way to steer he knew his death was close. But as flames licked around him, already blackening his face and hands, he had a choice in the matter . . . he could choose the way he died. In pain and already suffering terribly he chose the rocks below to the fire above. Spunner jumped, and his tormented body cartwheeled through the thin morning air and after long seconds smashed into boulders of stone that broke him into pieces and mercifully killed him instantly.

Trailing a plume of smoke, what was left of the balloon smashed into the front of the Cully house like a fiery meteorite. The wooden fabric of the house, tinder dry after years of exposure to the merciless sun, immediately burst into flame that eagerly engulfed the upper stories.

Flintlock had time to call out, "Lucy!" before the disaster struck. Then, as smoke and fire rose from the house, he yelled, "O'Hara, no!"

Lucy had vanished from the balcony as the relentless fire began to take hold and O'Hara ran to one of the front windows, flaming debris already raining down on him. O'Hara used the butt of his Colt to smash out the diamond-shaped panes until he had room enough to insert his arm to unfasten the window catch. Acrid smoke billowed out of the now-open window but O'Hara ignored the danger and began to scramble inside.

Flintlock sprinted to the window. "O'Hara, don't go in there," he said. He grabbed the back of the man's vest. "The whole damned building is on fire."

O'Hara ignored that and wrenched away from Flintlock's grasp. He vanished into the smoke, and Flintlock retreated from the intense heat and stood helplessly watching the place burn as ash fell around him like black rain. The panicked horses galloped from the crag and didn't stop running until they put safe distance between themselves and the house.

The acrid smell of smoke dominated the morning

and the feral roar of the fire was louder than Flintlock had ever imagined. The house burned like an Independence Day bonfire set with kerosene. Bright yellow and red flames had assumed the shape of a pillar of fire and a column of smoke rose into the air only to be tied up in bows by the north wind. All over the house windows blew out and showered shards of hot glass onto the stone top of the crag.

Flintlock watched the Cully house burn and feared for O'Hara's life. Nothing could live in such an inferno. But then a miracle of sorts. The front door slammed open and through a tunnel of fire and smoke O'Hara staggered outside and collapsed. Flintlock ran to him, picked up O'Hara's slim body in his arms and through a whirlwind of soot, smoke and sparks put a distance between him and the inferno. He laid O'Hara on a small, grassy area and looked him over. He was hurt bad. The skin of his face and hands was pink in color, very swollen and covered in weeping blisters. When Flintlock touched O'Hara's face or hands the man groaned in pain.

"O'Hara, can you hear me?" Flintlock said.

After a few moments, O'Hara's eyes fluttered open and through cracked, swollen lips he whispered, "I couldn't save her, Sam. I saw Lucy at the top of the stairs and I couldn't reach her because of the fire." O'Hara's burned hand grabbed the sleeve of Flintlock's buckskin shirt. His eyes were wild, haunted, remembering a horror no man should ever see. "I saw her burn, Sam. Her hair . . . her hair was on fire, Sam . . . like a woman with red hair. I saw that, Sam . . . I saw Lucy burn . . ."

"Easy, O'Hara, I'm going to get you to a doctor. Are you in pain?"

O'Hara closed his eyes and did not answer and Flintlock saw that he was unconscious and he considered that a good thing.

What was left of the house crashed in on itself, sending up sheets of flame, sparks and black smoke. Flintlock heard loud shrieks as nails tore loose and the structure collapsed, as though the house cried out in its death throes.

Leaving the unconscious O'Hara where he was, Flintlock rounded up the horses and when he returned there was no change, although O'Hara's skin had taken on a wet appearance from the weeping burns. Flintlock carefully lifted the injured man into the buckskin's saddle and then mounted behind him. With one hand he held O'Hara in place and led his paint with the other.

When he reached the trail that led to the mesa he looked back at the Cully mansion. It was no more, just a pile of smoking ash. Part of one wall still stood, black and ugly, and here and there stuck up thick beams of wood, blackened and charred by the flames. Flintlock saw the faint glow of still-burning embers, fluttering flames clinging to them like scarlet moths, and sooty dust hung in the air. Nothing had escaped the conflagration, shards of shattered glass littered the ground where the windows had blown out in the heat and the brass base of the grand chandelier that had hung in the entrance hall lay blackened and twisted on the ground.

Like the house, Lucy Cully burned away to ash and no trace of her was ever found.

In 1891 a letter written by a Mansion Creek matron named Cornelia Case to her sister in Boston mentioned that after a few weeks the ravens returned and flew around the ruin for several days before they left. But that cannot be verified since Mrs. Case was the only one to write about the phenomenon, and the return of the ravens was not reported in the *Apache County Herald*.

CHAPTER FORTY-THREE

"The prognosis is good, but I want Mr. O'Hara to remain here with me for the next couple of days," Dr. Theodora Weller said.

Sam Flintlock said, "What have you done for him, Doc? Me and O'Hara go back a long ways."

"I've given him morphine for pain and I will apply a poultice of goose fat and calendula on his hands and face twice a day," the doctor said. "The good news is that Mr. O'Hara will have no scars. His burns were not severe enough."

"What's that calendula stuff?" Flintlock said. "I've never heard of it."

Theodora smiled. "I'm not trying to poison your friend, Mr. Flintlock. Calendula oil is a member of the marigold family of flowers and it is used as a healing agent."

"Sorry, Doctor, I'm really worried about O'Hara is all," Flintlock said.

"He's asleep now, but he'll be just fine, Mr. Flint-lock. Mr. O'Hara will be up and around in a couple of days," the doctor said. She looked at Flintlock's face. "You have some burns yourself."

Flintlock shook his head. "No goose fat and marigolds for me, Doc. I'm a fast healer."

He thought Theodora Weller a very attractive woman in her brown, corseted dress that was tightly laced and revealed a deep cleavage. But the wide puffed shoulders and the row of buckles instead of buttons that closed the back of the dress gave her a slightly mannish look, as did the brown top hat perched on her swept-up hair. Flintlock figured that the good doctor would be a handful, in bed or out.

His pleasant speculations ended with the arrival of Marshal Slim Hart, who looked grim, his habitual expression. He looked at Flintlock with the cold eyes of a hanging judge and said, "I done two things before noon. I rode out to the Cully house, or what's left of it, and I spoke to that old poet feller . . . what's his name?"

"Walt Whitman," Flintlock said.

"Yeah, him. He told me what took place out there on the crag, murder, bedlam, strange cannibal folks, other high jinks too many to mention and you and the Injun always in the mix. Whitman never saw the house burn, Flintlock, but you did. Who burned with it? Tell me the truth now. A lie will not help you in your present situation. Oh, and I hesitate to mention it, I found a man's dead body at the bottom of the crag."

Hart was not a complicated man. Not overly intelligent, he saw things in black or white, legal or illegal, with no shades of gray in the middle. He was stubborn, intolerant of others and brave to a fault. His loyalty lay not with the lawman's star on his vest but out on the range with a hard, bitter old man named Hawk Collins who had taught him much about the frailty of human nature and the inherent evil in those who broke the law, knowingly or otherwise.

Flintlock said, "Marshal, did Whitman tell you about the flying machine or Jasper Orlov or the man with the knife and sharpening steel?"

"No, he didn't," Hart said, looking lost. "But I want to hear it from you."

Theodora Weller smiled and said, "I'll get us some coffee. This should be interesting."

Flintlock drank three cups of coffee as he sketched out the details of what had happened, from Tobias Fynes hiring him and O'Hara to guard Lucy Cully, through the cannibal horror and Roderick Chanley's murder, up to Lucy's horrific death in the fire.

Hart interrupted only twice, once to say that he'd heard about Whitey Carson, the albino shootist, and the other time to observe that flying machines were a danger to everyone and should be banned by every government in the world.

"O'Hara tried his best to save Lucy Cully but he was beaten back by the fire," Flintlock said. "I brought him here to Dr. Weller to get his burns treated, and that's the end of the story."

"Are you sure?" Hart said.

"Yeah, I'm sure. There's nothing else."

"It's a tall tale, Flintlock, but I doubt you have the wit to make it up," Hart said. He looked at Theodora. "How is O'Hara?"

"He'll be fine," the doctor said.

"When can he ride?"

"In a couple of days."

Hart nodded, and then said to Flintlock, "You'll leave town as soon as O'Hara can ride and I never want to see you back here again."

"Not much chance of that," Flintlock said.

"Good. Then we see eye to eye on that score." Hart touched his hat brim to Dr. Weller. "Thank you kindly for the coffee, ma'am," he said. He gave Flintlock a hard look and then stepped to the door. Before he opened it and without turning to face Dr. Weller he said, "Do you believe the story Flintlock just told us, Doctor?"

Theodora spoke to the lawman's back. "Yes, I do."

"Every word?"

"Yes, Marshal, every word."

"Then I'm much obliged," Hart said. He opened the door and walked into the sunlit afternoon . . . and he and Hogan Lord exchanged greetings as they passed each other on the gravel path that led to Dr. Weller's surgery.

"I heard you'd brought in O'Hara, Sam," Hogan Lord said. Then, to Theodora Weller, "How is he, Doctor?"

"He was burned but not too badly. He'll be up and around in a couple of days."

"Glad to hear that," Lord said. He swept off his hat, held it to his chest as he bowed and said, "And may I say, Doctor, that you look lovely this afternoon."

Theodora dropped a little curtsy. "Why, thank you, kind sir. You are most *galante.*"

Flintlock watched this exchange, slightly irritated at Lord's practiced ease around women, the perfect Southern gentleman in action. He knew that if he ever tried to bow and talk pretties he'd make a total hash of it.

"How did it happen, Sam?" Lord said after he'd regained his upright posture.

"You didn't hear about the fire and Lucy Cully's death?"

Lord's shocked expression answered that question better than words.

For the second time that day Flintlock told of the events that led up to the girl's death. "The house was destroyed, burned to ashes," he said. "Bad news for Tobias Fynes, huh?"

"Yes, it's bad news and I'll have to go break it to him," Lord said. "He isn't going to like it."

"Nothing he can do except comb through the ashes for his treasure map," Flintlock said.

"That, I'd love to see," Lord said. To Flintlock he said, "When O'Hara wakes give him my best wishes for a speedy recovery." He touched his hat to Theodora— "Ma'am"—and stepped out of the surgery, eager to give the fat man the bad news.

CHAPTER FORTY-FOUR

Tobias Fynes was enraged, furious at the little Cully whore for burning his house down and angry at Hogan Lord for bringing him the bad news.

The house was burned to ashes so the treasure map was gone. If it was written on paper it could not survive. A fortune in gold had slipped through his fingers—no, not that, *ripped from his hands*—and all Fynes had left was a pauper's portion, a miserable little bank in a miserable little town in the most miserable part of the whole damned country. Fynes slammed his fist onto his desk. Somebody would have to pay for this. He smiled. Yes, why not Estelle? He was in a foul mood and it was high time she vacated the cabin so he could move in his new ladylove, young, naive, eager to please and stupid, the way he liked his women.

Fynes rose from his desk, told his clerks he'd be back in an hour and waddled to Estelle's small cabin. No, it was his cabin, not hers. He'd bought the damned thing with his own good money.

When Estelle slid back the bolt and opened the door to his knock and saw him she did what she always did, smiled and then let out a little squeal of delight. Fynes pushed the girl away and stepped inside. Estelle seemed hurt but only for a moment or two. "Did you bring me anything, Toby tum-tum?" she said in a little girl's voice.

"Yes, Estelle, I have. A notice to quit these premises immediately," Fynes said.

The girl smiled, but the expression on her face was uncertain. "Don't tease me, Toby," she said. "I don't like it when you tease me."

Fynes grinned, a malevolent grimace that stretched his fleshy lips. "Who's teasing? I'm not teasing, Estelle. I want you out of here. Now! Gather up your things except the jewelry I bought you and hit the road."

Fynes had said it, he'd made it abundantly clear, but still Estelle couldn't believe him. She couldn't believe her ears.

"Toby," she said, "please stop funning." Estelle threw herself into Fynes's arms. "Say it's all right, that you're just funning me, Toby."

"Get off me, you worn-out whore," Fynes said. He pulled her arms off his shoulders and violently pushed her away from him. The cabin was small and it took only a couple of steps for Fynes to reach the clothes hanging in the open closet. He grabbed an armful, pushed Estelle aside and tossed the clothing out the door into a deep mud puddle left by the recent rains.

If Estelle Redway had any doubts, the petticoats and dresses slowly sinking into the mud outside dispelled them. After three years Tobias was really pouring the coffee on the fire and throwing her out.

Estelle experienced grief but reacted in anger. She picked up a crystal spray perfume bottle and pitched it at Fynes's head. Moving with surprising speed, the fat man stepped to his right but he was a split second too late. The bottle hit him just under his left eye, split him wide open and drew blood that instantly ran in scarlet rivulets down his cheek.

Hell hath no fury like a woman scorned, and Estelle was not done with Fynes yet. She backed off to the dresser, opened the drawer and pulled out the Forehand and Wadsworth .32 revolver. But Fynes was on the girl in a flash. He grabbed her wrist and tried to wrench the gun from her hand. But Estelle was surprisingly strong and she fought like a wildcat. She broke away from him and leveled the revolver. In a panic, Fynes grabbed the first weapon that was handy—a ten-inch-long letter opener made to look like King Arthur's sword, Excalibur. Estelle triggered the revolver but it clicked on a dud round. Desperately, Fynes swung the opener at Estelle and Excalibur plunged hilt-deep into her neck, three inches under the left earlobe. Blood spurted as the girl dropped to her knees without a sound.

When he saw what he'd done, Fynes was horrified. Estelle was choking on her own blood and he kneeled beside her and pulled out the letter opener and his hands and wrists were quickly covered in gore. Fynes grabbed the girl by the shoulders and, hysterical, pleaded, "Don't die, Estelle. Don't die. Think of me. Think of my poor wife."

But he was talking to a corpse.

Estelle's blue eyes were open, unblinking, and they stared at Fynes. In death they were not filled with fear but loathing and Fynes couldn't bear to look into them again. He staggered to his feet and lurched out of the cabin, holding up his glistening, crimson hands in front of him, staring fixedly at them in stark horror.

When Fynes reached the bank and staggered inside the clerks took one look at this blood-drenched madman and fled. The fat man made it to his office and collapsed into his chair. He put his elbows on the desktop and stared at his hands, his mouth working.

Tobias Fynes was still in this posture when Dr. Theodora Weller walked into his office, her right hand down by her side. "You did it, Tobias, didn't you? You finally killed her. You destroyed the woman I loved."

The fat man shook his head. "No, no, it was an accident. The letter opener was in my hand . . . she fell on it. Yes, that was it, she fell on the letter opener. It was a terrible accident."

Theodora raised the Colt and said, "Tobias, you're a piece of trash who can't be allowed to breathe the same air as other human beings."

"What are you going to do?" Fynes said. His face was gray, fear bright in his eyes.

"Kill you, like you killed Estelle."

Fynes shrieked, "No! Show mercy! Mercy for Tobias."

"What mercy did you show Estelle? You tired of that beautiful creature and killed her when you no longer had need of her. You're evil, Tobias, and I can't let you live."

"Nooo!" Fynes yelled. His cry for mercy was drowned out by the roar of Theodora's revolver. She pumped five shots into the fat man's chest, killing him five times.

Dr. Weller then left the bank and walked to her office. She poured herself a drink, lit a cheroot and waited for Marshal Hart.

CHAPTER FORTY-FIVE

Marshal Slim Hart inspected Estelle Redway's body. She'd been pretty and young, no more than a girl, and she'd died horribly.

"You sure it was him, Mrs. McGinty?" Hart said.

A shack dweller who did other people's laundry for a living, Rose McGinty said, "It was him, all right, Marshal. It was Tobias Fynes"—she spat as though mentioning the name left a bad taste in her mouth—"and I saw him clear. When he came out of Estelle's cabin his hands were covered in blood, the damned, dirty swine."

"Where were you when you saw him?" Hart asked.

She pointed across the dirt road to her frame-and-tar-paper shack, where a line of shirts waved, long johns danced and sheets billowed in a drying wind. "I was over there, hanging out my laundry as I always do on a Monday," Mrs. McGinty said.

She was Irish, hot tempered, and in half a dozen towns she'd fought a running battle with the Chinese for laundry rights. There were no Chinese in Mansion Creek and Mrs. McGinty said a rosary every night to ask that circumstances stayed that way. Currently her old man was down with the flu and she said a rosary for him as well.

"And then Dr. Weller showed up?" Hart said.

"Yes, she did, bless her, but Estelle was already dead and there was no need for doctoring."

"And after Dr. Weller left, you heard shots," Hart said.

"Yes. They came from the street somewhere." Mrs. McGinty laid a red, work-worn hand on the marshal's arm. "Find Tobias Fynes, lawman. Find him and hang him."

The clerks huddled together in a frightened group outside the bank when Slim Hart arrived. He ignored them and turned to one of the thirty or so onlookers, a respectable-looking man in a gray ditto suit. "What happened inside?"

The man stepped closer to the marshal and in a low voice he said, "From what I heard from the bank clerks, Dr. Weller walked into Mr. Fynes's office and shot him. At this time I don't know if he's alive or dead. No one does."

Hart nodded. "Much obliged. I'll go take a look."

"Marshal, I knew nothing good would come of having a woman doctor in town," the respectable man said. "I said that all along."

"Fynes murdered a young woman not thirty minutes ago," Hart said. "Nothing good will come of that either."

The respectable man was so stunned he couldn't

322   *William W. Johnstone*

speak and Hart left him there to adjust his attitude
and stepped into the bank.

Tobias Fynes was sprawled in his chair, his open
mouth trickling saliva, and his prominent dark eyes
stared into eternity. He had five holes in his chest that
could be covered by a playing card and any one of
them would have killed him. Marshal Hart felt no
sympathy for the man, just a twinge of disappointment. It would have been better if the doctor had just
winged the fat man and saved him for the rope.

Hart pulled down the office blinds and the office
was immediately suffused with an amber-colored light.
He reached inside the dead man's coat, did not find
what he was looking for, and then one by one he
opened the desk drawers. The bottom drawer on the
left side of the desk held what the lawman wanted, a
Colt Sheriff's model with a three-inch barrel in .44-40
caliber. Hart rotated the cylinder, checked the loads
and then pushed the little Colt into Fynes's blood-
crusted right hand.

"You were just too slow on the draw, fat man," Hart
said. "That happens sometimes."

The marshal stepped outside and faced the crowd,
including, he noted, Hogan Lord. Hart held up his
hands to silence the whispers and said, "Earlier today
Tobias Fynes murdered Estelle Redway by shoving the
blade of a letter opener into her neck."

There were cries of "Shame!" and someone yelled,
"Murder, by God."

Again Hart silenced the crowd and said, "According to the evidence I found inside, when Dr. Weller

confronted Fynes with his crime he drew down on her, but he was too slow. Dr. Weller, a brave woman, stood her ground, got her work in and shot him dead. As far as I'm concerned it was a clear case of self-defense."

This drew cries of "Huzzah!" and "Served him right!" Tobias Fynes was not a well-liked man in Mansion Creek.

"We need the undertaker here," Marshal Hart said. "One of you men see to it."

The crowd dispersed and the bank clerks hesitantly reentered the bank building and Hart immediately deputized a couple of loafers and told them to stand guard on the safe until he returned.

"Remember, boys, it's the town's money so guard it well," he said.

As the lawman crossed the street in the direction of the doctor's surgery, Hogan Lord caught up with him and Hart stopped, his hand dropping close to his gun. "Am I going to have trouble with you, Hogan?"

Lord shook his head, smiled and said, "Tobias Fynes was left-handed, Marshal. But don't worry, I fixed that little oversight for you."

"Damn, I never thought of that," Hart said.

CHAPTER FORTY-SIX

Sam Flintlock was with Dr. Theodora Weller when Marshal Slim Hart walked into the surgery. As always the lawman looked gloomy, like a perpetual bearer of bad news.

"Yes, I killed him, Marshal," Theodora said. She let tobacco and papers fall from her fingers. "And I'd do it again if I had to."

"It was self-defense, Doc," Hart said. "The murderer Tobias Fynes drew down on you and you had to defend yourself."

The woman was shocked. "But that's not how—"

"The murderer Tobias Fynes drew down on you and you had to defend yourself," Hart said. "Doc, how many times do I have to say it?"

Flintlock said, "Yup, that's how it was, Doctor. A clear-cut case of self-defense."

Then, as though it was the most natural thing in the world, Hart said, "How is O'Hara?"

"I'm just fine, Marshal."

O'Hara stood in the waiting room doorway. His

hands and most of his face were bandaged but his eyes were bright and he was solid on his feet.

Theodora, relief evident in her voice, said, "I badly need another drink. Anyone else?"

Heads nodded and Flintlock said, "I guess that's all of us, Doc."

"Wait, there's one more."

Hogan Lord stepped into the room and Flintlock immediately tensed, something the shootist noticed. He smiled and said, "I'm riding on, Sam. I hope we part as friends."

"Sure we do . . . until the next time," Flintlock said.

Lord laughed, raised the glass Theodora had just given him and he said, "I'll drink to that."

"And the rest of us," Hart said.

Theodora looked around at the three men and in a small, weak voice with a passable English accent, said, "God bless us, every one."

Only Lord knew where the quote came from. He smiled but remained silent.

Estelle Redway and Tobias Fynes were buried on the same day in the small Mansion Creek cemetery but their last resting places were far apart. Estelle's funeral was well attended but, according to the *Apache County Herald*, Fynes had no mourners. That same morning Ruth Fynes gave up her struggle, turned her face to the wall and died. Dr. Weller would later say that she died with a smile on her lips.

Flintlock and O'Hara rode out the following day and old Barnabas sat on top of the church steeple and watched them go, slowly shaking his head.

O'Hara's burns had not completely healed and he and Flintlock agreed that they should take it easy for the next few days. "Then once we get on a good trail south we'll be well on our way," Flintlock said.

"Promise me one thing," O'Hara said, drawing rein on his paint.

"Name it," Flintlock said.

"When we reach the Painted Desert we mind our own business and stay out of other people's troubles," O'Hara said.

"I'm with you on that," Flintlock said. "Yes, from now on we mind our own damned business."

"Do you mean that, Sam?"

"Yup, every word of it," Flintlock said. "Trust me."

Johnstone Justice. What America Needs Now.

*Bestselling authors William W. and J. A. Johnstone
continue the wild, epic saga of Tim Colter
with the building of the transcontinental railroad—
and the making of the American Dream . . .*

Twenty-two years have passed since Tim Colter and
his family were ambushed on the Oregon Trail,
forcing the young boy to find an unlikely ally in
one-eyed mountain man Jed Reno. Now a widowed
deputy U.S. marshal and Civil War veteran,
Colter is finally ready to remarry and settle down—
until a dangerous new assignment becomes
a life-or-death struggle for the soul of a town
and the heart of its people . . .

The Union Pacific Railroad is laying down tracks
connecting the great Northwest to the rest of the
country. But two rival factions have set their sights
on the town of Violet—aka Violence—to gain
control of the rails. It's Colter's job to tame the
rampant greed and rising tensions. But to do it,
he'll need to deputize his trusted old friend
Jed Reno—and wage a savage new war that will
determine the fate of the Dakota Territory
and the future of a nation.

THE EDGE OF VIOLENCE
A TIM COLTER WESTERN

Coming in October 2017
wherever Pinnacle Books are sold.

Live Free. Read Hard. www.williamjohnstone.net

CHAPTER ONE

Decades ago—by Jupiter, a lifetime, an eternity—Jed Reno had laughed at Jim Bridger. When the old (by mountain-man standards) fur trapper, scout, and guide had teamed up with Louis Vasquez to build a trading post on the Blacks Fork of the Green River, Jed Reno had jokingly told Bridger that Bridger's nerves had finally frayed. That Bridger was selling out. That he was calling it quits. That, pushing forty years old, he was too long in the tooth to be traipsing over the Rocky Mountains, trapping beaver and fighting the weather, the wilds, and the Indians. While sharing a jug of Taos Lightning or some other forty-rod whiskey seasoned with snakeheads, tobacco, and strychnine, Reno had slapped Bridger on the back, and told him, "Well, you just enjoy your life of leisure. I'm sure you'll be richer than a St. Louis whiskey drummer with this here venture of yours."

"Runnin' a store, ol' hoss," Bridger had told him, "ain't as easy as you think it is."

"Balderdash," Reno had said. Damnation, if Jim Bridger wasn't right.

As a bullet blew apart the copper-lined tin corn boiler, Reno ducked beneath the somersaulting axe handle that smashed the shelves behind him, sending metal-backed mirrors, salt and pepper shakers, scissors, axe blades, lanterns, baskets, jugs, matches, soaps, knives, forks, beads, containers of linseed oil, pine tar, and tins of tobacco flying every which way. He landed on the pile of pillow-ticking fabric and the woolen blankets he had not gotten around to stacking on the shelves, and he had to be thankful for that. At seventy years old, or something like that (Reno kept bragging that he had stopped counting after fifty), the onetime fur trapper wasn't as game as he used to be.

Which is why he had followed in Bridger's footsteps, and set up his own trading post about a dozen or so years ago on Clear Creek.

"You done a smart thing," Bridger had told him. "Make some money. Watch people go by. Drink whiskey. Smoke yer pipe. Easy livin'."

A hatchet fell with the axe handle, and the blade almost cut off Reno's left ear. A brass percussion capper bounced off his eyebrow. His good eye. An inch lower, and Jed Reno figured he might be wearing leather patches over both eyes.

Easy livin'? A body could get killed running a store.

He heard boots thudding across the packed earthen floor. His left hand reached up, found the handle to the hatchet that had almost split his head open, and jerked it free from the blankets and bolts of pillow ticking just as the bearded figure appeared on the other side of the counter.

A big man, bigger than even Reno, wearing fringed buckskin britches, black boots like those a dragoon or horse soldier might be wearing, collarless shirt of hunter green poplin, garnet waistcoat, and a battered black hat, flat-brimmed and flat-crowned. He also wore a brace of flintlock pistols in a yellow sash around his belly. One of those pistols was in his right hand.

Reno saw the hammer strike forward just as he flung the hatchet. Powder flashed in the pistol's pan, the barrel belched flame and smoke, and a .54-caliber lead ball embedded itself in the brown trade blanket rolled up on Reno's right.

"Horatio!" a voice yelled. Reno could just make out the voice as he sprang up, fell forward, and crawled toward the soon-to-be-dead Horatio, whose only replies were gurgles as he lay on his back as blood spurted from his neck like water from an artesian well.

The voice swore, and then barked at the third man who had entered Reno's trading post: "Sam, he's goin' fer Horatio's pistols. Get'm. Quick."

This time, Jed Reno heard clearly. The ringing from Horatio's pistol shot had died in Reno's ears. He dived the last couple of feet, ignoring the lake of blood that was ruining toothbrushes and staining wrapped bars of soap and the beads a Shoshone woman kept bringing him to trade for pork and flour, which, in turn, Reno sold to wayfarers from New York and Pennsylvania and Ohio and even Massachusetts who had been traveling so far that many of the ladies thought those beads from Prussia or someplace were prettier than rubies and garnets.

Reno jerked the second pistol from the dead man's sash. Horatio, Reno knew, was dead now because the blood no longer pulsed, but merely coagulated.

Footsteps pounded, but not only coming from Sam's
direction. The Voice was charging, too, and Jed Reno
had only one shot in the flintlock he had jerked from
Horatio's body. His left hand gripped the butt of the
.54 Horatio had fired just moments before.

Sam appeared on the other side of the counter,
where Reno had been refilling a barrel with pickled
pig's feet when the three men entered his store.

Sam was the oldest of the rogues, with silver hair, a
coonskin cap, and dark-colored, drop-front broadfall
britches—which must have gone out of fashion back
when Reno was a boy in Bowling Green, Kentucky—
muslin shirt, red stockings, and ugly shoes. A man
would have guessed him to be a schoolmaster or some
dandy if not for the double-barrel shotgun he held at
his hips.

The flintlock bucked in Reno's right hand, and just
before the eruption of white smoke obscured Reno's
vision, he saw the shocked look on Sam's face as the
bullet hit him plumb center, just below his rib cage.
With a gasp, Sam instantly pitched backward as if his
feet had slipped on one of the bar-pullers, tompions,
nuts, bolts, and vent and nipple picks that lay scattered on the floor. He touched off both barrels of the
shotgun.

One barrel had been loaded with buckshot, the
other with birdshot—as if he had been going out
hunting for either deer or quail—and the blast blew a
hole through the sod roof, and dirt and grass and at
least one mouse began pouring through the opening,
dirtying and eventually covering the ugly city shoes
the now-dead Sam wore on his feet.

Reno rolled over, just as The Voice leaped onto the

top of the counter. The pistol in Reno's left hand—the one he had jerked off the floor near the blood-soaked corpse of Horatio—sailed and struck The Voice in his nose. Reno caught only a glimpse of the revolving pistol The Voice held, because as soon as the flintlock crashed against the bandit's face, blood was spurting, The Voice was cursing, and then he was disappearing, crashing against the floor on the other side of the counter. Reno came up, hurdled the counter, and caught an axe handle on his ankles.

This time, Reno cursed, hit the floor hard, and rolled over, but not fast enough, for The Voice jumped on top of him and locked both hands around Jed Reno's throat.

Now that he had a close look at the gent, The Voice had more than just a rich baritone.

He had the look of a man-killer. Scars pockmarked his bronzed face, clean-shaven except for long Dundreary whiskers, and his eyes were a pale, lifeless blue. Those eyes bulged, and the man ground his tobacco-stained teeth. The nose had been busted two or three times, including just seconds ago by Horatio's empty .54-caliber pistol. Blood poured from both nostrils and the gash on the nose's bridge. One of The Voice's earlobes was missing—as if it had been bitten off in a fight. He seemed a wiry man, all sinew, no fat, and his hands were rock-hard, the fingers like iron, clasping, pushing down against his throat, and cutting off any air.

He wore short moccasins, high-waisted britches of blue canvas with pewter buttons for suspenders that he did not don; a red-checked flannel shirt that was mostly covered by the double-breasted sailor's jacket with two rows of brass buttons on the front and three on the cuffs. The black top hat The Voice had worn had fallen off at some point during the scuffle.

But he was a little man, no taller than five-two, and a stiff wind—which was predictably normal in this country—would likely blow him over.

Jed Reno figured he was forty years older than The Voice, but he had more than a foot on the murdering cuss, and probably seventy pounds. Jed kept rolling over, and The Voice rolled with him. They rolled like the pickle barrel Sam had knocked over with his right arm as he fell to the floor in a heap and ruined the store's roof. Rolled against an overturned keg of nails and knocked over the brooms until they hit the spare wagon wheels leaning against the wall.

The Voice came up, pushing off one wagon wheel, then flinging another at Reno, who blocked it with his forearm, and sat up, slid over, and leaped to his feet.

Staggering back toward the sacks of flour, beans, and coffee, The Voice wiped his mouth. The lower lip had been split. Reno tasted blood on his lips, but he didn't know if it belonged to him, The Voice, or the late Horatio.

"You one-eyed bastard." The Voice had lost much of its musical tone. More of a wheeze. But the little man was game.

He jerked a bowie knife that must have been sheathed behind his back. The blade slashed out, but Reno leaped back. Again. The Voice was driving him, until Reno found himself against another counter.

The Voice's lips stretched into a gruesome, bloody smile.

The knife's massive, razor-sharp blade ripped

through the flannel shirt; and had Reno not sucked in his stomach, he would be bleeding more than The Voice about this time. The blade began slashing back, but Reno had found the chains—those he sold to emigrants for their wagon boxes—and slashed one like a blacksnake whip. Somehow, it caught The Voice's arm between wrist and elbow, and The Voice wailed as the bones in the arm snapped, and the big knife thudded on the floor.

As The Voice staggered back, Reno felt the chain slip from his hand. He was tuckered out, too, and, well, it had been several moons since he had engaged in a tussle like this one.

The chain rattled as it fell to the floor, and The Voice turned and ran for the door.

Sucking in air, Reno charged, lowered his head and shoulder, and slammed into the thin man's side. They went through the open doorway, over what passed as a porch, and smashed through the pole where the bandits had tied their horses. Those geldings whinnied, reared, whined, and pounded at the two men's bodies. One, a black gelding, pulled loose the rest of the smashed piece of pine and galloped toward the creek. One fell in the dirt, rolled over, came up—and ran north, leaving its reins in the dirt and wrapped around the broken pole. The other backed up, reared, fell over, and came up. Reno couldn't tell which way he ran.

He was on his knees, spitting out dirt and blood, while wiping his eyes. He tried to stand, to find The Voice, when he tasted dirt and leather and sinew and felt his head snap back. Down he went, realizing that The Voice had kicked him. He landed, rolled, was trying to come up, when The Voice turned his body into a missile. His head caught Reno right in the stomach. Breath left his lungs. He caught a glimpse of the cabin he called a store flash past him as he was driven into the column that held up the covering over the porch.

The railing snapped. The covering collapsed, spilling more earth, debris, two rats, and a bird's nest. The two men kept moving. Past the cabin. Over dried horse apples. A fist caught Reno in the jaw. Then another. The Voice packed a wallop. Reno brought up his arms in a defensive maneuver, leaving his midsection open. A fist—it had to be The Voice's left, for his right arm was busted—hit twice. Three times. Reno fell against the woodpile, rolled over, hit the chopping block, and wondered if he had just busted a couple of ribs.

"Son of a bitch!" The Voice roared.

Reno blinked away sweat, blood, dirt, and dust. He saw the bandit standing next to the pile of firewood. He had a sizable chunk of wood in his left hand. Stepped forward, raising the club over his head.

Reno found the axe buried in the chopping block. Jerking it free, he flung it as he dived out of the way of the descending piece of wood.

He lay there, panting, played out, wondering why the devil The Voice didn't just finish him off. But that instant of defeatism vanished quickly. Reno rolled over, came up, and spit. He looked left, and then right, and saw his cabin, saw the woodpile, and finally his eyes focused on the moccasins and the ends of the blue pants on the dirt.

Neither the feet nor the legs were moving.

Wiping the blood and grime from his face, Reno limped to the pile. He had to lean against the wood for support, and breathing heavily, he looked down at The Voice, and the axe, and the blood.

"You . . . horse's . . . arse . . ." Jed Reno wheezed, and made a painful gesture at what remained of his trading post. "All three . . . of you . . . curs . . . dead . . . burnin' in . . . Hell. . . . Means . . . I gotta . . . clean this . . . mess . . . up . . . myself."

CHAPTER TWO

Jed Reno salvaged what he could from the three dead men. The guns he could resell, even the two flintlock pistols, a matched set of A. Waters with walnut grips—antiquated as they were. Reno also found a nice key-wind watch, and wondered who the dead man stole that from, but decided that the odds highly unfavored the victim—if the victim hadn't been murdered—coming into Reno's store and seeing his watch for sale. The boots and shoes might bring a bit of a profit, or he could trade them to the Shoshone woman for some more beads, along with the hats. Not much use with the clothes, especially now that they were all pretty much hardened and stained with dried blood. Reno was lucky. He even found a few gold coins and some silver in the outlaws' pockets. He was alive, and figured he had made a pretty good trade with the three dead men.

It was shaping up to be one passable, profitable day. But Reno certainly didn't look forward to cleaning up the mess.

He loaded the corpses onto his pack mule, saddled

his bay gelding, and led his cargo away from the post, crossing the tracks of the iron horse. He looked east at the town, still mostly tents, although a few sod houses and frame buildings had been put up. Then he looked west, following the iron rails and wooden crossties laid by the Irishmen working for the Union Pacific Railway. He could see black smoke puffing out of the stacks of a locomotive down the line. Back east, he heard the screeching and ugly hissing and saw more black smoke as another train made its way through the settlement, hauling more spikes, rails, crossties, fishplates, sledgehammers, and maybe even a few more workers.

It was a big undertaking, the transcontinental railroad, and as much as Jed Reno despised the damned thing, he had to admit it was progress. And had made him fairly wealthy.

He rode about five miles north, decided that was good enough, and dumped the bodies into an arroyo. Buzzards had to eat. So did coyotes. And one thing Jed Reno did not like about that railroad was the fact that since they had started laying track across this part of the territory, most of the game had left the country.

Reno could remember talking with Jim Bridger, Kit Carson, and other trappers. It hadn't been at one of the rendezvous because, the best Reno recalled things, those gatherings had ended by then. Maybe it had been at Fort Bridger. Talk had reached Bridger's trading post about a railroad being planned, one that would stretch across the country. Carson had shrugged.

Bridger had allowed it was true. Reno had laughed and called it a fool's folly.

"How you gonna get one of them trains across these Rockies?"

"Don't underestimate man's ingenuity," Bridger had said.

"Where, by thunder," Carson had said, "did you pick up that 'in-gen-yoo-ah-tee' word?"

"And in winter?" Reno had said. "Can't be done."

Of course, a few years earlier, Reno would never have thought he would be seeing prairie schooners by the hundreds crossing the Great Plains and then across the mountains, bringing settlers from New York and Pennsylvania and other places foreign to a man like Reno, bound for the Oregon country and later California. Farmers. Merchants. Women and children and even milch cows and dogs. One gent had been hauling sapling fruit trees to start some orchards in the Willamette Valley.

Born in 1796 in what was now Bowling Green, Kentucky, Jed Reno had seen much in his day. His father then apprenticed Reno to a wheelwright up in Louisville, and Reno took that for longer than he had any right to before he stowed away on a steamboat and went down the Ohio and Mississippi rivers. New Madrid. Then St. Louis. And then he signed up with William Henry Ashley and set out up the Missouri River and became a fur trapper. That had been the life, maybe the best years Reno would ever live to see, but . . . well . . . nothing lasts forever. Beavers went out of fashion. Silk became favorable for hats. Now fur felt had become popular. By Jupiter, Reno had a hat of fur felt on his head now, too.

So when Reno happened upon some men who said they were surveyors, and when they paid him gold to do their hunting and scouting for them, Reno decided that Jim Bridger was a pretty wise gent after all.

Reno had only one eye, but few things escaped his vision, and he had two good ears. And to live in the wilds of the Rockies and Plains since 1822, you had to see, and you had to hear. Reno listened to the surveyors. And he watched.

Apparently, there were a number of surveys going on. A couple were down south, which made a lot of sense to Reno. Weather would be warmer, less hostile, across Texas and that desert country the United States had claimed after that set to with Mexico. Another up north, somewhere between the forty-seventh and forty-ninth parallels north—whatever that meant. Reno wasn't sure England would care too much for that. Seemed to Reno that ownership of all that country up north was being debated between the king—or was it a queen now?—and whoever was president of these United States.

But the surveyors kept talking about a war brewing between the states. It had something to do with freeing the slaves or, to hear one of the men who spoke with a Mississippi drawl, it had to do with "a bunch of damn Yankees pushing us good Southern folk around." That got Reno to figuring that there was no way the United States would put up a railroad across country that might not be part of the United States in a few years. So he paid even closer attention to the surveyors.

Around 1853, some surveyors had been hauling their boxes and making their maps along what most folks called the Buffalo Trail, led by some captain named Gunnison. Something the surveyors called the Thirty-fifth Parallel Route. Reno figured that one died when Ute Indians killed some of the soldier boys, but he also met another one of those young whipper-snappers who called himself an engineer. Went by the name of Lander, Frederick W. Lander, who worked for some outfit called the Eastern Railroad of Massachusetts. Lander told Reno that there could never be a railroad in the South, but a railroad had to connect the Pacific with the Atlantic because if war came—not among the states, but against a European power with a strong navy and mighty army—the United States would not be able to defend California without "an adequate mode of transit," whatever that meant.

So Reno decided to throw up a trading post along Clear Creek in the Unorganized Territory, take a gamble that Lander was right, and that eventually he'd be selling items to greenhorns stopping for a rest on this transcontinental railroad.

The post was a combination of logs—which he had hauled down from the Medicine Bow country—and dirt. He had built it into a knoll that rose near the creek, digging out a cave that he knew would be cool enough in the summer and hot enough in the winter. The logs stuck out and made the post look more like a cabin, though, and gave it more of an inviting feel. Reno had never cared much for those strictly sod huts that looked, to him, like graves. This way, part log cabin, the post didn't seem completely like a grave to Jed Reno.

A few years later, Lander came back again, and this time he had some painter guy with him. That's when

Jed Reno began feeling pretty confident about his investment. After all, if you hired some artist to paint some pretty pictures of you working, then you had to think that this was being documented for history.

Besides, even if it didn't happen, if the railroad went north or south or never at all, well, Jed Reno still had a place he could call home, that would keep him warm in the winter and cool in the summer. He had a good source of water, and could fish or hunt or get drunk or just sit on his porch—if you could call it a porch—and watch the sun rise, the sun set, the moon rise, the moon set. By Jupiter, he was pretty much retired anyhow, like ol' Bridger.

Of course, the war came—just like everyone had been talking about—and the surveyors and engineers stopped coming. Poor young Frederick Lander. He joined up to fight to preserve the Union, and from the stories Reno heard, the boy took sick with congestion of the brain and died somewhere in Virginia in 1862. Wasn't even shot or stuck with one of those long knives or blown apart by a cannonball. Reno wondered if that gent with the paintbrushes—some gent named Albert Bierstadt, who had dark hair, a pointed beard, and penetrating eyes—ever amounted to much.

Most of the blood inside the trading post had been covered with more dirt, which Reno packed down with his moccasins. The merchandise that had been busted, or soaked or stained with blood, he tossed into a canvas bag and hauled to the smelly dump that the settlers, who had not moved on with the railroad, had started up and was already attracting vultures and rats and coyotes and flies. But it was far enough away from Reno's post that the smell seldom bothered him too much.

He salvaged most of the merchandise, not that it really mattered. Since the railroad moved on, Reno had not seen much business, and since the trains brought only supplies and more workers, it wasn't like settlers were stopping to spend money on trinkets and blankets and tin cups. Reno began to doubt if he could ever sell anything else—not that he really cared one way or the other.

Fixing the hitching rail was probably the easiest thing, since he had hammers and plenty of nails and even some spare ridgepoles, located behind the post, he could use. The roof and the porch, however, were another matter. He had to use another pole to replace the one he and The Voice had knocked down, and then secure that with another pole, nailing one end to the vertical pole and ramming the other between two logs, which he then patched with chink.

After that, he had to climb onto the roof and throw enough brush down to cover the hole one of the bandits had made with his double-barreled shotgun. He could hear some of the dirt sprinkling from his ceiling and probably dirtying up his bolts of fabric and those nice woolen blankets. But he could beat the dirt out of them later. It would give him something to do.

While he was still on the roof, he heard a couple of shots from the settlement, which some citizens were starting to call a town. Reno ignored that, kept busying himself with the roof, and then piled dirt on top of the hole. He was satisfied with his handiwork. Of course, he had built a few cabins in his day up in the

Rockies when he needed a place to winter, and some things Mr. Sneed, the wheelwright, had taught him back in Louisville still registered in his brain.

He had just finished, and was making his way to the ladder he had fashioned, when he spotted the dust. Reno remained on the rooftop, and checked the loads in the revolving Colt's pistol he carried these days—another sign of progress, he told himself. An Army Colt could shoot six times before you had to reload it. Back in Reno's day, a man had to do his job with only one bullet. Else he was dead.

Four riders, coming from the settlement. Four on horseback. A couple others followed afoot.

Tenderfeet.

Reno sighed. He hoped those fool city folks weren't coming to complain about him using their dump. Or maybe someone had found the bodies of the three men he had killed and were out to investigate another killing in Violence.

Connect with U s

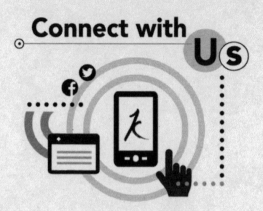

Visit us online at
KensingtonBooks.com
to read more from your favorite authors, see books
by series, view reading group guides, and more.

Join us on social media

for sneak peeks, chances to win books and prize packs,
and to share your thoughts with other readers.

f **y**

facebook.com/kensingtonpublishing
twitter.com/kensingtonbooks

Tell us what you think!

To share your thoughts, submit a review,
or sign up for our eNewsletters, please visit:
KensingtonBooks.com/TellUs.